"I was   **"**

"What?"
What's wrong?"

Sara took a deep breath and lied—a little. "I don't feel like we're connecting quite the way we should." Because I have a crush on you, she thought. "I'm wondering if someone else might be a better fit for you."

"Well, I won't allow anyone else in here. It's you or nobody, Sara." Damian had the nerve to smile as he spoke, though it sounded like a royal command to Sara's ears.

She bit her lip. "Now you're being unreasonable."

"No," said the prince, "I'm telling it like it is."

"But you didn't even want me at first!"

"I want you now."

RAYE MORGAN

has spent almost two decades, while writing over fifty novels, searching for the answer to that elusive question: Just what is that special magic that happens when a man and a woman fall in love? Every time she thinks she has the answer, a new wrinkle pops up, necessitating another book! Meanwhile, after living in Holland, Guam, Japan and Washington, D.C., she currently makes her home in Southern California with her husband and two of her four boys.

ROYAL
NIGHTS

RAYE MORGAN

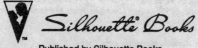

Published by Silhouette Books
America's Publisher of Contemporary Romance

SILHOUETTE BOOKS

ROYAL NIGHTS

ISBN 0-373-21832-X

Copyright © 2003 by Helen Conrad

This edition published by arrangement with Harlequin Books S.A.

® and TM are trademarks of Harlequin Books S.A., used under license. Trademarks indicated with ® are registered in the United States Patent and Trademark Office, the Canadian Trade Marks Office and in other countries.

Visit Silhouette at www.eHarlequin.com

Printed in U.S.A.

To Mary-Theresa, Susan and Kim.
Editors are like fairy godmothers—
they make the magic possible.

THE NABOTAVIAN ROYAL FAMILY

House of the White Rose
The Roseanova-Krimorovas
West Nabotavia

House of the Red Rose
The Roseanovas
Nabotavia

King Marcovo I
Royal House of the Rose
great-great grandfather

Peter
great-grandfather

Marcovo II
great-grandfather

Marcovo III
grandfather

Marie Kristiana
(Queen of
Nabotavia
deceased)

Marcovo IV
(King of Nabotavia
deceased)

m.

Jorgaro
grandfather

Trandam
(King of
West Nabotavia)

m.

Beatrice
(Queen of
West Nabotavia)

Tianna

David

Jannika

Marco
(*Counterfeit
Princess*
SR #1672)

Garth
(*Betrothed to
the Prince*
SR #1667)

Damian
(*Royal
Nights*
Silhouette
Single Title)

Karina
(*Jack and the
Princess*
SR #1655)

Prologue

The beautiful summer day gave no hint of what was to come. There was no message in the wind that shivered the tops of the trees around the lake, no sense of foreboding in the breeze that tousled the well-cut hairstyles of the spectators, no caution in the roar of the engines as the hydrofoils took the warm-up laps for the race.

If he'd thought about it, Prince Damian, youngest son of the Roseanovas, the royal family of Nabotavia, who had a strong sense of irony, might have taken warning just because the day *was* so bright with sunlight casting a golden hue over everyone and everything. But instead he felt good, strong, with just an edge of adrenaline that gave life that extra kick.

Things were definitely going his way. Thana Gar-

net, the film star, was cheering him on from the box
seats, and from the look in her beautiful green eyes
and the way she'd let her fingers trail down the inside
of his arm a few moments before, he was pretty sure
she was prepared to provide a very satisfying reward
for his success.

He knew he was going to win. Not that it would
be easy. No, his cousin Sheridan always made it
tough, mostly because he cared so much. They com-
peted at everything, and sometimes, Sheridan even
won. But not today. Damian could feel it in his blood,
that extra vibration, the special confidence that told
him he would come out on top.

Four hydrofoils paced impatiently in the starting
loop, engines revving, ready to run. The other two
were good enough, but the real race would be with
Sheridan. He glanced over at his cousin and gave him
a cocky grin. Sheridan didn't smile back. His jaw was
tight, his lips almost white.

"Lord, Sheridan," Damian thought with a chuckle.
"If you'd just relax, you'd be more of a challenge."

The spectator box was set out on the end of the
pier and he glanced up at it as they made the turn.
Thana waved to him and he gave her a nod. Penny
Potherton sat beside her, and Muffy Van Snook as
well, along with the usual crowd. He could see them
all yelling encouragement, though he couldn't hear
them over the noise the boats were making. All beautiful women. He'd dated each of them at one time or
another over the years. One of the advantages of be-

ing an eligible royal bachelor was you were always in demand. Life was sweet.

But it was time to get serious. He pulled down his helmet and settled in, focusing. They were coming up on the starting line. The race was run down the length of the lake and around a dogleg, then back. Adrenaline surged. He was ready, eager, but cool and confident. It was his day. He could feel it.

The signal came and the four boats surged forward. He took the start right on the nose, taking off like a jet from a runway. He was all speed, all sound, all spray, a force of will, a force of nature splitting the water, shattering the air—on a power speed high. He took the first turn and headed into the dogleg. He didn't shift his focus, but he could sense that he was pulling ahead of the others. He held back exhilaration. There would be time for that when he won. He was coming up on the hard turn and if he didn't slack off a bit, it would take all his concentration to make it work.

Slack off? Hah. He went for it.

The boat banked into the turn and he leaned against the centrifugal force, relishing that feeling of fighting fate.

And then everything went wrong. Suddenly, something ripped and the nose was heading for the clouds, much too high, then it slammed down and everything exploded. The sound was deafening. The boat shattered under him, like glass hitting stone. He was hurtling through the spray, hitting the water at a hundred miles an hour, torn, smashed, gasping. His mind was all question without words, but there was no time to think them. Because once he hit, there was nothing—nothing but cold, hard blackness.

Chapter 1

Sara Joplin was running late.

Why was it always on the days when she had an appointment that mattered that everything just fell apart? Things started to go bad early in the morning when her pregnant sister Mandy called, begging a ride to her obstetrician's as her car's battery had died. The wait at the doctor's had lasted forever and when she finally got Mandy home, she still needed to stop off at her office in the Sepulveda Atrium.

She'd barely had the papers she needed in hand before the building died. That was the way it had seemed as the frantically operating air-conditioning system fell silent and the lights dimmed, then went out, and the elevators stopped running. Another summer brownout. She'd had to take the stairs, down twenty-four floors, and then the door to the main landing was locked.

"That's illegal, you know," she mentioned as the lobby guard finally let her out.

By the time she got back in her car, she was already late for her appointment with Veronica Roseanova, duchess of Gavini at her home in Beverly Hills, but she was going to get later. Little did she know as she impatiently cruised up the on-ramp onto the Santa Monica freeway, that a police chase was in progress—the slow-motion sort that could tie up the freeway for an hour while television helicopters beat the air overhead and spectators lined the overpasses. It must have been about the time she came to a stop behind a truck belching black smoke and realized she was going to be there for a while that the cooling unit in her car went out. By then she was too whipped to swear.

Luckily the police chase moved on to some other neighborhood and it was only a little over half an hour later that she pulled into the driveway of the royal mansion, rolling down her window to talk to the gate guard. She even managed a smile, but it faded as he ushered her in but told her to pull over to the side, then took a call and spent the next five minutes arguing with someone on the telephone.

By then, Sara had just about had it. It was hot. Her silver-blond hair was coming out of the tuck she usually wore it in. Strands were plastered to her damp neck and her once-crisp blouse was beginning to make her look shrink-wrapped. She was tired. And embarrassed to be so late for her appointment. And annoyed with the world.

Giving the guard a fierce scowl, which he ignored, she got out of her car, grabbed her briefcase, and began the walk up the driveway toward the imposing house. She wobbled a little in the heels. They were only two inches, but she wasn't used to wearing them these days. She'd dressed up for this meeting, actually put on a skirt. After all, it wasn't every day she got summoned by royalty. She'd wanted everything to go so well.

She hated being late. She hated being in such a hurry. You tended to make mistakes when you hurried. And she hated making mistakes. Stopping in front of the house, she bit her lip. Here was a chance to make another one. How was she supposed to know which of the many entrances she could see on this huge house was the one she ought to use to find the lady of the manor? Old-fashioned vines covered everything and paths led everywhere. It was like facing a maze. Sighing, she started walking down one of the paths, only to stumble when a gap between paving stones caught her heel.

"Oh, damn it!"

"Such language for a young lady," someone said, his voice amused but mocking.

Whirling, she found that the voice was coming from the vine-sheltered porch she had just walked past. A male figure was leaning indolently against the post at the top of the low stairs, his hands shoved into the pockets of slacks that probably cost more than her week's salary. It was difficult to see him clearly; his face was shaded by the vines, and his eyes were pretty much hidden by a captain's cap set at a jaunty angle but pulled low over his face. Still, she could see that he was gorgeous. A spectacularly handsome man in incredibly expensive clothes lounging around in front of a mansion—it was all very *Great Gatsby*-ish.

"Oh, sorry," she said a bit sheepishly.

"Can I help you?" he replied.

"Actually, I'm looking for the duchess of Gavini," she said quickly. "I was supposed to meet her and I'm afraid I'm really late. Can you tell me where I can find her?"

His mouth twisted in a slight smile. "Don't worry. She'll find you."

"Oh. Well, but…"

"There's an empty chair here…why don't you have a seat?"

She glanced at the beautifully carved wood chair, only a step away. "No, you see, I'm very late and…"

"Sit."

Maybe it was something in his voice. Or maybe it was her harried state that left her more susceptible to orders than usual. Whatever it was, she sat. But she stayed on the edge of the chair, ready to jump back up at any moment. The man moved out from the shadow of the vines and came down one step toward her, stumbling a bit as he found his balance, making her wonder if he had an injury. But he seemed perfectly self-assured as he half leaned, half sat against the banister, his arms folded against his chest, his nicely bulging biceps on striking display.

"So tell me," he said casually. "Why are you meeting with the duchess?"

She looked at the opulent house, then back at him. He certainly belonged here. Already she felt as though she were traveling in rarefied air.

"She asked me to come and assess the situation with the prince. I understand he had some sort of boating accident which impaired his sight. She thought he might benefit from therapy."

"Therapy." The way he said the word spoke volumes. "How very considerate of the dear duchess."

She frowned, not sure she liked his tone. Maybe she shouldn't have said anything. Besides, though she couldn't really see his eyes, she had a hunch he was looking at her legs. Feeling awkward, she tugged on the hem of her skirt, trying to get it near her knees but failing utterly. Her legs were her best feature, but that didn't mean she wanted them gawked at. If that *was* what he was doing.

"I think it's important to make sure young people with a new disability get help right away so that they understand they will still be able to have control over their lives," she said, knowing she sounded defensive.

He seemed to be smiling, though she couldn't tell for sure. He had an odd way of seeming to look past her. "Just how old do you think the prince is?" he asked.

She blinked. "I don't know. From the way the

duchess was talking, I assumed he was about eleven or twelve.''

Now there was no doubt. He was laughing.

''I really think I should go and look for the duchess,'' she said, starting to rise from her seat.

''Don't bother,'' he replied shortly. ''She'll be here soon enough.''

She sank back down and looked toward the house again. ''Oh. I see,'' she said, though she didn't. She waited for a moment, tapping her foot against the grass, but he didn't say anything and she cleared her throat and ventured, ''It certainly is warm today.''

He nodded. ''That tends to happen toward the end of the summer,'' he noted dryly.

She made a gesture with her hand, then plunked it back down in her lap. She wasn't sure who this man was. Maybe he wasn't a part of the family at all. Another visitor, perhaps? Or maybe the prince's tutor? She wasn't sure why she felt so uncomfortable with him. Her usual bright, breezy manner seemed to have deserted her. She chalked it up to the fact that he wasn't particularly friendly, and was too darn good-looking.

Gorgeous men were not in her realm of normal experience, she reminded herself. *Let's face it. Lately I'm having trouble getting even average-looking men interested.*

Her thoughts flashed back to the dreadful day when the man she'd thought she might be in love with, Ralph Joiner, had walked out of her life. But even that now seemed trivial. They had worked together and dated a few times and she'd begun to feel there might be something there. But he'd taken another position in Colorado and she'd never heard from him again. Still, that ranked as her biggest disappointment in love, so she supposed she might as well hold on to it. How long ago had it been exactly? Two years? She wrinkled her nose. She could hardly believe it had been that long. It hardly even stung anymore. But there was a lingering sense of sadness. Though maybe hopeless resignation would be a better term for what she thought of it all now. Though trim and healthy-looking, with a mass of thick, wavy blond hair and sparkling blue eyes that were often smiling, she'd never been seen as a beauty. But it didn't matter. So she wasn't exactly guy bait. So what? She was busy and happy. Sort of.

The blue door behind the handsome man opened and an older gentleman stepped out, blinking toward the sunlight in a befuddled fashion.

"Oh, dear," he said, shaking his head as though impatient with himself. "I didn't mean to intrude. I'll get out of your way."

"You're not intruding, Your Grace."

But the older man retreated behind the door once again and closed it.

"Who was that?" Sara asked, reminded of the white rabbit in Alice's Wonderland.

"The duke."

"Oh! He might know where the duchess is."

"Trust me. He won't."

"But if he's her husband…"

"He never knows where she is. Nor does he want to."

"Oh." She frowned and looked longingly at the door the duke had used, wondering what would happen if she were just to get up and go knock on it.

But before she could put a plan into action, another man appeared, this one in his early thirties, looking rather handsome and debonair in a straw hat and white slacks.

"Ah, there you are," he said, approaching them rapidly. "I say, old man, have you seen the duke? He promised to show me an Etruscan artifact he received today."

"Just saw him. In there." He jerked a thumb in the direction of the blue door.

"Thanks. Oh, excuse me, miss." The newcomer smiled and tipped his hat, then hurried up the stairs and disappeared behind the door.

Sara felt laughter bubbling up her throat. This was all so unbelievable. "Who was that?" she asked.

"Count Boris. The duchess's younger brother."

Now she couldn't hold the laughter back. Hot and tired as she was, she had no resistance left. In fact, she was feeling a little punchy.

"What's so funny?" he asked.

"I don't know. All this royalty stuff. There's just something amusing about it."

"Don't tell me you're one of those antiroyalist people."

"Not at all. I have the utmost respect for royalty." Smiling she shook her head. "Just like every other

little girl, I once dreamed my prince would come."
She laughed again. "But that's not in my line any
longer."

"No prince in your life?" He asked it softly.

"None at all. And I don't expect one. I'm hardly
princess material."

She shifted her position. The laughter began to fade
and she was beginning to feel uncomfortable again.
She, of all people, shouldn't be talking about looks
to this good-looking man.

Still, it should be irrelevant if he was handsome.
For all she knew, he might be some sort of royalty
himself. No crown, she noted with a suppressed grin.
But then, they didn't walk around with them on their
heads these days, did they? Only in comic books, she
supposed, allowing herself a little silent chuckle.
Maybe she should go ahead and ask him. Why not?
He wasn't exactly offering up any small talk himself.

"Well, are you related to the royal family?" she
asked cheerfully.

He stretched back in a way that showed off his
nicely muscled chest right through the rich fabric of
his polo shirt, making her swallow involuntarily.

"Yes, actually," he said slowly. "I am. More's the
pity."

She nodded. She should have guessed it. "I suppose you know the little prince?"

His sudden grin was a stunner, all white teeth flashing against his wonderful tan skin.

Wow, she thought, taking a deep breath. For once,
she felt she could understand why men were so crazy

about looking at beautiful women. If more men looked like this, more women would be doing just as much looking.

"As a matter of fact, I know him quite well. Better than anyone else, I'd wager." He smiled at her. "You might almost say, he's me."

She frowned, not sure if he were making some sort of obscure joke. "What do you mean?"

"I'm him. I'm Prince Damian. The 'little' prince himself."

"But…" She shook her head, still confused. "You're not blind."

"No? You mean they've been lying to me all this time? Still, you should know. You're the expert." Tilting the captain's cap onto the back of his head, he squinted into the sunlight. "Nope, it still doesn't work," he said. "I can't see a thing."

"Oh!" Her face went crimson. What a jerk she was! She half rose from the chair, then dropped back down again. Now that she knew the truth, she realized she should have seen the signs. She was a professional after all. She'd seen him stumble on the steps and noticed that he seemed to look past her. Either of those things should have clue her in immediately. But she'd been expecting a young boy, not a fully developed and very virile man. "Oh, I'm sorry, I didn't…"

He flashed her another stunning grin. "Don't worry about it. I'm not the sensitive type."

"No, I really… I thought you were going to be a child. I can't tell you how…"

"Forget it." He pulled the cap back down. "We've got more important things to talk about." He seemed to be looking right at her. "In the first place, I don't need any of your therapy."

She didn't usually face much resistance from patients. Most were eager to learn how to deal with their problem, but now and then there was someone whose bitterness kept him from taking advantage of all the new methods. Usually, they just needed a little convincing.

"You may think that now," she said promptly, still having trouble adjusting to him being blind. He just didn't look it. "But you'll find that it's quite helpful once you get into it. I've had quite a bit of experience with the sight-impaired and—"

"Call it 'blind,'" he said bluntly.

She hesitated. So he was going to be one of those, was he? "All right, if you prefer that. As I was saying, I've had a lot of experience with the blind and I've found that one of the things they hate worst about their condition is the feeling of helplessness and having to depend on others just to go through normal daily life. With therapy, I can help you get beyond that."

"I'm not a fan of psychobabble solutions."

"That's not what I do," she said, trying to keep the indignation out of her voice. "I'm not a psychologist. I'm not here to mold your mind in any way. I'm an occupational therapist."

He shrugged. "I don't need a new occupation. Being a prince is taking up all my time."

She swallowed hard, trying to keep her temper in check. "As an occupational therapist," she explained carefully, though she was sure he already knew this and was just tweaking her, "I help people learn to deal with disabilities. It's all very hands-on and practical. No psychobabble involved."

"Whatever." He turned to face her again. "Bottom line—I don't need you."

She drew in a sharp breath. "Well, your aunt seemed to think you did."

"My aunt is wrong. Look. There's no point to all this. The blindness is only temporary. I should be back to normal soon."

She hesitated, feeling a flash of sympathy despite being thoroughly annoyed with this arrogant man. She found it highly unlikely that anyone had promised him a speedy cure. "Well, I only got your case history from Dr. Simpson's office today and I haven't had a chance to look over the records yet."

"I'm glad to hear that. If you'd already checked out the records and still thought I was a twelve-year-old boy, I'd have to question your reading skills."

Despite everything, she had to smile. "True."

"To save you the trouble of looking it up, I'll tell you. Doc Simpson gave me a fifty-fifty chance of getting my sight back within the next couple of months."

She grimaced, trying to be careful. "That sounds encouraging, but it's hardly a guarantee."

"Fifty-fifty?" He shrugged. "I'm a winner, Ms. Occupational Therapist. I'll take those odds." He tapped his temple with his forefinger. "Six weeks, tops."

"Well, good luck," she said reflexively, then grimaced, wishing she could recall the words. They were awfully close to mockery, weren't they? Prince Damian seemed to be bringing out the worst in her. She took a deep breath, prepared to make amends somehow, but before she could think of anything nice to say, a voice hailed them from the driveway.

Chapter 2

"Well, there you are!"

Sara turned to see a woman she assumed must be the duchess hurrying to join them.

"So sorry to have kept you waiting, Ms. Joplin," the older woman was saying as she came forward, her hand outstretched. "My limousine was caught in one of those horrible chase tie-ups on the freeway."

Sara stood and shook hands with her, realizing she was no longer the one who was late and she didn't have to worry about making all those embarrassing excuses. That in itself was a huge relief.

"I see you've met the patient. I hope he's been… kind to you." She glanced at her nephew, then gave a rather brittle smile as she looked Sara over. "No obvious wounds, I see."

"Only to her ego," Damian muttered, dropping to sit on the top step after reaching out to feel his way.

"Yes." She gave Sara a long-suffering look. "Well, as you can see, he is not going to be an ideal patient for you. But I'm sure you'll get used to each other."

Sara hesitated, then decided to get it out in the open. "I do have to let you know that the prince is not exactly what I was expecting. You see, my experience is largely with children."

"Believe me, you'll hardly notice the difference," she purred, and managed to make a shrug look elegant and continental.

"That's my beloved auntie," he said coolly. "So supportive in my hour of need."

"Sorry, Damian, but you have been acting almost like a child of late, and you know very well that that is the truth."

Sara winced. Relations between these two didn't seem to be as rosy as one might hope. Was that going to be a problem? Possibly.

She glanced at Prince Damian. His handsome face didn't reveal any resentment at his aunt's words. In fact, he looked amused, if anything. And awfully sure of himself for a man who had recently lost his sight.

The duchess was a handsome woman with a look of cool intelligence, but around her mouth there seemed to be a tension that hinted at a certain dissatisfaction. Still, she seemed friendly in her aloof way, chattering on about the room Sara would be using and what her living arrangements would include. But Sara was hardly listening. She was much more interested in the man sitting across from her, the man she would be working with for the next few weeks—if she could convince him that she could help him.

The duchess seemed to assume that everything was set up and ready to go. She looked at her watch and gave a little sound of exasperation.

"You know, I do have to get into the house and take care of some loose ends. I'm just worn to a frazzle in this heat. Why don't you two continue to get to know each other for another half hour? I'll have tea sent out. Then, Ms. Joplin, come to the green door and ask for me, and I'll have you shown to the room you'll be using while you're here. Dinner is at six, we're used to an early meal. That will leave time for you two to have your first session later this evening." Her smile was perfunctory but she shook hands once again. "I will be expecting you in half an hour."

And she hurried off.

"She'll map out the next five years of your life if you let her," Damian said, stretching his long legs out in front of him.

Sara couldn't help but laugh. "Do you feel manip ulated?" she asked.

"Damn right. I don't have much recourse right now, considering my condition. But I do enjoy needling her." His mouth twisted in a slight smile.

And might that be one reason you seem to want to send me, your aunt's bright idea, packing? Sara smiled.

"I'd say it runs in the family," she said aloud. "She needles you back pretty effectively."

He laughed, nodding. "You got that right." But his amusement quickly faded and he frowned. "You know, it would probably be best for all concerned if you would just get back into your car and head out of here," he suggested quietly.

She was back on the edge of her chair. Did she want to fight for this job? If so, now was the time to do it. Just the thought made her a little nervous. She wasn't used to this sort of opposition. The one thing she liked about her job was its transitory nature. She came, she provided assistance, she gathered her things and went on to the next assignment. Her job was to initiate therapy, get the patient going on the road to self-confidence, then call in someone else to take over for the long haul. No commitments, no emotional entanglements, no lasting relationships. The situation was ideal for her.

But this case had earmarks of the sort of emotional baggage she usually avoided. There were tensions here, edgy undercurrents. The patient was almost at daggers drawn with the woman who wanted to hire her. Signs were not good. Should she stay or should she go? In many ways, going seemed a real possibility. After all, she had other things in her life that needed attention, such as a sister undergoing a difficult pregnancy. What she didn't need was a mess at work taking up valuable time and effort.

"You don't think I can do anything for you?" she asked.

He put his head to the side, considering. "Not unless you can rustle me up a willing woman and a very large bottle of whiskey. That would help make the wait go faster."

She frowned. "The wait for your eyesight to come back?"

"Bingo."

Her frown deepened. "What if it doesn't?"

"That's not going to happen."

He said it so firmly, with such confidence, she was tempted to believe him. But if she did that, she would be as deluded as he was. Mentally, she shook herself. Who was the professional here, anyway?

"Mr.... Prince Damian," she said firmly. "I can help you understand what has happened to you. I can show you ways to gain control over your life despite your disability. Your attitude will change, along with your independence. And I will guarantee you one thing. Once I'm through with you, you'll be glad you put yourself in my hands."

"Ms....Joplin, was it?"

"Sara," she said quickly.

He nodded. "Sara. I don't doubt your sincerity. And your talented hands."

She blinked, just a little startled by the way his tone made that sound somehow provocative.

"But I'll take a pass. Thanks just the same."

She ought to go. Why not? He didn't want her here. And she usually had a horror of being where she wasn't wanted. The easiest thing would be to get up and leave.

Instead, she found herself making one more argument.

"You'd be making a big mistake," she told him. "You'll only end up having to hire someone else eventually. Why not try my methods for a few days and see if you don't think they're worth it?"

"No, thanks." His tone was clipped. "I may be blind, but I'm not helpless." He turned his head.

She was being dismissed. Usually, that would have sent her striding for the door. But something in the way he was acting put her back up. He couldn't treat her like this! Still, she was going to have to work fast and forget good manners if she was going to make any headway.

"If you wanted to go back to your room right now, how would you get there?" she challenged him.

"I'd buzz for someone to come help me," he said. "The place is crawling with servants. There would be no problem getting help."

"How convenient for you." Rising from her seat, she took a few steps closer to where he sat on the stairs. "But something tells me you're not the kind of guy who is used to depending on someone else for the little everyday maneuvers of life."

"What I'm not is the kind of guy who needs some therapist holding his hand," he said shortly.

"Really. You like to make the world think you're entirely self-sufficient, don't you? But I'm guessing you get a small, deep anger every time you have to sit and wait for someone to come help you. Am I right?"

His face was hard. "Get out of here, Sara Joplin," he said, ice in his tone.

That was as good an admission as she could hope for. She licked her lips and went on. "I'm guessing you feel a little helpless right now."

Anger was simmering in him. She could see it in the way his jaw tightened and she wasn't surprised when he swore, softly but obscenely. She ignored it.

"And if someone were to begin to taunt you, poke at you, torment you, you'd feel even more helpless. Wouldn't you? Because you wouldn't be prepared to do anything about it. It's all about preparation, you know."

To prove her point, she took a quick step closer and reached out to touch his cheek, then drew back, meaning to step quickly out of range.

But she should have known he would be too fast for her. His hand shot out unerringly, grasped her arm and yanked her so that she tumbled right into his lap.

"Is that prepared enough for you?" he asked, his face so close she felt his warm breath on her neck.

"Oh!" was all she could manage for the moment. She was flailing awkwardly in his arms, feeling clumsy and out of control.

But then she realized his hands were sliding down her sides, one of them barely grazing her breast, and she made the effort to jump back onto her feet, turning on him indignantly.

"What do you think you're doing?" she demanded, regaining her balance, hardly able to believe what had just happened.

"Getting to know you, of course," he replied calmly. "Using my hands as my sensory guide. Isn't that the sort of thing you want me to learn to do?"

"You…!"

The sound of people approaching stopped the words of outrage in her throat. Whirling, she found a group of young men coming up the drive toward them. Laughing and calling out, they looked like a party in search of a setting.

"Looks like I've got company," the prince noted, rising to meet them, one hand on the banister for stability. "You're going to have to excuse me, Sara Joplin. It's been nice knowing you. I'm sure you can find your own way back to your car."

She looked at him, then at his approaching friends, and a mad mix of emotions churned in her soul. She felt angry and insulted, dismissed and challenged, all at the same time. But she knew one thing. She wasn't leaving.

"Sara, you watch yourself. You know what those people are like. They've got thousands of years of entitlement bred into them. They think they can grab any milkmaid and toss her into the hay."

Sara had a quick vision of what she must have looked like when the prince had grabbed her an hour or so ago—into his lap rather than the hay—but she laughed into the telephone receiver at her sister's worries. "I'm not a milkmaid, Mandy."

"No. But you're not royal, either. They use people and you know it."

"I want them to use me, use me for what I'm trained to do. That's what I'm here for."

But she hadn't called her sister to complain about her job. It was Mandy's troubled pregnancy she was worried about. She was seven months pregnant and after some unexplained contractions and a little bleeding, she'd been ordered into bed for the rest of the wait. "Tell me, how are you feeling?"

"Oh, I'm fine, Sara. Really. Just a twinge now and again."

"Is Jim coming home tonight?" Jim was Mandy's husband. They were both in their early twenties—much too young, it seemed to Sara, to be going through all this anxiety.

"I just talked to him. I'm afraid he's going to be stuck in San Diego again tonight."

"Darn. I don't like you being alone. Tell you what, I'm coming out to see you as soon as I can get away."

"Don't you dare. Really. Mrs. Halverson from next door offered to bring over a casserole for my dinner. I'm going to be fine."

"Oh, not Mrs. Halverson and her health foods!"

"Don't worry. I made her swear to stay away from those wheat germ croquettes."

Sara shuddered at the memory. "And none of that mulled lentil cider, either," she advised.

In the end she agreed not to try to get to her sister's that night as long as Mandy promised to call her, no matter how late, if anything at all seemed to be wrong. She hung up, not sure if she were doing the right thing. After all, on her list of priorities, Mandy was right up there at the top. She was going through a rough period right now, and Sara wanted to be there for her. So why was she fighting so hard to keep this job, which was bound to keep her away from her sister for days at a time?

She'd gone to the green door, as the duchess had asked, and been welcomed inside and shown to the room that had been prepared for her. Small but nicely furnished, it looked out over the grounds. From her window, she could see the swimming pool and the extensive rose garden with its arbors and walkways covered with sprays of red and white roses.

Though she was getting ready to go down to dinner, she paused for a moment, gazing out over the estate. She could hardly believe she was here. This was so different from what she was used to. All her life it seemed as though she'd been scrambling to keep up, wearing hand-me-downs, getting by with the cheapest versions. Over the past few years, of course, she'd made a good salary and could afford a few luxuries.

But nothing like this. Everything in sight, from the smooth-as-silk paint job on the windowsill to the lush terry cloth robe in the bathroom to the embroidered fabric of the bedspread, was the best, the most deluxe, the sinfully indulgent. She already felt pampered and spoiled and she hadn't even begun to take advantage of all this luxury.

But maybe she ought to enjoy it while she could. If the handsome prince had his way, she'd be out on her ear in no time. Funny, but it had become very

important for her to keep this job. She couldn't have
said why in words.

She'd showered and changed into a dress. A dress!
She never wore dresses. Blue jeans and tailored slacks
were more her style. But at last she was ready to go
down to meet the rest of the family for dinner—and
to face the prince again. What if he ordered her out
of the house? What if he flew into a rage? What if
he threw things?

"You throw something at me, I'll throw it back,"
she muttered in warning to him as she gave herself a
last look in the mirror before leaving the room. *Oh,
sure, and get caught throwing things at a blind man.*
She groaned at the thought. *That would look great on
your permanent record.*

Whatever happened, she was going to enjoy seeing
real royalty interact up close and personal. She'd
never been a tabloid fan and had never followed the
exploits of the jet set, but she'd read her share of fairy
tales as a little girl. Deep in her heart somewhere there
was a soft spot for royalty, right next to the affection
for unicorns and the Easter bunny. Royals were something special, from another world. And now here she
was, about to have dinner with some. She had to
laugh at herself.

Still, she could see that it was going to be difficult
to keep her equilibrium in this place. She'd worked
for wealthy clients before. The smell of money could
be intoxicating. But this was different. There was
more than money here. There was background and

history and a sense of destiny that set these people apart.

Was she going to be able to keep her head on straight? Sure. She had no doubt about it. But facing Prince Damian again was going to take a little more nerve than she usually had to display. Taking a deep breath, she opened the door and looked out into the hallway.

"Okay, Prince Damian," she whispered. "Here I come."

Chapter 3

"Ah, Ms. Joplin. Just in time. We are just going in to dinner."

Sara came down the stairs and into the formal living room, joining a small group. The first thing she noticed were two huge portraits hanging over the fireplace. She assumed the images must be of the king and queen of Nabotavia, the parents of Prince Damian and his siblings. Painted in lush oils, the handsome pair stared down at their heirs with the proud superiority of their time and place and their royal presence dominated the room.

But the real live people were the ones she was going to have to deal with. Looking at the group, she saw Damian, this time without the captain's cap. His hair was thick and dark, his facial features cut as clean and strong as the product of a classical sculptor. But what she saw on that face told her he hadn't realized she was still here. No one had told him. He didn't look pleased and her heart rate made a quick gear shift, going into overdrive, leaving her just a little breathless.

The duchess was waiting to introduce her to the rest of the family. "Let me present you to Crown Prince Marco, Prince Damian's older brother. And Princess Karina, his younger sister. And Count Boris, my younger brother."

"I'm so pleased to meet you all," she murmured, wishing she were better schooled in the proper way to treat this sort of introduction. Her smile felt stiff and phony but she clung to it. She would have preferred a life preserver. She was feeling a bit in over her head.

The entire family were intimidatingly beautiful, every one of them, straight out of a magazine piece on the rich and famous. They seemed very gracious, but still, they were royal! Was she ever going to be able to treat them like anyone else? But then, maybe she wasn't supposed to do that.

She found herself with her hand slipped into the crook of Damian's arm as he escorted her into the huge room—though she wasn't sure if it weren't *her* escorting *him.*

"What are you still doing here?" he asked her, his voice low but icy.

"I just couldn't bear to leave you," she answered, trying to keep her tone light.

The dining room was stunning with its high ceiling and high-backed chairs. Sterling silver glowed with quiet dignity and crystal glasses sent sparks of light and color all around the room. Floor-to-ceiling windows displayed the beautiful gardens outside. Servants moved silently around the fringe, making sure everything was taken care of.

"Ms. Joplin," the duchess said helpfully. "Why don't you sit right next to Damian so you can begin giving him pointers."

"Oh..." She sat down where the duchess indicated, but didn't get her response out as the others were all talking while they pulled out chairs and sat down themselves.

Damian leaned close and whispered in her ear. "I've got a pointer for you," he said. "My food is off-limits. Unless, of course, you want to prechew it for me."

She put her napkin to her mouth to hide her smile from the others. "Don't worry," she whispered back. "I'll pass. This time."

The soup was a light creamed asparagus and utterly delicious. She noticed Damian did very well with his, though he didn't try to eat more than a few spoonfuls. The conversation was quick and pleasant, and everyone made sure that she was included. Crown Prince Marco filled her in on the background of Nabotavia, the little European nation they had all escaped from twenty years before when the government was overthrown by a rebel force. Most of the family had taken refuge in the United States, some in Beverly Hills, others in Arizona. During the past year or so the rebels had been defeated and now the royal family was preparing to return to their birthright.

"When we all gather at the Red Rose Castle we will have a grand coronation," Karina told her. "And Marco will be king. Our parents would be so proud."

Her eyes shone with love and pride for her brother.

"And Garth, our other brother, who isn't here, will be the minister of defense," she added. "He's spent many years as an officer in the American army, learning every aspect of military affairs."

"Boris will be taking over as the minister of commerce," the duchess put in quickly. "He is such a good businessman, you know."

Sara waited expectantly to hear what Damian's job would be, but the conversation had gone on to something else. Had they forgotten, or had his blindness made them less confident in his ability to take a job in the new administration? She glanced at him. His face was expressionless. He seemed unconcerned. But she knew very well that still waters could run deep.

She wanted to say something but she hesitated. After all, she didn't know what the dynamics were here. Maybe it was one of those situations where it was better not to ask a question if the answer wasn't obvious.

The others were in an animated argument about a soccer game score and she took the opportunity to offer Damian help, should he want it.

"I just want to say, if you'd actually like me to help you with anything..."

"No." The pulse at his temple seemed to throb. "I would not like it. I would hate it." He leaned a little closer and said, his voice hard as diamonds, "In fact, I'm not sure why you're still hanging around. I thought I made it very clear that I didn't want you here."

That stung, but she should have expected it. She took a deep breath. "I think you're wrong."

"What in God's name gives you the delusion that I care what you think?"

The suppressed anger and frustration in his voice told her he was on the verge of losing his temper. She could either shut up or she could make her case. Either way was dangerous.

"Listen," she said earnestly, speaking very quickly but trying to keep her voice low enough so that the others didn't hear their conversation, "You're blind. I'm trained to work with the blind. You need me, whether you admit it to yourself or not. In fact, you're just lucky that you've got me here. Take advantage of what I've got to give and your life will change for the better, mister."

Whew. Was that really her, Sara Joplin, notorious for her modest demeanor and retiring personality? Well, that might be laying it on a little thick, but the fact was, she didn't usually stand up and fight this way. Ordinarily, she was never one to hang around where she wasn't wanted. She usually avoided rejection at all costs. But something in her was making a stand here. She was staring rejection in the face and she wasn't running. That in itself was a victory of sorts.

Too bad the prince didn't seem to see it that way.

"What is it about the words 'go away' that you don't understand?" he virtually snarled at her.

She was saved from having to answer that by the timely arrival of the servants with the next course. The entrée was served—rack of lamb with saffron wild rice and baby bok choys. She stared at it, not sure she would be able to swallow much if she couldn't calm her heartbeat down. She tried slow and careful breathing, and that began to do the trick.

Glancing sideward, she noticed that Damian was having some trouble manuevering his knife and fork into position. She bit her lip, wanting to help him, knowing she could give him a couple of tactics that would make eating a lot easier for him, but knowing he didn't want to hear any of that from her right now.

"Well, are you going to give him some advice?" the duchess demanded suddenly, sounding like a woman who didn't think she was getting her money's worth.

Sara looked up, startled. They were all looking her way expectantly. *If you only knew,* she thought giving the duchess a weak smile, *what you're asking here.* But aloud, she said calmly, "I'm afraid not, Your Grace. Not with an audience listening in."

"Oh." The duchess looked startled. "Well!"

Karina laughed. "Oh, Aunt, come on. Of course she can't launch into lessons with us all sitting around watching them. Besides, can you imagine a more contrary student than Damian if we were all involved?''

''He seems to be doing pretty well as it is,'' Sara added, being generous.

''Showing that I really don't need any help adjusting to my new reality,'' Damian said, coolly using her intended compliment against her underlying argument. ''I think you'll have to agree that any lessons you could come up with for me would be a waste of time. So give it up, Sara Joplin.''

His audience sat in stunned silence, then everyone began to talk at once. But he went on eating, ignoring them all. He'd made his statement. Now everyone knew exactly where he stood.

Alone. The way he liked it.

The entire situation was a pain in the ass, of course. He was frustrated and trying hard not to show it. It was all he could do to keep his temper in check and stop himself from lashing out. It wasn't their fault he was blind but he had to guard against taking it out on them. Though he would certainly like to take it out on somebody. Preferably the bastard who put him in this position.

His mind flickered over his suspicions, but he filed that away in the To-Be-Dealt-With-Later folder of his brain. The prime order of the evening was to get rid of Miss Bright-and-Shiny here next to him.

This was the first time he'd come down to eat with the family since the injury. It was humiliating that he couldn't see his food. Just getting it to his mouth, and then trying to identify what the hell he'd just put in there, was exhausting. Still, so far, it was working out pretty well, as far as he could tell. Now and then the fork arrived empty and he still didn't know when food fell, or when something was hanging from his chin. In front of his own family, that was bad enough. But now, to have Sara Joplin here to witness his ignominy...

But what did he care about Sara, anyway? He was going to make sure she found reason to leave as soon as he could. He didn't want her here. Why would a woman stay in a place where she was so obviously not wanted?

The funny thing, though, was that she'd been right about the anger deep inside him. It wasn't little however. It was large and getting bigger by the day. He knew what anger could do, how it could eat away at your guts until you were a hollow human being. He was guarding against letting that happen, fighting it all the time.

Marco was excusing himself to take a telephone call, but Damian barely noticed. He was still thinking about the woman sitting beside him. What was that scent she was wearing? It was fresh and clean and somehow yellow, like sunshine. But it was sweet, too, and a little spicy. He couldn't place it, but he knew he would never forget it.

"Now I do have to warn you," his aunt was saying as he tuned back into the conversation swirling around him, "that we are going to have to see a lot of improvement by a certain deadline."

"A deadline?" Sara echoed.

"Yes. The Foundation Ball in two weeks. The whole thing is Damian's production. He must be presentable by then."

Sara hesitated. "And by presentable, you mean…?"

"Ready for prime time," he interjected. What was the matter with these people? Didn't they realize he had basically fired the woman? "She's worried that I'll embarrass the entire family by staggering around and falling into the punch bowl. She's afraid all our plans will fall through, alliances will be severed, conspiracies will be sparked, and we'll all begin to spiral downward into the slime." He was dying for a drink of water, but he wasn't going to reach for his glass and risk knocking it over at this point. "She's a gloomy Gus, our duchess is. Always sure the worst is going to happen."

"Damian!" Karina protested.

"Look here, old man," Boris said at the same time.

But the duchess brushed them off with a wave of her hand. Leaning forward, she directed her speech to Sara.

"It is imperative that Damian be able to present a strong and confident presence for the new regime. Ruling a country is partly a psychological construct. When confidence crumbles, the entire structure may come tumbling down. And we can't provide anyone with an excuse to back away from promised funding." Her eyes narrowed as though she were trying to see if Sara really understood how important this was. "They have to have complete faith in him."

Sara cleared her throat. "These people do know that he is blind, don't they? They've heard about the accident?"

"Oh, yes, of course. They don't know details. We've kept things pretty close to the vest. But they know something happened. The point is not to try to pretend he's not blind. The point is to show he can manage perfectly well regardless of his sight condition. We can't have him knocking over flower pots and stumbling into the cake."

"Oh, Aunt," Karina said with a nervous laugh.

"At the same time," the duchess went on, "he must be up and moving around, looking vigorous and on top of things. He needs to exude confidence. That's the only way this will work."

"Aunt," Karina interjected, trying to be helpful. "If all this is so important, perhaps it would be better if Marco or Garth—"

"No," she said firmly. "Everyone knows Damian is slated to become the minister of finance. He is uniquely qualified for the position. The ball is a fundraiser, and as the host of the ball, he is the one who must take on this task."

"Of course it's my responsibility." Damian raised his head and seemed to be looking at them all. "There is really nothing to get in such a panic about. My eyesight will very likely be back in time for the ball."

The duchess rolled her eyes significantly. "Yes, but just in case, you know…" She turned to Sara. "I do hope you have some paces to put him through. There is not much time, and he will have to appear as normal as possible."

"That's a little hard to do," Sara noted.

"But are you prepared to try?"

"Well, if the prince agrees to cooperate, I can try, but two weeks is hardly enough time—"

"You see, there's no point to all this," Damian interjected dismissively, pushing his chair back away from the table. "Pack your bags, Sara Joplin. Your work here is done."

Sara looked at the other faces and saw uncertainty. They all seemed prepared to give up, if Damian was so sure nothing could be achieved. In another moment, they would be repeating what he'd said and waving goodbye. For some reason she didn't understand, she couldn't let that happen.

Silence stretched awkwardly while she tried to think of something that might save the situation.

"You know, I do have an idea," she ventured at last. "Something I've heard about."

"What?" said three voices at once, everyone but Damian.

The trouble was, she'd only heard about it, never actually tried it. "I'm not sure it would work," she said, wondering if she should go on with this. "We'd have to test it out."

"What is it?"

She took a deep breath. "I've heard of instances where people used little transmitters in the ear."

After a moment of puzzled silence, the duchess nodded. "Go on."

Sara turned to Damian. After all, he was the one who would make or break this. "I'm talking about a special one-time strategy for the ball. You see, you could wear it like a hearing aid. Someone could be concealed in a place where they could oversee all your movements and give you constant instructions. 'Take two steps to the left, there's a large man with a walrus mustache coming up behind you, the woman in front of you is trying to shake hands.' Things like that."

Everyone stared at her. Even Damian seemed to be staring, speechless.

"Well, it might work," she said, just a little defensive. "We won't know unless we try."

"It sounds crazy," Damian said. "It'll never work."

But inside he was thinking it was the best idea he'd heard yet. In fact, it was downright intriguing. Maybe he'd been a little hasty here. Why not do a bit of reevaluating before he tossed it out completely?

After all, what if his sight didn't come back in time for the ball? Much as he hated to admit it, his aunt was right. It was very important that he come across with strength and conviction as the representative of the new Nabotavian regime. There was no way that he was going to be able to hide the fact that he was blind, but he had to present an image of competence in spite of that. If there was a way for someone to guide him unobtrusively so that he seemed to be in better control, that would help a lot. In fact, the very idea was beginning to make him feel more optimistic than he'd felt in days. No one else had come up with an idea of how that could be done.

Besides, the whole proposal appealed to the experimenter in him. Think of the possibilities.

"I think it sounds wonderful," the duchess cried, beaming. "Sara my dear, you are going to be our miracle worker. We will put our fate in your hands."

He was hardly ready to do that, but her idea was worth pursuing. He supposed he could put up with her for a few days, just to see if things worked out. After all, he didn't have much else to do these days, did he?

He heard Sara laugh softly and the sound seemed to curl through his system like smoke. And that brought up another question. Blind or not, he was a normal man and his reactions to women hadn't been muted by the accident. Was he ready to put up with being run through lessons by a woman who might prove a distraction? Wouldn't that create its own problems?

"Would you be willing to let me hang around for a few more days to give it a try?" she was asking quietly, leaning toward him.

"I suppose it's worth a test run," he allowed reluctantly.

"But I have a condition," she told him.

"*You* have a condition?"

"Yes, I do."

He frowned in her direction. She had spunk of sorts. That could get annoying. "What is it?"

"I'll help you learn to use the transmitter in order to act properly at the ball if you agree to go through the exercises I'm sure will help you deal with your lack of sight."

"Blackmail," he said in soft accusation, realizing he was going to have to keep a tight rein on his relationship with this woman or she would actually think she was in charge. "Is that all you want, Sara Joplin? How much larceny do you have in that sweet little heart of yours?"

She didn't say anything in response and that irritated him. He wanted to know what she was thinking, but without sight, he had no clue.

"Damn it," he muttered. He hated being in this box, with only his hearing, taste, smell and touch to count on. Sight was so important. Without it, he was...well, blind. Unable to judge people. Unable to discern truth. Anger simmered again, just barely below the surface. He was like a man living half a life.

Sara was staring at Damian. His last comment about her having a larcenous heart had shocked her. In a small way, it had revealed something she was sure he didn't want exposed. There had been something in the deep chords of his tone when he'd said it. How many people had cheated him, tricked him, used him and his royal status for their own selfish ends? It could be that she was assuming too much, just from a tone and a few words. But she didn't think so.

Here Mandy had been worried about him using her. Instead, it seemed he was the one who needed protecting. At least, in the spiritual sense. Silly, she supposed, but somehow that appealed to her. Still, she had to wonder what the heck she thought she was doing here. She hadn't even wanted this assignment, and now here she was promising the moon in order to keep the job. Could she pull this off? Gritting her teeth, she vowed to do it and do it well.

"Well?" she asked. "Do we have a deal?"

He nodded slowly. "You've got me over a barrel," he said, with only a trace of sarcasm. "All I ask is that you be kind as you wield your power."

She smiled, feeling pretty sure this was settled, though not sure enough to celebrate. "Compassion is my middle name," she quipped. "I suppose we ought to get started."

Rising, he held out his arm for her. "Shall we go up to my room?"

"Your room?" After nodding to the others, she rose to join him, but she was suspicious. "Isn't there someplace more neutral where we could work?" she asked as they started to leave the dining area.

His free hand covered hers, strong and warm. "Afraid of the blind man, are you?" he murmured.

"Of course not," she responded quickly.

"Don't worry," he said, one eyebrow arched in cynical disdain. "I'm annoying but harmless."

He started for the door but misjudged and hit the

wall sharply with his shoulder. He corrected quickly, but she could see the tightening of his mouth and she knew it cost him. He hated making a mistake like that in front of her after he'd claimed he was getting on so well. And she cringed for him. Still, it might help make her point.

Just before they reached the stairs, Crown Prince Marco returned from taking his phone call.

"That was the county inspector," he said, and Damian came to a stop, listening. "I'd asked him to contact us when the investigation on your accident was wrapped up."

"And?" Damian asked.

"He wanted to let me know they haven't been able to complete their work as yet. They've dredged the lake, but parts of the hydrofoil are still missing."

"Are they going to dredge again?"

"He didn't want to. The expense…"

"They have to," Damian said, and Sara could feel the tension in his arm. "Tell him we'll pay for it."

The crown prince looked pained. "Damian," he began.

But his brother cut him off. "I mean it, Marco. I have to know."

Marco sighed, glanced at Sara, and said, "We'll talk about it later," before bowing to her and taking his leave.

"What am I supposed to do when he bows?" she whispered to Damian.

He turned as though to look at her and a faint smile lifted the corners of his mouth. "Hold your head up high and nod, ever so slightly, like a natural born queen," he said. "Act like royalty and you'll be treated like you deserve it."

She smiled, but she knew she would never take his advice. Deep down, she was a blue jean girl and there just wasn't any help for it.

A blue jean girl, heading into the private quarters of a prince. Suddenly, her mouth was dry. What exactly was she getting into, anyway?

Chapter 4

"Mind if I put on some music?"

"Music?" Sara gazed at Prince Damian blankly.

"Music. That thing with melody and a bit of a beat. Surely you've heard of it."

"Go right ahead," she said, not bothering to respond to his quip. She was still trying to adjust to being in the private rooms of a prince. It wasn't quite what she'd expected.

He used a remote to start a compact disc player. Light jazz filled the empty spaces of the room, and there were a lot of them. The living room area of the suite was large with big, comfortable pieces of furniture, including a computer desk and floor-to-ceiling bookcases. But there was a stark, impersonal quality to it, like a college dorm room on move-in day. She glanced around for evidence of sports teams, favorite souvenirs or family pictures, but didn't see anything of that sort at all. Strange. Either he was a very private, careful man, or he was only passing through.

He was sitting on a couch and she was in a chair. A heavy, glass-topped coffee table sat between them. She'd started their session by filling out the standard questionnaire she'd developed through years of dealing with all sorts of people. It gave her a quick way of getting to what she'd found was most important. So far she'd pinned down the prince's age to twenty-eight years and noted the fact that he was the youngest boy in the family, that he'd been born in Nabotavia but grew up in the States. Now it was time to get into what was often a touchy area—the relations with his mother and father. She decided to edge into it a little sideways.

"The portraits of your parents downstairs are very impressive. They look so majestic. Quite imposing."

"Of course. They're meant to be. If you can't be bigger and better than the norm, what's the point of being royal?"

She smiled, looking at him. His tone was droll but she suspected that was a smoke screen to hide his true feelings of pride and affection. "So as a royal yourself, you're bigger and better than the norm?" she said, letting her voice turn slightly toward teasing.

The corners of his mouth twitched, but no actual smile emerged. "Well, bigger anyway." He leaned back against the plush upholstery. "We royals do our best to live large. Visit swanky watering holes, decorate exclusive clubs with our presence, wear more jewels, drive fancier cars, be better dressed.''

''Be more beautiful,'' she murmured, really to herself.

He only half caught it but his mouth twisted. ''Don't be fooled by beauty, Sara,'' he said softly. ''It's only a mask.''

She paused, pencil to her cheek, and regarded him with interest. ''Are you really this cynical, or did I just catch you on a bad day?'' she asked lightly.

He shrugged and didn't answer. ''At any rate, you asked about my parents. My mother was an angel. My father was a pretty good ruler, but a little more problematic in the morals department. I probably take after him more than her, unfortunately. Now, are we finished with the inquisition?'' he added hopefully.

''We've barely begun,'' she responded primly, while he groaned. ''I assume that your parents are no longer living. May I ask what happened to them?''

He was quiet a beat too long and she looked up at him.

''They were both killed during the rebellion,'' he said at last, his voice as expressionless as his face.

''You mean…?''

''When I was eight years old.''

''Oh, I'm so sorry.'' Her throat closed with dismay. Why hadn't she found time to research his background better before she started asking questions? ''I didn't know.…''

''Don't worry about it. It's part of the package.''

His sudden grin was humorless. "There is always a price for living bigger. You get to die bigger, too."

"I should have known, though. I'm sorry to have sprung it on you so casually."

He turned toward her, his dark eyes shadowed. "Your sympathy is appreciated, but a little over the top. Sad it may be, but it has very little to do with the fact that I'm blind."

"Maybe," she said pensively, watching him with what she hoped was professional detachment. "And maybe not."

He threw his head back, groaning again. "Here we go with the psychobabble. I knew it."

"No," she said quickly. "I promise I'll hold that back. I may think a few 'psychobabble' thoughts. When it comes down to it, I have to admit it does sort of come with the territory." She knew she was contradicting what she'd said to him before, but she was only being as honest as she could be. "But when I do make those connections, I'll keep them to myself. I won't tell you."

He half turned toward her, his handsome face bemused. "Unless, of course, it's for my own good," he said.

"Of course," she replied, then bit her lip to keep from laughing. He didn't miss anything. He was so aware of every nuance. She was really going to have to watch her step with this one. "Seriously, I will try to tamp those instincts down, since you object so strongly."

"I'd appreciate that," he said wryly.

She nodded and went back to her list. "Well then, who raised you? The duchess?"

"No." He gave a short laugh. "The duchess raised Karina, but my brothers and I were mostly raised by another uncle at his castle in Arizona."

"A castle in Arizona?" She had visions of cupolas and spires among the cactus strewn mesas and the picture was an odd one.

"You'd have to see the place."

"Interesting. So your schooling consisted of...?"

"Tutors, private schools, prep school, university, London School of Economics, Harvard Law."

"Well. I'm impressed." And she was.

He nodded, taking it as his due. "You see, I actually do know what I'm talking about."

Her eyes sparkled. "Oh, I don't know if I'd give you a blanket concession on that one," she said. "On economics and law, maybe, but—"

He laughed out loud, and suddenly he looked more relaxed than she'd seen him look before. She stared at him, astonished by how a touch of humor lightened the darkness that lurked in his face, how it made him even more attractive. But it was gone quickly, though this time his usual frown didn't take its place.

"Sara, you surprise me," he said softly. "It might not be such an ordeal to work with you after all."

She flushed with pleasure and tried hard not to. Professional distance, she reminded herself silently. That's what's called for here. And don't you forget it.

But she knew that wasn't going to be easy to maintain. There was a thread of anger and resentment running through him. How could there not be? But there was a lot more to this man. Maybe she would get to see some of what made him who he was as they worked together. Or maybe not.

Suddenly, he held up his hand. "Wait for it," he ordered, and she turned toward the CD player, since that seemed to be the object of his command. "This is the good part. Here it comes."

The smooth, aching sound of a saxophone solo cut through the soft night air, high and sad, full of regret, the sort of sound that curled around your heartstrings and gave a tug you couldn't ignore.

"What's it called?" she asked as the solo faded.

"'Take a Walk Down Lonesome Street.'"

She nodded. Lonesome. That was the emotion it evoked. Something told her he would be playing that piece again tonight, when he was alone. She studied him for a long moment. Here he was, rich, famous, gorgeous, royal. It didn't seem fair that one man should have been granted so much of life's bounty. It made Sara think that the rest of mankind should be allotted something extra in their gene pool to make up for the inequity of it all. But she knew that wouldn't even begin to balance the ledger.

Of course, there was one thing he didn't have. He didn't have his sight. And that was exactly why she was here. Pursing her lips, she got back to business.

"What are you doing for yourself at this point?"

"Nothing," he said, looking restless.

"Nothing?"

"They bring me my food. I sit here and eat it. They take away the empty plates." He shrugged carelessly. "I sit here and listen to the radio or put in a CD. And wait for my eyesight to come back."

She frowned. "You expect it at any moment?"

"Sure." He straightened, turning toward her. "My bruised collarbone and the ribs I cracked are getting better every day. Why wouldn't my eyesight get better, too?"

"It's a totally different situation. From what I've read about your case, there is no physical reason that they've found—"

"As I told you, the doctor claimed my chances were good," he interrupted calmly. "It could even be some deep-seated hysterical reaction I'm not consciously aware of, something that could change in a heartbeat. At any rate, I'll get over it."

She sighed softly, shaking her head. "You're awfully confident."

"That's the secret of success. Confidence." He almost smiled. "And that's my life for now. Waiting. I feel like I'm in a sort of twilight zone."

She hesitated, but finally she had to say it. "I suppose I've made my opinion clear, but I'm going to say it one more time. I think you should face the fact that you might never get your sight back, and begin preparing, just in case."

He moved restlessly and his answer was short and quick. "*You* face it, if you want to. I won't."

She opened her mouth to say more, then closed it again. This was probably not the time for hectoring him. Looking down at her list, she went on with her questions. "Can you get to the bathroom by yourself?"

One dark eyebrow rose. "Why? You volunteering to help me?"

"No," she said carefully, "I'm trying to get a clear picture of how much you can actually do for yourself. What you already know and what you need to know."

"Well, don't you worry. I can handle the bathroom on my own."

She ignored the steely hint of resentment in his voice and pressed ahead. "How do you do it? Get there, I mean."

His lips thinned but he answered her. "I put one foot in front of the other."

"Yes, but how do you know?"

"I count the steps." He said it almost as though he hated to admit making such a concession to his disability.

She nodded, pleased. "Exactly. That's how it's done. You're already on your way to self-sufficiency. But there are many other things you need to consider. There are so many options for the blind today."

He nodded. "Great. I'm happy for them."

"You are one of them."

"But not for long."

She threw him a baleful look she knew he couldn't see, but she felt better having made it. His constant retorts were beginning to annoy her. Maybe he needed a reality check. Maybe it would be better to confront his resistance instead of trying to ignore it and hope it would wither away.

"Dr. Simpson's report does seem to indicate there is a chance you'll recover at least somewhat, but..."

His head whipped around at her use of that word. "They promised me my sight back, damn it!"

"They did no such thing," she told him, trying to be gentle. "No one can promise that."

"It'll be back. If not in time for the ball, soon after."

His attitude was beginning to look less like confidence to her and more like obstinacy.

"The doctor told you there was a fifty-fifty chance you'd get it back. That means there is also a fifty-fifty chance you won't."

"No."

She drew in her breath, tempted to let it drop. But she'd started this and maybe she'd better finish it. "Yes, Your Highness. You're going to have to face it."

His face gave no evidence that he agreed. "If it's not coming back, there's got to be a reason. They should be able to figure out what and take care of it."

"If anything can be done surgically, I'm sure Dr. Simpson will tell you." She bit her lip. A rebellious tightness around his mouth let her know he was simmering with resentment. She tried for a light tone.

"You know those people who are always waiting for their ship to come in? Or for that big insurance settlement to come through? They waste their entire life waiting for something to happen and miss out on all the good things they could have had.''

She knew as soon as she said her piece that she should have kept quiet. She sounded like a school-marm giving a lecture, even to herself. And she couldn't really blame him for the look that crossed his face in response.

Grimacing, she quickly picked up her notebook and began to go over some of the procedures she planned to introduce him to the next day. But he wasn't really paying much attention and she dropped the notebook and sat up straight in her chair, forcing a cheerful tone.

''Well, let's move on. How about this? Could you please get up and walk to the door of your suite for me?''

He turned his head slowly in her direction. ''Why?''

''I'd like to see how you handle it.''

He was quiet for a moment too long and she felt herself getting tense as she waited for his answer.

''There are a lot of things I'd like to see, too,'' he told her coldly. ''But I don't get to. Life is funny that way.''

She swallowed and pasted on a smile. ''In order for me to evaluate your progress—''

''You don't need to evaluate anything,'' he inter-rupted. ''Just train me to use the earpiece.''

Closing her eyes, she counted to ten, her jaw clenched. But it hardly helped at all. ''Your High-ness,'' she began crisply.

"Lose the formality," he said. "My name is Damian."

She drew in a long breath. "I prefer to keep a little formality if you don't mind," she told him, an edge to her voice because she was getting really angry.

He shrugged. "If you must."

She hated his tone. She wanted to tell him so, but she held herself in check. "You are not cooperating."

"Ah, so you noticed."

Her hands were clenched into fists in her lap. "You know, I feel bad for you being in this position, but that doesn't give you license to be rude."

"Rude? You think I'm being rude?" He put his head to the side, considering. "A little short, perhaps. But I wouldn't call it rude. I've been much ruder in my time."

"Oh, yes, I'm sure you're a master at it," she snapped.

She wanted to snarl. She wanted to throw things at him. She wanted to leave. *That* she probably could do. Rising to her feet, she grabbed her things.

"After all, you're some high-and-mighty prince." She stopped in front of where he sat. She was livid. "You seem to think that gives you the right to lord it over people who are only trying to help you. Well, you know what? I don't have to put up with this. I have certain minimum standards and, royalty or not, you're not meeting them. I don't think I can do anything for you. I don't think I *want* to do anything for you."

Turning on her heel, she strode quickly to the door.

"Goodbye," she threw back at him. It was supposed to be a dramatic statement but the effect was pretty much ruined when she couldn't turn the knob. "What…?" She turned on him in fury. "Did you lock this door?"

"No." He was rising off the couch and coming toward her, reaching out to feel his way along the wall. But the infuriating thing was, he was laughing.

"No, Sara, I did not attempt to lock you in my lair. The door sticks sometimes." He gave the knob a twist and it opened.

"But wait a minute," he told her. "Don't go yet." He ran a hand through his thick hair and grimaced. "Okay, listen. I've been acting like an idiot. I'm…" It seemed to take a lot for him to say the word. "I'm sorry. Really. I'll try to behave better."

She shook her head, still simmering. "I don't know if that will help. You are so angry. It comes out in everything you say and do. I don't know if I have the ability to deal with that."

A look of pain contorted his face for a brief moment, then he tried to smile. "I'll work on it. Please stay."

She took a deep breath and began to calm down. She could see that he was struggling. But was it enough? And would he just revert back to the behavior she couldn't tolerate as soon as he had her where he wanted her? "You know, this will only work if you put in some real effort."

"I know." He stood with his weight evenly balanced, seeming to look right past her. "It's not fair to take it out on you. I won't do it again."

Searching his face, she believed him. At least, she believed that he would try. And that left her with mixed feelings. She had almost escaped. If she just kept going, she could be at her sister's in under an hour. Still, to get this man to lower his walls and find ways of freeing himself from his self-imposed prison would be so satisfying. And wasn't that what her choice of career was all about?

"Will you stay?" he asked quietly.

She nodded slowly. "I'll see you tomorrow," she said abruptly. "Nine o'clock good for you?"

"Yes," he said.

She gave him one last look. His head was turned in her direction and she could have sworn he could see her. Shivering, she walked through the open doorway.

"Good night," she said as she left him.

Once out of sight and hearing range, she sagged against the banister of the stairs, closing her eyes for a moment and struggling to get a grip. Her emotions had been on a roller coaster and she felt as though she'd been through the wringer. Some of the things she'd said to him had been so very unprofessional.... Sighing, she had to admit that she should have been able to keep a better leash on her anger. She'd let his baiting get to her and that was her own fault. But he was so impossible. What a man. He was the one with the disability, but she was the one who had doubts about survival.

Taking a deep breath, she straightened and looked at her watch. A flash of stinging guilt made her shoulders sag again. It was eleven, much too late to call Mandy. She should have called her earlier. How could she have been so selfish? Somehow she'd let a handsome man beguile her into losing track of anything other than him. And all for nothing.

Chapter 5

Damian stirred. A deep cold chilled him to the bone. Something had woken him—maybe a dream. He wasn't sure what had roused him, but it was still so dark, he reached for the bedside light. And then he remembered.

A wave of emotion choked him before he could stop it. Anger and resentment mixed with grief. The feeling was ugly and he didn't like it.

Waking up blind, after the accident, hadn't been so bad. He'd been in a lot of pain and at first, the blindness had just seemed a part of it all. He'd been sure it would fade away given a little time and rest. Just a few days, he'd thought. But it had been weeks now, and weeks were turning into months.

From the beginning, he'd refused to give in to de-

spair. His life had been put on hold, every plan in
abeyance, every thought existing with the statement
"when I'm not blind anymore" tagged onto it. That
had been one way he'd held off self-pity. But he was
getting impatient. This was lasting too long. Too
long...

But he wasn't going to let himself think about that.
He had something else to think about now. Sara Joplin had arrived and blown out the cobwebs. For too
long he'd been obsessing about the way his world had
gone dark, playing all the angles over and over in his
mind. How had it happened? Why had it happened?
Who had made it happen? It was good to have something to think about other than the accident for a
while.

Most of his friends and relationships had drifted
away lately. At first, people had been horrified and
sympathetic and had come by to comfort him. But he
hadn't been very receptive and pretty soon the visits
had become fewer and farther between. Yesterday's
surprise from a small group of old friends had been
unusual. But it hadn't captured his attention half as
strongly as had the visit from his new occupational
therapist.

Why?

Because it was something new, he supposed. The
days had been so dreary lately. He'd thought he
wanted her gone, but she'd hung on and as the evening progressed, he'd found that her presence at least
put a little life into things. He'd taken his anger out
on her and she'd called him on it. He couldn't fault

her for that. And he had to admit, it was good to anticipate something in his day besides the darkness.

He felt for the talking clock his sister Karina had given him, pressing down the button.

"The time is seven-fifteen and thirty seconds," the clock told him in its colorless monotone.

Past time to get up. The cold in the room had to come from someone turning on the air-conditioning too strong. If he could see, it would be nothing to go to the control and adjust the temperature, but as it was, he was liable to crash into all manner of things before he found it. Throwing back his covers, he swung his legs over the side of the bed and pulled himself up, testing his positioning for a moment before he started off toward the bathroom, counting every step. Even so, he cracked his ankle against the curved leg of a chair and swore in frustration. That made him lose count, but he made it into the bathroom and turned on the water in the sink, splashing water on his face and gasping at the cold.

That woke him up. Another day. Another long day of waiting. But at least he had a meeting with Sara to look forward to. He felt his way to the shower, turning on the water and testing it for warmth, dropping the light pajama bottoms he wore to the floor. He was going to get clean and fresh and hope for the best. Why not? Maybe Sara would turn out to be a miracle worker. Just in case he needed one of those.

An hour later, after fifteen minutes on his treadmill and another half hour on the stationary bicycle, he sat restlessly in a chair beside his radio, trying without success to find a station broadcasting something interesting. He tried to remember what he used to do in the morning in the old days. Read the paper. That was it. The loss of the ability to read was probably what bothered him most.

He switched off the radio and at the same time, heard someone coming up to his door. It wasn't Sara, but he couldn't identify the visitor from his footsteps, nor from his knock on the wood.

"Come in," he offered anyway, slightly on edge.

"Damian?"

He recognized the voice of his uncle, the duke, and relaxed.

"Hello Uncle," he said. "To what do I owe the pleasure of a visit from you?"

The older man chuckled. "So you know me by my voice, do you?"

The remark wasn't as odd as it might seem. The prince and the duke had never been close. Damian couldn't remember ever having had a conversation of any consequence with his uncle. He thought of him—when he thought of him at all—mainly as a henpecked man skulking in the shadows in order to stay out of the reach of the duchess.

But the duke was his father's half brother, and as such, he was actually his uncle. The duke's mother had been a lady-in-waiting to Damian's grandmother. And his father had been Damian's grandfather. He'd been born illegitimate, a part of the royal family, but not the genuine article. And Damian was pretty sure he could see resentment of that status in the duchess all the time.

But not in the duke. The old man seemed to harbor no anger toward anyone or anything.

"Yes, I recognize your voice," Damian told him. "I'm told I'll soon learn to recognize you by the sound of the breeze in your hair if I study hard and play my cards right."

The duke chuckled again. "I don't doubt it, my boy. You've always been a quick study. Quite a bright little lad you were, in your time. Oh, how your father did dote on you. You being the youngest boy and all."

Damian stiffened at the mention of his father. "I hardly remember him," he admitted softly.

The duke opened a package, paper crinkling loudly. "I brought you something." He pressed a small rectangular plastic box in Damian's hand. "It's a book on tape I thought you might enjoy."

"What is it?"

"It's a reading of the poetry of Jan Kreslau, the Nabotavian poet."

Damian drew in his breath. "That was my father's favorite, wasn't it?"

"You know then. I was afraid you boys didn't really know enough about your father."

Know enough? There had been a time when he'd devoured information about the man, searching the archives that had been salvaged during the escape, reading up on anything he could find in libraries, asking old servants for their memories. His father, the

king, and the most important emblem in his young
world. He'd idealized and idolized him.

But that had been long ago. Maybe he'd learned
too much about the man at too young an age. He
knew he didn't want to learn any more.

"I think I know all I need to know," he told his
uncle firmly.

"He was a great man, you know."

Damian turned toward him. "You can say that?
After the way you were treated?"

The duke was silent for a moment and when he
spoke again, his voice was sad. "You know nothing
about it, my lad. Someday, when you're ready to hear
the truth, I'll tell you a few stories." He rose and
began to shuffle toward the door.

"But right now, Annie has a breakfast waiting for
me, and I feel in need of a little sustenance. Come
and visit me in my office when you feel like chatting.
I'll be expecting you."

Damian sat very still as he listened to his uncle
leave. Then he began turning the cassette over and
over in his hands. If he were Marco or Garth, or even
Karina, he would put in the tape right away and listen
intently, hoping to gain insight into his father's life.
He supposed by listening to a poet the old man had
loved he would come to understand more of how he
had thought. But he wasn't his brothers or his sister.
He already knew more than they did, and he didn't
want to learn more. As he'd told his uncle, he knew
all he wanted to know.

If he could see, he would try for the trash can near

the door. But since he couldn't he stuck the tape under a pillow.

"Bring me something my mother loved," he murmured to himself, "and maybe I'll listen."

Sara made a morning call to her sister and was reassured to find all was normal. She still felt guilty for having forgotten to call the night before, but Mandy didn't seem to have noticed. They had a nice chat, and then Sara dressed in crisp linen slacks and a soft cotton pullover, brushed her hair back into a twist, and paused before opening the door, preparing herself for what was to come.

"Back into the lion's den," she murmured to herself, then shook her head in exasperation. No, it was going to be better today. He would be more used to the situation between them. He'd be ready to learn something. She could do him a lot of good if he would only let her. This was what she was trained for. She could do it. And it was only for two weeks.

Two short weeks of lots of work with a businesslike attitude and things would go fine. She really didn't doubt it. And—she had to admit—it wouldn't hurt to have such a magnificent specimen to work with. She would probably never get to spend so much time with a man like this again in her lifetime. So why not take it for what it was worth and enjoy it?

But her heart was still beating with anticipation. Who was she kidding? Why try to deny it? The little altercation the night before had shaken her more than she had realized at the time. Raw burning anger was not her style. She still wasn't sure just where all that had come from. Something about the man had brought it out in her. She only hoped things went better today.

But before she faced him again she planned to have breakfast, though she wasn't sure where it was served. Her first try in the dining room where they had eaten the night before came up empty, but as she turned away from the doorway, she found Marco coming down the hall toward her.

"Good morning, Ms. Joplin," he said. "I hope you slept well."

"I did," she told him with a smile. "Thank you."

"I'm off to a meeting, but I did want to tell you how much we appreciate your working with my brother. I know he can be difficult, and if you have any problems with him, I hope you'll come to me about them. I'll do my best to see that you are accommodated in any way."

"Oh." She was rather startled by his concern. "I'm sure we'll do fine."

"I hope so." He did one of his royal bows again. "Good day to you."

She watched him leave, so tall and regal and so unlike Damian. And then she remembered she still didn't know where breakfast was. For a moment, she felt lost, but a coolly efficient-looking servant noticed her and came to her rescue.

"Come this way, please," she told Sara, after introducing herself as Annie. "Most of the family has already been and gone, but I believe Count Boris has just arrived. I'm sure he'll keep you company.''

"Thank you," Sara said, following her into a beautiful room rimmed with tall windows and hanging plants. The morning sun turned the atmosphere golden and she took a few seconds to marvel at how real sterling silverware and crystal, set against a hand-woven lace cloth thrown over a table of highly polished cherry wood, created a feeling that could only be described as luxurious.

The rich really do live differently from the rest of us, she reminded herself with a sense of chagrin. Lucky them!

The lone occupant of the room stood and smiled at her, making her feel instantly welcome. He was a tall man, very blond and very handsome, looking as though he'd been sent in from central casting to fill the role of the perfect royal.

"Count Boris," she said, nodding to him. "Good morning."

"Just plain Boris will do, my dear," he said, wiping his mouth with his linen napkin and gesturing toward the sideboard where the food was presented in silver chafing dishes.

She laughed as she picked up a plate for herself. "There's nothing 'just plain' about any of you people," she told him as she began to serve herself.

He looked stricken. "Why? What's wrong?"

"Nothing," she said quickly, taking a sweet roll and putting down the sterling silver tongs. "You're all just so very…royal."

He made a sound that was halfway between a snort and a cough. "Oh, no we're not. We have as many hounds and hedgehogs as any other family."

"Do you?" she said politely, filling her plate with scrambled eggs and buttered toast, though she wasn't really sure what on earth he meant.

"Oh, my, yes. Take my aunt Gillian." He helped her into her seat and sat at the place beside her. "A good sort, really, but she thinks the paperboy is spying on her for the Mafia. Then there's my cousin Kyle who gave up a lucrative legal career to run a small newspaper in Vermont. The town only has thirty-two residents old enough to read, and the cognitive abilities of some of those are somewhat suspect. And, of course, there's Beanie, the family hippie. She's living with a caravan of circus performers on a beach in the south of France."

He poured himself some fresh coffee, frowning when what was left in the pitcher didn't quite fill the cup. "So you see, royal doesn't always mean much. We're people just like everyone else."

"I'll keep that in mind," Sara said with a suppressed giggle.

He nodded as though he felt he'd made his point, and they both looked up as Annie came back into the room with a pot of newly brewed coffee.

"Ah, here she is," the count said with satisfaction. His handsome but rather angular face lit up. "You can count on it. Nothing stays empty for more than a few seconds. It's like she has a sixth sense about these things."

Annie ignored his lighthearted compliment, as any good servant would, and asked, "Can I get you anything else, sir? Ms. Joplin?"

Boris and Sara both demurred and she turned to leave. Boris sighed, his gaze lingering on her trim figure as it disappeared through the doorway. "You don't find many like that anymore," he confided. "She's really taken this staff and pulled them into shape. It was chaos when I first arrived." He took a long sip of his coffee. "My own staff in London are hopeless as well. A surly bunch, the lot of them. All except my man, Egbert. He's a gem, but I had to give him a long holiday, so he's not with me right now." He frowned thoughtfully. "I do hope he comes back."

Sara murmured her sympathy on his servant situation, having to fend for himself in the wilds of Beverly Hills, but his comment gave her a thought. These people did tend to have valets.

"Does Prince Damian have someone to attend him?" she asked.

"Damian? No. He somewhat scorns that sort of thing." He shook his head. "Oh, but they have assigned a young man to help him since the accident," he added as though just remembering. "Young Tom, I believe his name is. Haven't seen him doing much, but now and then he does escort Damian out onto the grounds for a walk and such."

"I see." She gazed speculatively out the window. Why hadn't she thought of that before? Young Tom could be a big help if Damian learned how to make proper use of him.

She'd finished her breakfast but it seemed rude to eat and run, so she lingered, trying to think of something to extend the conversation a few more minutes before she excused herself. "So, you're a wonderful businessman," she noted, remembering the duchess's statement from the night before.

"Am I?" he responded, looking suddenly cornered.

"Well, yes. Aren't you going to be the minister of commerce in the new government?"

"Oh. Yes, that is what they say." He didn't look especially excited at the prospect. "Though I am looking forward to the return to Nabotavia. They say the fishing along the upper Tannabee river is extraordinary."

Before she could respond, an older man entered the room and she recognized him as the duke who had made his brief appearance the day before when she'd first met the prince.

"Your Grace," Count Boris said, rising to bow.

Sara rose too, just in case it was customary, but the duke gestured for her to sit again as he muttered his morning greetings to them both.

"Your Grace, allow me to present Ms. Sara Joplin. She's working with Damian on the blindness thing."

"Ah, Ms. Joplin." The duke was very handsome, his hair a beautiful shade of white and slicked back in the style of an old-fashioned dandy. But his attitude was sweet rather than lascivious, and Sara thought right away that she was going to like him. "Come from a very musical lineage, haven't you?"

Sara blinked. "I'm sorry, I don't know…"

He waved a hand. "Scott Joplin, the turn-of-the-century composer. Janis Joplin, the very loud singer. Are they in your background?"

"Oh." Sara smiled. "Not that I know of. And we don't have many signs of musical talent. My parents are travel writers. The Joplin books?"

"Oh, of course. You see them everywhere."

"Yes." The books were always around. Her parents never had been. Sara sighed silently, wishing she hadn't brought them up.

"What an interesting life you must have had growing up in that family. You must have been dragged all over the world. I'll bet you went everywhere."

"No, actually, my sister and I were usually left behind." Her smile covered the evidence of an old, hardened-over ache where happy family memories should have been stored. "But it's fun to think that we might have ties to some other famous Joplin," she said, to change the subject.

He frowned at her thoughtfully. "You must look into it, my dear. You never know what you may find."

Sara murmured something agreeable and looked to Boris for help. He quickly obliged, changing the subject and she rose to excuse herself and get on with her day. Both men gave her formal bows, which she had to admit made her feel special as she hurried off.

A duke and a count had joined her for breakfast, and now she was on her way to see her very own prince.

"Alice in Wonderland's got nothing on me," she said with a chuckle. What a world.

Damian turned down his stereo as Sara entered his room. He'd been listening to that lonesome sax solo again. He didn't know why it soothed him. Music was a mystery. Its appeal was so visceral. And it was the one art form you didn't need eyes to enjoy.

He thought that the first thing he caught was a hint of her scent, but that couldn't be. She wasn't all the way in the room yet. He knew he must have imagined it. Or maybe she traveled with an ambiance that floated around her like the auras one young New Age girlfriend of his had always insisted people had.

"Good morning," she said.

Interesting. He could tell she was trying hard to sound breezy and casual, but that she was nervous about seeing him again. He had to admit this was the sort of thing he would never have paid any attention to before he'd lost his sight. His universe had shrunk, but in some ways seemed more brightly colored.

"Good morning to you," he said. "I hope you slept well."

"Very well, thank you." He heard papers rustling and knew she was sitting in the chair across from him and spreading out her supplies, ready to launch into her work. The slightly stiff quality in her voice told him she was determined to keep her distance from him today. She was trying to erect barriers. That made him speculate about what she might be trying to protect. And he knew himself well enough to know he would be challenged to break down the walls as fast as she put them up.

"I've just had breakfast with Count Boris and your uncle, the duke," she told him. "Very congenial people. Very nice breakfast. Have you eaten?"

He shrugged. "I don't usually eat breakfast," he said. "And since I'm sitting around all the time, I figure cutting back on eating is a good thing."

"Breakfast is the most important meal of the day," she said, and he groaned.

"When it starts including steak and baked potatoes, I'll think about agreeing," he said lightly. "In the meantime, I'll continue considering it expendable." He paused, then asked, "Did you get the ear transmitter?"

"I called the company that makes them. They're sending a setup over by courier later today."

"Great." He shrugged again. "So we might as well wait until..."

"Oh, no, you don't," she said, as though she'd caught him out and it was just what she'd expected from him. "You remember our deal? You're going to begin to learn a few important things today. News you can use." She shuffled through her papers and he couldn't help smiling, enjoying her willingness to confront him, despite the impulse to protect herself that he could still hear in her.

"I'm also having a white cane sent over," she informed him, and his smile faded fast.

"No," he said firmly. "Absolutely not."

"The white cane is fundamental. Once you learn how to use it, it will give you a freedom you haven't had in weeks."

Interesting. To her, the cane represented freedom. To him, it meant giving in to fate and giving up hope.

"Do I get to wear dark glasses and tap my way along?" he asked. He tried to keep his voice light, but he couldn't hide the sarcasm. "Wonderful. Get me an organ and a monkey while you're at it. I can beg for pennies in the park."

She hesitated. He could feel her looking at him, wondering if he was going to be a problem today, and somehow it rankled. "I know this is hard for you…" she began.

"Hard!"

"But if you plan to fight me every step of the way, this is going to be a long drawn-out process."

He wasn't fighting her. He was fighting himself. And the battle was getting bloody. "I'm not fighting you. I'm just being…"

"Cynical and bitter," she provided when he paused.

He raised his head, resentment surging in him despite all his efforts to quell it. "You find me bitter? I don't know why I should be bitter. Do you?"

She sighed. "You have a right to be, of course."

Her voice was warm with compassion, understanding, even pain for his misery. He felt a prickly sensation in his eyes and realized to his horror that her sympathy was releasing his own for himself. If he didn't watch out, he was going to start tearing up. He groaned, letting his head fall back. Here it was. He'd sunk deep down into the muck with self-pity oozing all around him.

Don't give me any slack, Sara Joplin, he thought, though he didn't voice it. Don't give me permission to feel sorry for myself. I just might take it.

"But the cane is wonderful," she went on, ignoring his reactions. "Using the touch cane travel technique, you'll become so sensitive with it, you'll be able to feel your way along streets and tell what is a curb, what is a building, where cars are...."

"I thought they gave you Seeing Eye dogs to do all that."

"Getting a guide dog is a major commitment," she told him earnestly. "It's not something to be done on a whim. You have to bond with your dog. You can't just get one and then toss it aside. Keep it in mind for the future, along with lessons in Braille, but for now..."

"Do they have Seeing Eye chimpanzees?" he asked, regretting the severity of his tone a moment before and trying to make up for it with a touch of humor. "I'd rather have a chimpanzee. I could train him to mix up Mai Tais and dial phone numbers for me."

She barely hesitated long enough to show that she was ignoring his pathetic attempt at a joke. "Another method to consider is echolocation, using sound shadows to locate obstacles around you. This is rather controversial and usually works best for people born blind, but you might want to try it. You learn to make a clicking sound with your mouth, or with a clicker of some sort, and listen for the echoes that come back from the structures around you in order to 'see' your surroundings. It's using sonar, like bats do.''

Interesting. He had hazy memories of having heard of this before. ''And it works?''

''Some people swear by it. They claim they can almost see the landscape once they get used to it.''

''Yeah? I'll bet they still trip over cracks in the sidewalk.''

She didn't answer and he wondered if she was taking offense at his tone. He didn't want to offend her. But he did want her to realize that, despite what it might seem, this wasn't something he really took all that lightly. The humor was there for a reason. He would rather laugh than cry. But maybe she didn't understand that. Maybe she thought he was just being a jerk.

And—damn it—maybe he was.

Okay. This was it. He'd promised he would try and he was bound and determined to do just that. He was going to make every effort to be good for her. She was trying to help him and despite all disclaimers, he knew he could use a little help. Hard as it was to admit it. Looking into his own soul, he knew he didn't want her to leave. Taking a deep breath, he stared out into the darkness and forced himself to smile.

''Okay, therapist lady,'' he said as lightly as he could manage. ''I'm a captive audience. Do what you will with me. I'm all yours.''

Chapter 6

Sara had to take a nap before their afternoon session. She was exhausted. She didn't know which was more tiring, Damian fighting her or Damian cooperating. Either way he involved her totally. It was hard work but the time flew.

Damian cooperating. What a concept! But she had to admit he was trying. There were times when she felt it was working, and times when she felt nothing would work. Had they made any real progress? She wasn't sure.

She'd spent most of the morning filling him in on options he might want to explore, including some new software programs for the blind, and carefully starting him on a few experimental exercises in maneuvering through his own suite of rooms more easily. She

moved a few chairs and a small bookcase into better
positions, made him listen to certain sounds and identify them, and generally introduced him to the methods she was going to use with him. For the most part,
he'd held back the skeptical comments she could see
forming in his brain at every step. But the thoughts
were there. He couldn't seem to shake the cynicism.

And she couldn't seem to shake the way he affected her. At first she'd assumed it was his natural
beauty that made her insides quiver when he got too
close. But very soon she'd realized it was a lot more
than that. Something in his bitterness touched her, and
something in his pain appealed to her instinctive com-
pulsion to make things better. The night before, his
angry manner had made her furious, but now when it
cropped up, she saw it as a symptom of his need. It
was her job to help him with that. But it was also
becoming her preoccupation.

The tension between doing what she'd been hired
for and letting that overlap into an all too spontaneous
attraction to the man was what kept her on her toes.

So she'd felt a measure of relief when she'd left
him. She'd called her sister to make sure Mandy's
husband was on his way home, then she ate the light
lunch Annie had brought up to her and went over
research and medical papers she'd had sent over from
the agency's library. She was meeting her supervisor
at her office later that evening to report her progress,
and then going to dinner with another therapist she
often worked with, hoping to get some good advice
from either one or both of them. She could use advice.

This was by far the toughest case she'd ever taken, for a number of reasons.

The transmitter hadn't arrived and she put in a call to the manufacturer. A nice young woman assured her it would be delivered within the hour.

The hour came and went and no transmitter arrived. As the time for their next session came closer, she began to realize she wasn't going to get the transmitter in time for it, despite the promises.

"I'm sorry," she told Damian as they met for the afternoon session. "No transmitter as yet. But we have plenty of other things we can work on."

"Work." He pretended to shudder. "That word again."

She looked at him speculatively. He had worked awfully hard that morning and until they got the transmitter, all they could really do was go over the exercises again. Twice in one day for the same old thing might just tax his patience to the breaking point. Maybe it would be the better part of valor to try something else.

"How about if I read to you for a while?" she offered. "Here. What are you interested in?" She picked up one of several magazines littering his coffee table and read off a few headlines. "'Archeology's Greatest Hoaxes,' 'Telling the Truth about Global Warming,' 'The Monkey Man of Borneo,' 'Arizona Mirages, Cities in the Sky.'" She looked up expectantly. "You choose."

He chose one and she began to read but he wasn't really listening to the words. Just the sound of her voice was enough. Funny thing about voices—sometimes they affected him the same way music did. The sax in the jazz piece he loved cut straight into his soul. No words were necessary. And in a similar way, Sara's voice was beginning to get to him. Similar, but different. The sax made him feel that there was someone in the universe who understood the kind of bleak loneliness he'd been living with. Sara's voice made him feel something else. And maybe it would be just as well not to analyze what that was too closely. Still, he could sit back and enjoy it, let it run over him like a warm spring breeze.

"Interesting article, wasn't it?"

She seemed to have finished. He tried to look alert. "Yes, very," he agreed, though he couldn't remember which one he'd chosen.

"Shall I read another one?" she asked.

"Please," he said. "This time you choose," he added quickly, hoping to avoid the embarrassment of choosing the very one she'd just read.

She read about mirages in Arizona and he actually listened to parts of it. Fascinating stuff. Still, there was something more fascinating going on in the room. Her voice was forming images in his mind, like the faint manifestations of a hologram. He could see her and feel her in ways he'd never experienced before, ways that had nothing to do with color or feature outlines. She was becoming almost a spiritual being to him, like an angel. And suddenly that made him uncomfortable. He needed something more substantial to anchor the new emotions he was beginning to feel for her.

"I'm trying to 'see' you," he said suddenly, as she paused for a moment. "What color is your hair?"

"My hair?" Involuntarily, she reached up and pushed a stray strand back into the band that held the rest of it. "Light blond."

"Really?" He shook his head, his lower lip in a pout. "There goes that theory. I thought you had dark hair."

She smiled, shaking her head. She was surprised that he was being so casual, almost friendly. Could it be that he was finally warming up to her and her program? "Why?"

"I don't know. Something about the rich tone in your voice. It made me think of Mediterranean skies and mandolins. I imagined olive skin and silky midnight hair."

She laughed softly. Usually, talk about her features left her feeling self-conscious. She'd never been a beauty and incidents in her childhood had brought that home painfully. But this was different, and she rather liked it. "Readjust your screen and set it for the canals of Holland and snowscapes of Scandinavia."

"Blond hair and blue eyes?"

"Exactly."

There was a pause before he asked the next question. "Are you pretty, Sara Joplin?"

Suddenly her pulse was pounding and old ghosts

were nipping at her heels. "Why should that matter to you?"

"Even a blind man reacts to a pretty woman. It's in our nature." He waited a moment, and when she didn't comment, he went on. "I see you as pretty. Quite beautiful, in fact."

Her breath caught in her throat. She couldn't lie to him. Still, to put her on the spot this way was completely unfair. Swallowing hard, she kept her tone light. "If that makes you happy." But being honest, she had to say more. "Just remember how far off you were with the hair color."

His wide mouth twisted. "Now you think I'm superficial."

Her laugh sounded a little stiff to her own ears. "I didn't need new evidence to convince me of that."

"Ouch." But he laughed, too.

She closed the magazine and started to collect her things. Suddenly she felt it was high time she went back to her room. There would be plenty of time for more of this tomorrow.

"Is it true that the blind use touching the face as a way to get to know people?"

She stopped and looked at him. His face was calm, almost bland. But her heart was beating in her throat again. "Sometimes."

"I've never done it. And I suppose I should learn how. Why don't I start with you?"

She'd known this was coming. It had been obvious. Still, she gasped softly. "Oh, I don't think…"

"Come on," he said, smiling in her direction. "It's

not a big deal, is it? You're my teacher. I need to know what you look like.''

She glanced toward the door, tempted to make a run for it. But that would be silly, wouldn't it? He was right. It wasn't a big deal. In fact, she'd often let new students run their hands all over her face to get to know her. Why was she afraid to let Damian ''see'' her?

She wasn't. Drawing in a deep breath, she squared her shoulders. She could do this. No big deal.

''All right,'' she said. ''I'll just come on over next to you.''

Her palms were sweating and her mouth was suddenly cotton dry. The steps around the table felt as though her feet were being dragged down by quicksand. He looked so incredibly handsome, a lock of dark hair falling down over his forehead, the classical cut of his features emphasized by the shadows thrown from the lamp. She glanced at his hands. They were beautiful, the fingers long and gracefully shaped, but strong. He was going to use those fingers to touch her.

I can't do this!

Ridiculous. She was being a wimp. This was nothing. For heaven's sake, soldiers slogged through leech infested jungle swamps carrying M16s on their backs to save the free world and she was balking at a little touching?

You can do it! And you will!

''Here we go,'' she said, trying desperately to sound calm and cheerful and praying her voice didn't come across as shaky to him as it did to her. She sank on the couch next to him and reached for his hand—only after wiping hers quickly on her slacks. "I'll guide you."

He didn't put up with that for long. Very quickly she found herself submitting to his exploration, her own hands lying useless in her lap. His fingers moved curiously, hooking around her ear, sliding down her cheek, softly testing the length of her eyelashes, tugging playfully on her nose. One minute she was laughing, the next, she was closing her eyes and drinking in his touch. And all the time he was pulling her closer.

"You're softer than you sound," he told her.

She opened her mouth but couldn't think of a thing to say in response.

"And you smell like daisies."

Opening her eyes, she found herself within inches of his lips. "I'm not wearing any scent."

"Do you suppose I'm imagining it?" he asked her softly.

"I—I don't know."

"I'm telling you, you smell like daisies," he said firmly.

"I...daisies have no scent."

"Whatever. The fragrance I get from you puts pictures of daisies in my head."

It was embarrassing how much pleasure his words gave her. She'd never been the type of woman to wear scent. To be thought of that way was new—and very nice.

And then one hand cupped the back of her head. "Come here," he ordered, pulling her close. "Let's test this out." And suddenly his face was nestled into the sensitive line of her neck, behind her ear.

For one long second, she couldn't move. First it was the shock of what he'd done. Then because the feeling was so sublime, warm and tantalizing, full of a certain sweet sensual promise. For just a second or two, she had an image of tangled bodies, long limbs wrapped around each other, smooth skin and crisp hair, and she knew, from the deep, throbbing ache inside her, that one kiss could send her into a spiral of desire such as she'd never known before. A shocking image. A wonderful one. But it was what finally gave her the strength to jerk back away from him.

"You are outrageous," she cried, half laughing, half truly outraged as she quickly moved out of his reach.

He smiled lazily, looking like the embodiment of the instant dream she'd just had. "I aim to please."

Pulling herself together quickly, she retreated to the chair and went back to collecting her papers, glad he couldn't see how her fingers were trembling. "How did you almost manage to turn this counseling meeting into a make-out session?" she demanded. She looked up at him, her papers in hand. He was so gorgeous. "This is not going to happen again," she said, hoping she sounded stern rather than desperate.

"Really? That's disappointing."

He looked adorably regretful. The audacity of the man. She laughed silently, shaking her head. How had

she let him get her in this position? She had to be
more careful in the future. She did have to keep the
upper hand, after all.

But he was so appealing, so attractive, so charming…so sexy. And he was using all those character-
istics to flirt with her. She felt thoroughly compli-
mented in a way she surely wasn't used to. How on
earth could she ignore the rush of euphoria his flirting
gave her?

That made her smile, but gave her warning as well.
He was a man used to a lot of female companionship,
and she was the woman most available to him right
now. What would be a casual flirtation to him could
be devastating to her.

And he *was* flirting, wasn't he? Her heart was still
pounding. What if she let herself go for a change?
What if she responded? Had he sensed how much
he'd affected her breathing? Her pulse rate? Did he
expect her to fall into his arms when he'd nuzzled her
neck? She'd been tempted alright—tempted as she'd
never been before. She had to get out of here before
she did something supremely stupid.

"I'll be calling the company that makes the ear
transmitter first thing in the morning," she told him.
"In fact, unless they can guarantee a quick delivery,
I may run over there and get it for myself. I know
you want to get started on working with that right
away. You'll need a lot of practice to learn how to
use it before this fund-raising thing you're going to."

"The ball. Yes, that's the goal." He nodded. "It's

also my engagement party, you know,'' he noted casually, as though it were a common thing to say.

She stared at him, frozen in time. Could he really have said what she'd thought she heard? ''Your engagement...'' Her voice trailed off into nothing.

''Party. Yes.''

All the blood drained from her face and she was suddenly intensely glad he couldn't see. The man was engaged to be married. Why hadn't anyone told her? It was deeply humiliating to know how much she hated to hear this news. Taking a deep breath, she forced herself to steady before she dared speak again.

''Who is the lucky girl?'' she said at last, thankful that her voice was sure and clear. It was going to be okay. She wasn't going to let him know how much his words had shocked her.

And she knew darn well they shouldn't have had any real effect on her at all. As if she had ever had any reason to think... Well, she wouldn't even let her mind articulate what she'd thought, what she'd let herself feel. It was all so unbelievably ridiculous.

''Her name is Joannie Waingarten. Daughter of the industrialist, Bravus Waingarten. You may have heard of him.''

''Of course.'' Princes, industrialists, heirs to huge fortunes, lords of the manor. What did they all have in common? They inhabited a rarefied plane of existence that was far out of her reach. ''Wasn't he just in the news for—?''

''Investment fraud. But he's going to beat the rap.

No worries. His mother was Nabotavian and he is a big supporter of the return.''

"Of course." She'd said the same thing twice now. That meant she was either dead tired or losing her mind. In either case, the best thing she could do for herself was to get the heck out of here. Rising unsteadily, she looked down at him, trying to think of something pithy to say and failing miserably.

"I'll be going now," was all she could come up with.

"So you're going to leave me alone." He said it coolly, without emotion, but the words cut anyway.

She hesitated. "Don't you like being alone?"

He shook his head slowly. "It's already too lonely here in the dark."

He said it matter-of-factly and without self-pity, but her heart lurched anyway. She wanted to take care of him, to comfort his angst, to dull his anguish. Biting her lip hard, she shook her head. Where on earth had this new urge to nurture him come from? She headed for the door, in a hurry now, anxious to get out before she found herself giving in to it.

"See you tomorrow," she told him, then shut the door behind her. Gasping, she headed for the stairs. How could she have let herself get so entangled in her own emotional responses?

"This is not going to happen again," she promised herself out loud. "Never!"

Damian sat and listened to her leave, frowning, slightly puzzled. He wasn't sure what had happened here, but he knew something had. Not being able to see people's faces, read what was going on in their eyes, was the worst part of this whole ordeal.

It had been a long time since he'd had a woman in his arms who hadn't melted at his touch. He didn't kid himself. He knew it was often the prince in him they were melting for, not necessarily the man. That had never really bothered him. But Sara hadn't melted. She felt so good and smelled like life itself— and yet, she'd pulled away.

Playing around between men and women was common in the set he usually ran with. No one thought much about it, or took it very seriously. There had been signs that she liked it when he touched her, but then again, there had been signs that she didn't. Probably she thought it besmirched her dignity as his therapist or some such rubbish. Too bad.

She'd resisted him. It was just too trite to think that was what had aroused this sensual response he was feeling, but there it was. He was beginning to feel a definite fascination for her. The fact that he hadn't had relations with any woman in months probably had something to do with it. Certain appetites didn't die away just because they were unused. But he was going to have to watch out. He didn't want to risk offending her. Yes, it was true. She was making a difference and getting him to deal with things more realistically. But more than that, having her here was something he was beginning to look forward to, just because...well, just because of who she was.

But right now, he had other things to worry about.

He was still mulling over his suspicions about the accident. So far he hadn't really told anyone else how strong they were.

There had been no evidence of foul play. No one else seemed to think the circumstances were all that suspicious. But the certainty was growing in him. Someone had done this. That hydrofoil had been in perfect shape and had responded like a dream to his touch. What happened when he went into that turn could only be explained by sabotage. There was no other answer.

Or was there? A part of him was suspicious as hell. And another part wondered if he was just being paranoid.

Paranoid? You're a blind man, sitting in the dark, sure that someone is out to get you. You feel helpless, defenseless and very much alone. Who wouldn't feel a little paranoid?

Had it really come to this? Was he a victim? He swore harshly. If there was anything he hated it was to be thought of as a victim. He was no damn victim. And yet here he was, sitting in the dark....

"Today is going to be different."

Sara stared hard into her mirror, trying to convince herself. Today she would be all business. Somehow she would make herself ignore the fact that she'd acted like a complete fool last night. She would try to convince herself, along with everyone else who might be interested, that she really hadn't fallen for the prince like a ton of very unstable bricks, that she hadn't actually allowed herself a momentary dream at his expense, that she hadn't been shocked silly to hear him casually announce that he was marrying some other woman.

A sudden thought occurred to her. For all she knew, he might have told her of his engagement in order to warn her, to keep her from doing anything too embarrassing. Her cheeks felt hot as she imagined he might have been trying to save her from herself.

But on second thought, she dismissed the idea. No. He wasn't trying to gently warn her to keep her head. He'd told her because he hadn't thought it would make much difference. She had to know he could never be seriously interested in a woman like her. All she could hope to have with him under the best of circumstances would be a sexy little one-night stand, like some royalty groupie. So what could it matter to her?

Taking a deep breath, she opened the door and stepped out into the hall. Now she was good and mad at him. Better. Much better.

She found Count Boris in the breakfast room again and she'd barely filled her plate and sat down to join him when the duke showed up, too. They all greeted each other, commenting on how they were forming a happy little breakfast group among themselves.

"I have a surprise for you," the duke told her, smiling merrily.

"Really? What is it?"

He looked startled that she would ask. "Why, if I

told you, it wouldn't be much of a surprise, now would it?''

She bit her lip to hide a smile, thoroughly chastised. "No, I suppose you're right." She did like the old man. His sweetness seemed to shine from his pale blue eyes.

"You're out and about early again this morning," Boris said to the duke. "That must mean that your duchess is gone."

"Yes." The duke picked up a croissant and smiled happily. "She and the princess have gone off to dedicate...oh, a tea room in Dunkirk or some such thing. They won't be back until late afternoon."

"Aha." Boris frowned. "But if they are going all the way to Dunkirk, I doubt they'll be back in time for tea."

Annie had appeared with a special package for the duke, and she gave them all a look. "The duchess and the princess are addressing the Nabotavian Ladies Tea Society in Downey," she said crisply. "They will be back by three at the latest."

"She's right, of course," the duke said, taking the package from her with the guilty smile of a child caught stealing cookies. "Bless you, Annie."

Leaning closer to the two seated, he said conspiratorially, "Annie has fixed me a special snack to take back to my laboratory. That's just between us, now. You'll not tell tales, I'm sure."

Boris raised an aristocratic eyebrow. "We wouldn't think of it, would we Sara?" He waved his fork in the air. "What the duchess doesn't know, etc."

Sara nodded, but her mind was wandering. She was seeing this scene as an outsider might, knowing it must look like an illustration for an article in *Town and Country Living* or a similar magazine. And she was a part of it. No wonder her head had been so easily turned the night before.

But there would be no more of that. No, she was made of sterner stuff. She straightened her shoulders, mentally preparing herself for seeing the prince again.

"If you gentlemen will excuse me," she said, rising from the table after eating very little. "I must make a few calls before I meet with Prince Damian."

"Of course."

"Oh, and Ms. Joplin," the duke said just before she made it through the doorway. "Please tell Damian that his cousin Sheridan arrived during the night. I'm sure the two of them will be getting together without much delay. They are the best of friends, of course."

"I'll be sure to tell him," she said, giving them both a quick smile and hurrying off.

Damian heard her step on the stair. He knew it was Sara right away, but he wasn't sure why he knew it. Still, there was a warm glow at the knowledge, and a slight, barely perceptible stirring of his blood. Rather pleasant, he thought. So his mood was bright as she entered the room.

"Hello," she said.

"Good morning," he replied. "You're late."

"I had to make some calls." She sighed. "Those darn transmitter people! Now they say they are out of the unit we need and it will be at least this afternoon before it arrives.''

Damian's good mood dimmed. ''We've got to get going on that,'' he said.

''I know. If they don't come through today, I'll call another company.''

He nodded, but impatience was nagging at him, along with a deep restlessness that had bothered him since he'd woken that morning. In the old days when he felt like this, he went for a good run to shake the discontent from his system. He was going to have to develop some new way of doing that.

He winced, realizing what he was doing. Sara must be getting to him. He was beginning to let the possibility that this situation was permanent seep into his thinking. He'd sworn he wasn't going to do that.

''So what do you have planned for today?'' he asked her, trying to keep the impatience from his voice.

''First I'd like to go over some things with you. I talked to Dr. Simpson last night, and consulted with some other occupational therapists about your case. They all had interesting things to say and I thought I ought to share them with you.''

He sat stony faced while she went over the various theories her colleagues had given her. He knew it was somewhat irrational, but he didn't want to hear from other occupational therapists. It had taken him time to get used to Sara knowing all the intimate details of his disability. Now she was a part of his world and that was okay. In fact, he knew he would be better for her being there. But he didn't want to share that new relationship with anyone else.

And here she was, telling him things others had said about how he should be reacting, what he should be doing, how he should feel. He took all of it he could stand, and finally he stopped her.

"Sara, I know these people are experts on blindness, but unless they've been there, they can't really understand." He turned toward where he thought she was. "I'm really not interested in their theories about it. But I'll tell you how it really is, so you'll know."

He paused for a moment, then went on. "It is so damn lonely here in this darkness, there are times you feel you'll go crazy. But worse than that, not having sight robs you of your confidence. You have no idea how many goblins rise up to bring you down when you're blind. There is no longer any such thing as dignity, or grace under pressure. Everything around you is conspiring to knock you flat on your ass. Or even worse, on your face." His voice lowered even further. "Do you know how much I hate being laughed at?" he said softly.

"No one is laughing at you," she said reflexively, but she could tell right away that wasn't the right thing to say. He didn't believe it, and he wasn't going to believe her any longer if she kept saying things like that. He didn't want his situation whitewashed. She made a quick and silent vow to tell him nothing but the truth from now on.

She thought she knew what he was trying to tell her. He was a prince, after all. He was royal and used to feeling a certain arrogance, a certain sense of superiority. It killed him to risk making a fool of himself in front of those he considered his "inferiors." It wasn't politically correct to point this out in so many ways, but she knew that was behind a lot of his anguish. His sense of self was being challenged.

"Okay, tell me this," Damian said, moving restlessly. "I know you're primed to get going on 'helping me adjust,' but I want to get rid of this blindness thing as quickly as possible. We haven't really discussed any ideas on going for the cure. Do you or your expert friends have any eye exercises I can do? Any brain food? Magic potion? Harebrained schemes? Quack remedies?" He spread out his hands. "Whatever. I'll try it. I've *got* to get rid of this."

There was passion in his voice, and something close to desperation. Her heart ached for him, but she knew she couldn't hold out false hope and expect him to go on trusting her. "No," she said softly. "There's nothing you can do."

She bit her tongue. She felt like apologizing, but she couldn't do that. She had to maintain a distance. On this journey they had embarked on she had to get him to do things he didn't want to do. He had all the strength and power of his wealth and royalty—not to mention his pure masculinity. She had only the authority of her profession and her dignity. She had to keep it. She had to keep the upper hand.

A pulse throbbed at his temple but he didn't say anything. She looked down at her papers. *Be professional,* she ordered herself. *Stay right here and stick to the matters at hand. Don't let yourself get side-tracked.*

Then she looked up again. He was sitting very still, but she knew emotion was raging inside him. He was like a big beautiful animal that had been wounded and didn't know what to do about it. The old lion with a thorn in his paw scenario. If only fixing things were as simple as stepping up and pulling out the thorn. It wasn't so easy, but she ached to do something. Her heart overcame her sensible side and she couldn't stop herself. Abruptly, she abandoned all common sense. Rising, she went to him, sinking onto the couch beside him and taking his hand in hers.

"Damian, I'm sorry. I know it is almost unbearable for you to just sit and wait. You're used to taking action. When you don't like your circumstances, you change them. That's the way you are. But this is different. You can't make this go away just by your own effort. You've got to give it time."

"Time." Turning toward her, he raised his free hand and touched her face, his fingers trailing lightly over her cheek.

Suddenly she was overwhelmed with awareness of him, of his masculinity, of his magnetism. Her heart began to thump a little harder and she looked at his mouth. He had such beautiful lips, full and clearly defined. She wanted his kiss, wanted it with a surge of urgency that took her breath away.

This was new. She'd never felt things like this for a man before. She'd had boyfriends, dates and one little love affair in college. It didn't work out, but still,

she knew what it was like to get a bit out of control.
But this was different.

Was it just because he was so good-looking? Was
it just because his mouth was sexier than any mouth
she'd ever seen before? No. That was all part of it.
She couldn't lie to herself about that. But there was
more. She was sure there was more. Something in her
yearned for him in a way she'd never yearned for
anyone before.

And he felt it, too—or felt something, anyway. She
could tell. He leaned toward her, cupping her cheek.
"Sara," he began softly, his voice like a provocative
touch.

"No."

The word came out of her mouth before she
thought it in her head and she knew right away that
at least one of her instincts was still running on all
cylinders. She backed away. What she'd almost let
happen here, couldn't. He was engaged for heaven's
sake. And she was his therapist. This was all wrong
and she wasn't going to let herself fall into the trap.
Jumping up from the couch, she stood looking down
at him.

"You are just like a kid who thinks he can get out
of the test by distracting the teacher," she said
briskly, hoping to mask the beating of her heart. "It's
not going to work, mister. We're going to go over
these exercises."

It took a moment, but finally a slight smile tilted
his gorgeous mouth and he responded.

"Lead on, Macduff," he said. "I'm ready to learn."

She felt relief, and a sense of affection for this troubled man. She only hoped she could find a way to reach him and convince him that what she had to give would help him in the long run. Because Damian needed help. And she could give that to him.

They got to work and quickly found a pattern that seemed to supply the sort of repetition he needed. And all the while, she managed to maintain her reserve, mostly through sheer willpower. And though she still sensed a thread of underlying turmoil in him, he was good-natured and cooperative. So why at the end of the session did she feel drained and exhausted, as though she'd just run a marathon?

She stopped and looked at him for a moment. This was so much more difficult than it should be and she wasn't sure why. She'd had worse cases before. She'd had monsters who threw themselves on the floor and screamed and kicked until she put them under a cold shower to get their attention. She had one little girl who mimicked everything she said until she thought she would go mad. She'd had a six-year-old boy who spit his food at her. This should be a cakewalk compared to that. But somehow it wasn't.

In every other case, she'd always found a way to get through to the core person and begin the process of give-and-take that was so essential in therapy. So why was she feeling so uncertain with Damian?

Maybe because, despite his moodiness, he charmed the socks right off her, and that set off all her alarm

systems. She was having a very hard time remaining
reserved and objective with him and she realized that
given a chance, she could get too close. She closed
her eyes and sighed. It was true. She couldn't deny
her growing attraction to him. She could make all the
promises she wanted, set up all manner of vows, but
she couldn't really predict what might happen if she
stayed near him.

So—should she go? Should she admit defeat and
get out of here?

Chapter 7

"**W**hy the heartfelt sigh?" Damian asked Sara, frowning in her direction.

She hesitated. She'd sworn she was going to be honest with him. Here was her first chance to prove it.

"I was just trying to decide if I want to stay, or if I should get someone else to come out and take over for me."

"What?" One dark eyebrow rose in consternation. "Why? What's wrong?"

She took a deep breath and answered carefully. "I don't feel like we are...connecting quite the way we should." Okay, she was fudging a little, but she couldn't tell him she had to go because she was afraid she was getting a crush on him. That much honesty

was just a little too much to ask of her. "I'm wondering if someone else might be a better fit for you."

"We'll never know," he said simply. "Because I
won't allow anyone else in here. It's you or nobody,
lady." And he had the nerve to smile when he said
it.

She bit her lip. "Now you're being unreasonable."

"No. I'm telling it like it is."

"But you didn't want me at first."

"I want you now."

His words hung in the air between them. She swallowed hard, glad he couldn't see her face turning
bright red. Clearing her throat, she began to gather
her papers.

"Well, by this afternoon, we should have that darn
transmitter. We'll see how things go with that."

"Things will go well," he predicted. "I'm counting on you to make this crazy scheme work for me."

She nodded. "I hope so. But you do know that
once we have that mastered and you launched with
your exercises, I'll be moving on. You'll be assigned
a new therapist."

His face darkened. "I thought we just got through
with that topic. I don't want anyone else."

"Damian, you have to understand. I don't do long-
term. My specialty is establishing a routine, developing a course of study, and then I hand the patient
off to someone who is better at the day-to-day stuff.
That's the way I work."

"You'll stay until after the ball."

He said it like a royal command. She looked up at

him and the sight tugged at her heart. He thought he was going to change her mind. Well, he was wrong.

"I'll do my best to help you get through the ball," she promised. Then she remembered what his interest in the ball was all about and her emotions churned. "I know how important this engagement party is to you."

She winced as she heard her own inflection, especially after she saw his head come up in reaction. Great. She didn't have to put her reservations in words. Her own voice was betraying her.

"I've got to get married, you know," he said, the corners of his mouth tilting as though he saw some secret joke here. "It's time. I'm heading for thirty."

"You make it sound so romantic."

He gave her a look that said it was hard to believe she could be so naive. "But it's not romantic at all. It's dollars and cents."

She blinked, sinking into the chair and looking at him curiously. "I'm afraid I don't understand."

"It's purely a business arrangement. She'll go on with her life and I'll go on with mine." He leaned forward, his elbows on his knees, his hands clasped together. "We barely know each other, Sara. I know you better than I know Joannie Waingarten. It's a marriage arranged by lawyers and financial planners. She wants my title, I need her money."

"Her money?" That didn't make any sense. Wasn't he rich? And even if he wasn't, did he really think playing gigolo was a good idea? The idea repelled her. Maybe these people really were more different than she'd thought at first.

"What do you need her money for?" she asked him. "You're young and smart. Go make your own money. Get a job. Lots of blind people do, you know."

He looked surprised, then laughed. "I'm a prince, Sara. I don't go to work. It's not like that. I'm given positions where my name and title are worth a lot to someone. I get offers all the time."

Okay. She could understand that. Sort of like famous athletes and movie stars doing endorsements. But couldn't he do that without the lifetime commitment? "Then take one of those offers and make them give you a lot of money for it," she suggested, still bent on thinking of ways he might avoid this crazy marriage.

He laughed at her. "You have a comical way of seeing the world."

"I like to think of it as a practical way."

"I'm as practical as the next man, believe me." He sobered, turning her way. "And I think you're getting the wrong idea of what is really involved here. The money that I need, the reason I'm marrying Joannie Waingarten, is for Nabotavia and the return, not for myself personally. It's going to take a lot of money, a lot of very big money, to set up a new government successfully. As minister of finance, it will be up to me to secure a lot of the financial backing."

That made her feel a bit better about his motives, but it didn't help keep him out of the clutches—and

that was how she couldn't help but think of them—
of Ms. Joannie Waingarten. In her mind, the girl had
taken one look at Damian and said, "Daddy, buy that
for me!" The fact that Damian was for sale as a ser-
vice to his country, rather than to support a playboy
lifestyle, was some consolation. Still, she thought the
whole deal reprehensible. Not to mention moldy—as
in out of the dark ages. No two ways about it—she
disapproved. But who was she to say so?

"You're awfully young to be a finance minister,"
she pointed out, changing the subject.

"We're all young, all of us going back. The old
ones are tired. The middle ones were mostly wiped
out in the rebellion. So it's up to us, to Marco and
my other brother, Garth, and Boris and Karina and
me. As well as assorted others you haven't met."

She pictured the group of them returning together,
all so beautiful, so tall, so noble—or so it seemed.
The entire situation made a romantic portrait in her
mind, like something out of myth and legend. She
could see them crossing the drawbridge into the castle, banners flying....

"Oh, by the way," she said, suddenly remembering. "I was supposed to tell you that your cousin
Sheridan is here."

"Sheridan?"

His reaction surprised her. There was nothing spe-
cific she could put her finger on, but somehow he
suddenly seemed more alert, almost as though poised
for action.

"Did you see him?"

"No. The duke told me to tell you he had arrived during the night. He seemed to think the two of you would be getting together very soon."

Damian sat still for a moment, obviously thinking. Then he reached for his cell phone and flipped it open.

"Kavian," he said as he reached the butler. "Can you tell me where Lord Sheridan is at the moment?" He listened for a moment, then said, "Ah. Thank you, Kavian," and rang off.

"He's gone out," he said slowly, his brow furled.

Sara waited, watching him, wondering why he seemed so intense.

He turned toward her. "He's gone into L.A. to see his lawyer about something," he told her. "He'll be back about two or so. What time are you planning for our afternoon session?"

She hesitated. "I thought about two, but if you'd like to put it off until…"

"No, not at all," he said firmly. "Come at two. I want you here when he comes up to visit. I need your eyes."

"My eyes?" She stared at him blankly.

"Well, I can't use my own, can I? So I need some help. I want you to watch Sheridan for me."

She shook her head. "I'm not sure I understand."

"I need to know what his reactions are. I want you to watch him and observe his reactions, and when he's gone, I want you to tell me what they were."

This was a little crazy, as far as she was concerned. She didn't know the man. How was she going to judge his reactions? She wished she knew what Damian wanted to see, what he seemed to worry about. But something told her asking wouldn't get much of a response. So she began putting her things together in preparation for departure, and she said lightly, "Where did you get the idea that I might have a photographic memory?"

He raised an eyebrow. "You don't?"

"No."

His mouth twisted. "Develop one, quick."

She stood, her books in her arms. "Aye-aye, sir. Any other orders while we're at it?"

"No. Just don't stay away too long. I'll miss you."

"I'll miss you."

Oh! She could scream. Blind or not, he knew how to push the buttons that set her off. Probably through much practice, she told herself cynically. Don't fall for his tricks!

She wouldn't. She was too level-headed for that. And she had too much work to do and things to think about. She ate her lunch while going over some abstracts, then read some references in a medical journal. With almost two hours to go before she had to be back at Damian's room, she lay down for a rest and promptly went to sleep.

She awoke an hour later, her head still full of dragons and unicorns and damsels in distress, all of whom had just been running amok in her dreams. But all that quickly faded as she thought of Damian. Just thinking of him gave her much the same feeling she got when she set lit candles around her tub and filled it with fragrant water and bubbles and took a long, luxurious bath. Somehow he made her heart beat faster and made her feel lazier at the same time. That didn't work in the real world. But in dreams...

Going downstairs, the house was eerily quiet. No one seemed to be about. She had an urge to take a look at the library and she was just wondering where it was, when a sound to her right caused her to whirl in surprise.

"*Psst!* Ms. Joplin. Come this way. Quickly!"

It was the duke gesturing to her from down a dark hallway. As she started down it, he disappeared around a corner. She walked carefully, wondering why he'd vanished, feeling her way in the gloom.

"Ms. Joplin," he said, opening a door right beside where she stood.

"Oh!" she cried, jumping. "You startled me."

"Sorry, Ms. Joplin, but I did want to show you something and I would prefer that the servants not know about it." He gave her his sweet smile. "Some of them do tell the duchess everything, you know, and somehow once something is whispered in her ear, it takes on a whole new aspect that was never meant to be. If you take my meaning."

"Of course," she murmured, though she wasn't absolutely sure and was feeling a little shaky about all this herself.

He opened the door a little wider and beckoned. She slipped inside the room and found herself in a combination lab and library, with books open and papers littering the floor. Along the wall, just under the low windows, were a variety of mice in cages. Some sort of blue liquid gurgled softly in a beaker on the counter. A computer hummed on the desk. The entire atmosphere was that of an old-fashioned scientist's laboratory.

"Oh, my," Sara said, for lack of anything better to say.

She looked down at a large leather-bound book lying open on a sort of writing easel. The pages seemed to portray family trees, but the lettering was old-fashioned and illuminated, like bibles from the Middle Ages.

"Oh, just let me take care of that," the duke muttered, hurrying to close the large book and lock it with a key on a chain around his neck.

"Now look here," he said, jamming rimless reading glasses on his prominent nose and pulling papers out of his printer. "I've found your Joplin ancestors back to Jonathan Joplin who brought his wife and family to America on the good ship *Fair Maiden* in 1759. They settled in New Jersey. I'm afraid I can't find any ties to the musical Joplins for you. Such a pity."

Sara was astonished. She leafed through the papers, noting the diagram of a good part of her family history on her father's side. "How did you find all this so quickly?"

His smile would have done a Cheshire cat proud. "A lot of it is on the Internet, if you know where to look. I'm just starting on your mother's family. The name is Harkinora from what I've been able to gather in her biography. I'll let you know what I find there.''

Sara was speechless. She looked down at the names on the pages. These were all hers. People she was tied to. People who carried the genes that made her who she was. Her family. A lump rose in her throat. What a wonderful thing the duke had done for her.

Looking at him, she tried to put her gratitude in words, but they failed her. Impulsively, she leaned forward and planted a solid kiss on his leathery cheek.

''Oh, my.'' He looked almost bashful. ''My dear, it's nothing. I enjoy this sort of research. It's my life to delve into the unknown.''

''You're a dear, sweet man to do this, regardless of your motives,'' she told him, and only a tiny little voice inside said, You're talking like this to a duke? ''This is one of the nicest things anyone has ever done for me.''

He told her to expect more results by dinnertime and she left his office in a joyful mood. That dimmed when she found the transmitter still hadn't arrived. Resigning herself to waiting until evening to begin work with it, she made her way back toward the main entryway to the house. Suddenly there were people everywhere. The butler nodded to her in passing, and then she saw Count Boris striding up the walk from the garage area, and a young man was coming toward her down the stairs from Damian's rooms.

''Hello,'' the redheaded stranger said, giving her a friendly grin. ''I'm Tom. You must be Sara Joplin.''

"*Ms.* Joplin to you young man," Boris said as he approached them, his brow furled in disapproval.

"Whatever," the youngster responded with a good-natured shrug.

"You're the prince's attendant, aren't you?" she asked him.

"Sure." He stuck out his hand and took hers in a friendly shake, while Boris groaned in the background. "It's a really cool job. He doesn't need me much, and all kinds of neat people come to visit him. Including movie stars." His green eyes sparkled and Sarah laughed.

"I may call on you to help the prince learn some new methods," she warned him.

He shrugged again. "I'm available. Call me any time." Turning to go, he called back over his shoulder, "Nice to meet you, Ms. Joplin. See ya' later." And he pretended to throw a friendly punch the count's way as he passed him.

"Did you see that?" Boris asked Sarah, mournfully shaking his head. "There's no hope for these young servants. They just don't have the right attitude."

"He may be missing a forelock to tug on, but I think his attitude is going to be just what I can use." She gave him a wave as she turned to go up the stairs and realized at the same time that he probably thought *that* was a bit too familiar as well.

Damian was ready for her. He was disappointed that the transmitter hadn't arrived, but he had no hesitation in going on with other methods and they launched into work right away. She'd brought along a compact disc of sound exercises, with graduated complexity, meant to help train the ear to pick up aural clues and thereby help the blind gain a fuller picture of their surroundings. He seemed to catch on very quickly, and in some ways, he seemed more focused than he had been before, a bit more intense. They worked on echolocation techniques and clicking, and he understood the concepts with no problem at all. But twice he asked her for the time, and she knew he was wondering where Sheridan was.

It was almost four when they declared the lesson over for the afternoon.

"Your cousin never showed up," she noted as she packed her things away.

"He'll get here."

She looked at him. He was turned toward the doorway, listening for footsteps.

"Tell me why you're so interested in your cousin's reaction to seeing you again," she asked at last, curious.

He was quiet for a moment. She assumed he was thinking over whether to tell her or not. Finally, he patted the couch next to where he was sitting and said, "Come here. Sit by me for a moment. I'll try to explain."

She dropped beside him and he reached for her hand, sliding his fingers down the length of hers before holding it tightly. She understood right away that he wasn't being provocative. He needed contact with her response, and since he couldn't get it by sight, he was going to try to read her reactions through touch.

It was a good way to try to re-create the normal give-and-take of everyday conversation. That made her smile. He was learning fast.

"Okay. I'm going to tell you a little bit about Sheridan." His fingers laced with hers. "His mother was my mother's twin sister. We're the same age. In some ways, he's been more of a brother to me than a cousin, closer than Garth and Marco. For the first few years after my parents died, I was considered a little too young to go live in Arizona with the others, so I was sent to live with Sheridan's family. We were inseparable. Even after I was sent to Arizona, I spent a lot of time with Sheridan and his family, and he spent most of the rest of the time with me and mine. We were roommates in prep school, and in college. We studied at the same graduate schools. We're as close as two men can be." He paused, then smiled. "And at the same time, we're as competitive as two men can be, too. We're always trying to beat each other at everything. We were racing each other when I had the accident."

"Oh." She knew instinctively that this was an important bit of information, though she didn't have enough background yet to pinpoint exactly why.

"I haven't seen him since, and I've been wondering why he stayed away so long. I don't know if there is some reason...." His voice trailed off and he looked troubled.

She glanced down at their clasped hands and felt the warmth of his. Heat was spreading through her from his touch and she began to worry that he could

feel her pulse beginning to race. With effort, she kept
her breathing deep and slow, trying to keep calm. But
she knew she couldn't stay here like this much longer
and keep her feelings under wraps.

"I don't know if Sheridan is going through something that he's keeping from me." He turned toward
her, his eyes shadowed. "It's so frustrating not being
able to see faces. You get a lot of your information
about life and love and everything else from faces.
Voices can tell you a lot, but faces hold the complete
story. That's why I want you to watch Sheridan when
he arrives. I know he'll never tell me if there is something wrong. Ordinarily, I would be able to tell by
looking into his eyes. But this time, you're going to
look into them for me."

"I'll do my best," she said. "Though I can't promise I'll know what his face is trying to say, even if I
see it."

He nodded. "I know that." Before he got another
word out, steps could be heard on the stairs. His hand
tightened in hers and she looked at him, surprised
again. Surely there was more to this than mere curi-
osity.

"Here he comes," he said. He rose to greet his
cousin, and she stepped away from the couch, planning to open the door for the visitor. But she never
got the chance. Sheridan beat her to the door and
came bounding in like a large and very enthusiastic
puppy.

"Damian!" he cried, lunging forward and throwing

his arms around him. "It is so good to see you at last!"

"Sheridan." Damian's greeting was more tepid. "How are you?"

"I'm great, but you…" Sheridan drew back and looked at his cousin, his eyes filled with tragedy. "I can't believe you like this. This just wasn't meant to be."

"Accidents happen," Damian said dryly.

"At least you're alive." Sheridan's voice was choked with emotion. "When I looked over and saw your boat breaking up, I thought you were a goner, man."

"I had a few thoughts along those lines myself." Damian moved restlessly. "So…where have you been? Why'd you leave?"

Sheridan grimaced. "You know I didn't want to leave you at a time like that."

Damian was standing rather stiffly. "I heard you took off for Europe right away."

Sheridan nodded, glancing at Sara and giving her a fleeting smile. "I didn't want to bother you with it, with all you've got to worry about, but…well, they contacted me the day after the accident and told me Mum had suffered a stroke."

Damian's face changed. "A stroke! Why didn't someone tell me?"

"Hold on. She's okay. It turned out to be a false alarm, really. She's been sick, but it's not that bad any longer. I stayed with her as long as I could. You know how she is. She doesn't make it easy."

"Damn." Damian looked troubled. "I suppose I should call her."

"She may come out to see you soon. She's so upset about what happened to you. I'm sure she'll be here as soon as the doctor lets her travel."

Sara watched the exchange between the two of them with keen interest. She'd been assigned the job of watching Sheridan's reactions, but she found Damian's much more interesting. Sheridan seemed genuine and openhearted, a man without guile or hidden motives. Damian, on the other hand, looked stiff and slightly suspicious. His face was guarded, his manner cool. She wished she knew what the problem was. And she knew darn well there was one.

They talked on. She was introduced after a few minutes and Sheridan gave her a very warm smile. Gradually, Damian's stiffness was melting. It was evident he couldn't resist Sheridan's impulsive charm. Sara was pretty sure there were few who could have.

"Tell you what," he said at last. "I'm taking you down to the Areo Club for dinner. Most of the old gang will be there. They'd love to see you."

Reluctance was plain on Damian's handsome face. "I don't know. It's pretty hard for me to maneuver in public."

"Come on. You need to get out of here. We should be able to handle it, the two of us. Don't you think I can do it, Sara?" he asked her.

"I'm sure you will do fine," she said calmly. "But if the prince takes Tom along, it will be that much easier for both of you."

"Take Tom along?" Damian's face cleared. "What a good idea. Yes, I'll take Tom along." He began to look enthusiastic about the outing. "Thanks, Sara."

It warmed her heart to see him begin to look happier. She was trying to ignore a faint little stirring of jealousy—after all, *she* was the one who was supposed to be helping him—but once he began to show some excitement, all her reservations faded away. She hoped he would have a good time.

Still, something about the meeting between these cousins bothered her. Both men were exceptionally handsome, and both could charm birds out of trees. But there was something about Sheridan that struck a strange note with her, and she couldn't put her finger on what it was.

"Jealousy," she decided at last as she left the two of them to go back to her room. "You want Damian all to yourself, don't you Sara Joplin?"

Talk about pipe dreams. She laughed at herself and put it all behind her.

Chapter 8

"Crown Prince Marco had to make a sudden trip to New York," Count Boris told Sara as they waited to go in to dinner that night. "He asked me especially to tender his regrets to you and his apologies for not saying goodbye in person. He also wanted me to tell you that Kavian has numbers for where he'll be staying in case you need to get in touch with him about anything."

About Damian, he meant. She smiled and thanked the count, but all the time she was wondering why Marco would think she might have enough trouble with his youngest brother to feel the need to call him in New York.

They had a quiet meal. The duchess and Princess Karina were back from their sojourn to Downey and they, along with the count, were Sara's only dining companions. The two ladies were tired from their day, so conversation was polite and low-key, though she did learn a bit more about Marco's past.

"It's a tragic story," Karina told her sadly. "He married Princess Lorraine, his childhood sweetheart, and they had two children, a boy and a girl. They were the perfect family in every way, so very happy. Then Lorraine was killed two years ago in a traffic accident in France. Marco has only barely begun to come out of the shock of it."

"What happened to the two children?" Sara asked. She hadn't noticed any young ones in the halls.

"They are spending most of the summer with their grandmother, Lorraine's mother. She's been a god-send to Marco. I don't know what he would have done without her."

"She's a bit of a busybody if you ask me," the duchess said, giving her niece a significant look. "He's going to have problems when he marries again."

"Oh, Aunt!"

"I mean it. It's been arranged that he marry Prin-cess Illiana who has been living in Texas. Well, when that happens, do you think Lorraine's mother is going to hand her daughter's precious children over and walk off into the sunset? I hardly think so. There's trouble ahead, mark my words."

The two women discussed the issue for a few more moments, and Count Boris got in a comment or two, but Sara was thinking about the haunted look she'd seen in Marco's eyes from the first time she'd met him. And then she remembered that she'd heard a few whispers that hinted that Princess Karina had an unhappy romance in her past as well. She glanced at the young woman. Her face was so pretty and so very animated. Could she be hiding a broken heart?

Hearing Sheridan's name mentioned, she asked about him.

"Sheridan is a live wire," Princess Karina said. "It's never boring when he's around."

"Sheridan and Damian were born just days apart," the duchess explained. "Their mothers were twin sisters, you know. And the boys were raised together after the escape."

"Once those two get together, there's usually hell to pay," Count Boris noted dryly. "I doubt you'll see the prince back tonight."

"Oh, Boris, I think you're overstating the case. They just like to have a little fun." Karina turned to Sara. "They're practically twins," she added with an affectionate smile. "Did you notice how alike they look?"

No, she hadn't. She wrinkled her nose, thinking back and still not really seeing it. Both were tall with dark hair and blue-gray eyes, both were exceptionally handsome men, but Sheridan had something of a superficial look, in her opinion. He looked like a playboy. And Damian, despite his reputation, didn't—at least not to her. Damian had a strain of unhappiness in him, which seemed only natural considering what he was going through. But he also had a warmth and a humor that reached out and touched the person he was with. She had a feeling that the right word or sentiment would make him smile at any moment— smile with an understanding and a regard for what that person was thinking and saying....

Oh, good grief. She stopped herself cold, staring down at her plate. What on earth was she doing? Of course the mythical ''person' she was thinking about was herself. She was building castles in the air, wasn't she? Building Damian up into some sort of paragon who understood her as no one else could. Her ideal. Pretending something could happen between them, when she knew very well that was impossible.

A small kernel of panic nestled into the depths of her stomach. This couldn't be happening. She never got close to her clients. She knew it only led to disaster and heartbreak. And here she was, playing with fire. After only two days on the job.

She looked around quickly to see if the others had noticed her private internal drama, but they were arguing about the pronunciation of a Nabotavian word and were paying no attention to her. Relieved, she calmed herself. It was going to be okay. She was levelheaded. She'd never gone off the deep end before and she wouldn't let herself do it now. The prince was just a client, like any other. Very soon, she would be moving on.

She was surprised a few hours later when she got word that Damian was back and waiting for her. Grabbing the box with the transmitter, which had arrived just before dinner, she made her way toward his room, embarrassingly buoyed by the fact that he'd returned in time for their session. As she came around the corner and looked up, she saw Sheridan just leaving Damian's doorway and starting down the stairs. Lost in thought, he didn't notice her until they passed one another, and his face was drawn and serious, as though he had a problem with no solution. That fell away quickly with his smile as he greeted her. But it seemed a little strange.

Still, she forgot all about it once she'd opened Damian's door and found him lolling on the couch, listening to music.

"Hey," he said, looking up almost as though he could see her. "We went out looking for gorgeous women, and then I remembered I had one right here at home. So we came back."

She could see right away that he'd been drinking. He was sprawled back as though his bones were made of butter. His shirt was unbuttoned low on his chest and a lot of dark, shiny hair had fallen over his forehead. He was so impossibly stunning-looking, her heart made a leap into her throat and stayed there, beating hard.

"I'm…I'm glad you did," she said when she could manage it. "The transmitter arrived. Would you like to try it out?"

"No." He rose to his feet more smoothly than she would have thought possible in his condition. "I want to dance." He reached for her and suddenly she found herself in his arms. "They're playing our song," he told her as he pulled her closer and began to sway.

She didn't recognize the tune. It was something with a soft Latin beat. But that hardly mattered, because her senses were already on overload, full of the feel of his muscular body, the smell of expensive liquor on his breath, the sound of him humming near her ear. Caught off guard, her normal defensive reactions were slow to respond and in a moment, he had her so wrapped up in his embrace, and the music, that she didn't want to pull away.

"Daisies," he murmured leaning down to nestle his face against her neck. "No doubt about it. How could I ever have imagined dark and dusky looks for you? Daisies go with blond. I see it now."

He dropped a kiss on her tender skin and she gasped. His body was pressed against hers in the most erotic way imaginable. She could feel every muscle, every sinew and especially the evidence that he wanted her. He was all male hardness against her female softness, and that sensation was intoxicating. Something was quivering deep inside, desire—long suppressed—was stirring in her, rising through her like heat. She was going to have to stop this right away, before it got out of control. But it felt so good.

"Nordic. Viking, even," he muttered, his breath hot on her neck as he nuzzled just behind her ear. "Maybe a Valkyrie."

"That's German," she told him breathlessly. Her muscles were melting. If she didn't move fast, she was going to lose all ability to stop him—or even to stop herself.

"Ah, yes, of course." His face drew back, as

though he was trying to see hers. ''The maidens of the great god Odin.'' His beautiful mouth hovered very near hers and she looked at it longingly for a moment, already imagining what his sweet heat would taste like. Then she took a deep breath, shook her head sharply and jerked out of his arms.

''Okay, that's enough,'' she said in her best drill leader voice. She had to close her eyes for a moment, and steady herself, but then she was okay. Her knees firmed up and she wasn't going to crumple to the ground. She was going to be all right.

''But we've only just begun.'' He looked lost standing there on his own, his arms empty. ''I thought a little romance might be in the air.''

''You only thought that because a little alcohol is in your brain,'' she told him firmly. Amazing how strong she could be once she conned herself into trying. ''And since you don't want to get down to work, I'm leaving.''

''No.'' He turned toward her, reaching into the air as though to take her in his arms again, but not coming anywhere near where she stood. ''Don't go.''

Something in his voice made her hesitate. Was she imagining it? Probably. But some sound resonated with her, like a note to a tuning fork, and made it impossible for her to walk out on him. ''I should go,'' she said, feeling a little trapped. ''I think we'll get along better once you're back to normal.''

''I'm perfectly fine,'' he protested, taking a step toward the couch and wavering.

''You're perfectly sloshed,'' she told him. Still, she

couldn't help but smile. He looked very cute as a befuddled prince. Reaching out, she helped guide him to the seat. And she sat beside him instead of heading for the door. Her nurturing instincts seemed to be taking over. "I hope you don't do this often."

"I haven't done this in years," he assured her. "But sometimes a man needs something to help break through his inhibitions and let his true feelings out."

She laughed softly. "If you got any more candid, we'd have to call the local hospital and book you a room. I haven't noticed you holding back on anything yet."

"What are you talking about? I'm always very sensitive to your feelings, aren't I?"

She laughed aloud. "Oh, Damian," she said, "you are funny."

He reached for her hand and got it on the first try, raising it to his lips and kissing the center of her palm. "Come on. Confess. You've considered the possibility that we might conjure up a little flirtation, haven't you?"

"No!" She said it emphatically, but she didn't pull her hand away and he pressed it to his cheek.

"Liar," he said softly.

"We have a professional relationship," she protested. "It would be completely unethical for...for me to take advantage of you that way," she added mischievously.

His head came up in surprise, and then he laughed aloud.

Watching his face, she felt a surge of affection that

choked her. She wanted to brush back his wayward hair and touch his skin and kiss his lips. She wanted it so badly, she couldn't breathe for a moment.

"You could look at it as a part of my therapy," he suggested hopefully. "After all, I'm a grown man. I need the occasional ministrations of a good woman."

That was like a cold splash of water and as she realized what he probably meant, it woke her up. For just a second, she was thankful for that. She'd needed a wake-up call from reality and here it was. He was a man. He needed a woman. Simple as that. And just as impersonal. She breathed a sigh of relief as she straightened and got her good sense back. Saved from folly again.

He needed a woman. Every now and then.

"Sort of like haircuts and manicures?" she said crisply.

He smiled in acknowledgment. "Yes. Pretty much."

She pulled her hand away and prepared to leave.

"Do you not understand how insulting that is?" she noted dryly.

He looked shocked. "I'm not talking about you."

"I know. But you're talking about my gender." She rose and stared down at him. "You're talking about women being disposable, rather like facial tissues."

"Am I?" His face scrunched in thought. "Maybe I am. Well, there are some women who don't want anything more than to be disposable."

She shook her head. "I don't think you know

women very well. Every woman wants to be loved."
Her voice shook a little as she said it, but she didn't
care. It was true. "Every woman wants to be that one
special one to any man she makes love with."

He frowned in her general direction, as though trying hard to understand. "Really?"

"Yes. Really."

"But what about *my* gender? What about…men
and our needs?"

"Needs. Hah." She rolled her eyes and was sorry
he couldn't see the gesture. "With all due respect,
that is a bunch of bull. Plenty of very decent men
spend lots of time in celibacy, and so can you."

He frowned speculatively. "You don't buy the
'natural male urges' argument?"

"Not for a second."

"Damn."

He looked so sad about it, she almost had to laugh.
But she wasn't going to put herself in a vulnerable
position with him again. It was time to go.

She turned, but he reached out and took hold of
her hand before she could get away.

"Sara," he said softly. "I know you're not disposable."

Oh, she did like this man.

"Guess what," she said back. "Neither are you."

She leaned down and dropped a kiss on his cheek,
then hurried from the room.

He was waiting for her when she arrived for their
session the next morning, standing just inside
the door.

"I'm really sorry," he said simply before she had a chance to say a word. "Will you forgive me?"

"Oh," was all she could say at first. She was surprised. He did look repentant. What had happened to the arrogant prince she knew so well?

"I know the way I treated you last night was unforgivable, but I'm asking for a reprieve, and I'm ready to do penance. Just tell me what I can do to make it up to you."

She gazed at him for a moment, thrown off balance and not sure how she was going to handle this.

"Do you actually remember what you did?" she asked.

He looked chagrined. "Unfortunately, yes. I wasn't wasted, just high enough to let me jettison my manners, and morph into the ugly beast you saw last night."

She laughed softly. "Not so ugly," she told him. "A little worse for wear, maybe. But still pretty darn…" Her voice faded. She was going to say "appealing," but realized in time that might be a little too honest.

"So you forgive me?"

"Of course."

He stuck out his hand and she took it in hers, as though sealing some sort of bargain. His hand was warm and as she looked into the beautiful gray eyes that couldn't see her, she had an overwhelming urge to melt into his arms. She could see the same impulse developing in him and she dropped his hand and stepped back quickly.

"I've brought the transmitter," she said with forced cheer. "But I have something else I want you to try first."

"What is it?"

The suspicion in his voice was justified, but she tried to keep a steady tone. "A cane."

"No." He shook his head, making a face. "Not the long white cane."

She turned to look at him, one hand on her hip. "Didn't I hear something about a willingness to do penance?" she reminded him. "Here's your chance."

He hesitated, looking rebellious, then sighed. "All right," he grumbled. "Give me your fricken stick."

Sara smiled with relief. This was actually turning out to be easier than she'd thought. She'd expected a battle royal to get him to try it, and in her experience, it was so important for the sight-impaired to learn its use.

They spent the next hour working with the white cane. Damian was cooperative, but hardly enthusiastic at first. She made him practice using it to negotiate the passages of the upper floor of the house, learning how to tap in a sweeping motion that took in everything from one side to the other.

"The biggest hazards are stairwells and low-hanging objects," she warned him. "The cane can help with the stairwells if you pay close attention to changes in tone, but the low-hanging objects are hard to guard against. If you have a suspicion one may be nearby, you can use your cane to test the passage, but

usually, you just have to hope someone will warn you
before it's too late.''

She took him out into the garden to try a wider
area. He quickly became adept, and as the cane
worked for him, telling him more about his environ-
ment, he began to see the value of it.

''I've got to admit, this could make me much more
confident about getting around by myself,'' he said.

She sighed happily. What could be better than a
man who could admit when he'd been wrong?

''But I still hate the thought of how I must look
using this thing,'' he added.

''Bigot,'' she said softly.

He turned toward her, frowning. ''What was that?''

''Nothing,'' she said quickly.

His frown darkened with mock menace and he
tapped out her position with the cane. ''You called
me something. Did you say I was a bigot?''

She pretended complete innocence despite all the
evidence that would appear to convict her. ''Who,
me?'' She stepped back as he took another step toward her. ''Well, I might have said something along
those lines,'' she admitted.

He grabbed her by the front of her shirt, pretending
anger and making her laugh. After all, he could have
misjudged badly and ended up embarrassing both of
them with that move. She loved the look on his face,
loved being so close to him. Everything about him
made her shiver inside.

''Listen lady,'' he growled in his best gangland impression. "I'll have you know..." he hesitated, then grimaced "...that you're right." His hold on her loosened and his sigh was heartfelt. "I guess I do need an attitude adjustment." He touched her cheek in a seemingly careless gesture. "But like the psychologists always tell us, that can't happen overnight. We're going to have to work on it, long and hard. Just you and me."

Just you and me. He was teasing, but his tone was provocative. Her skin still tingled where he'd touched it. If only...

"Just you and me and your fiancée," she said emphasizing the last word. "We mustn't forget her."

His face fell. "Oh, yeah," he said. "Good old what's-her-name." He turned toward her. "The engagement isn't official yet, you know," he said. "I think we could ignore it for now."

"I don't," she said, feeling a little wistful but not letting it show. She smiled and slipped her hand into the crook of his arm. She loved touching him, getting this close, and the trip up to his room gave her an excuse. "Let's go up and start playing around with the transmitter," she suggested, hoping her voice didn't betray the affection she felt for him.

The transmitter turned out to be complicated to set up, but easy to use once installed in place. Damian was frustrated at first because he knew he was better with gadgets than Sara, who was all thumbs, and yet he couldn't help much when he couldn't see what he was doing. But she finally got it rigged up and once

he began to use it, he was amazed at how helpful
it was.

"We'll still need a lot of practice to get coordinated
with each other," he noted. "But once we get that
down, I think this is going to work." He turned toward her. "All praise Sara Joplin for bringing us the
miracle thing."

He pretended to be leading applause and she took
a bow, murmuring, "Thank you, thank you, I couldn't
have done it without the backing of all the little people."

He laughed. "Watch out for those little people.
Sometimes their bite is as strong as their backing."

"Ouch." She grinned, feeling utterly happy. She'd
had good rapport with clients before, but this was by
far the best. And then she sobered as she had an
epiphany. The problems she'd thought they were having from the first weren't due to a lack of the ability
to connect. The problem had been they connected
only too well.

Beware, she reminded herself quickly. Beware.

Turning, she began to gather her things together.
The afternoon session was over and it was time for
her to go. Pausing, she looked up as she remembered
something.

"Are you ever going to want my report on Sheridan's reactions?" she asked.

He turned toward her, looking surprised and a little
embarrassed. "No," he said dismissively, shaking his
head. "That was stupid. I was being paranoid. Forget
I ever said anything." He turned away.

For some reason, his dismissal bothered her. But if he didn't want to know... She shrugged.

"Why?" he asked, suddenly turning back. "Was there something you noticed?" He sighed, exasperated with himself. "Okay, tell me what you thought."

"About what?"

He looked uncomfortable. "About Sheridan's reactions, of course. Did you detect any...wavering?"

She frowned. "I have no idea what you mean by wavering."

"Well, then just tell me what you noticed."

She shrugged. "Not much. He seemed genuinely happy to see you. It's obvious you and he are very fond of each other. All in all, I'd say he was very open and friendly."

He nodded, looking relieved. "Of course."

She frowned, studying him. "What were you expecting?"

He shrugged. "Exactly that. Don't give it another thought."

But she couldn't wipe his on-again, off-again interest out of her mind that easily. And then she remembered the look on Sheridan's face when she'd seen him coming out of Damian's room. There had been something there that she hadn't liked, but she didn't know how to explain or describe her feeling.

She went back to putting things into a pile and her attention was caught by something coming out from under a pillow on the couch. Reaching in, she pulled out an audiocassette recording of a book of poetry in Nabotavian.

"What's this?" she asked, describing what she'd found.

"Nothing," Damian said shortly. "The duke brought it up for me to listen to."

"Do you want me to put it in—"

"No. Throw it away."

His cold tone startled her. "Why?"

"Because I don't want it."

She looked at the English translations of a few titles on the back of the box. The poet's name was Jan Kreslau, and his titles were things such as "Faithfully," "Truth is the Sun, Lies are Shooting Stars," "Trust."

"Sounds like a philosopher," she noted, slipping it into her pocket. "Same time this afternoon?"

He turned back toward her. "Can we make it a little earlier? Sheridan and I are going to visit a friend down in Laguna later."

"No problem."

"Sheridan will be leaving at the end of the week, but I'll probably be doing something with him every afternoon while he's here."

"Good," she said stoutly, despite the tremors this scenario gave her. She couldn't help it. The thought of him rocketing about the Southland with his cousin, looking for gorgeous girls, as he'd described it the day before, gave her the willies. But they were willies she had no right to have, so she was going to ignore them. "It's good for you to get out. Just don't forget to take Tom with you."

"Yes. I'll take Tom."

"Good."

Why was she lingering? Come on girl, get going! One last look. He was so strong and attractive. If only she were a princess. A very rich princess. She sighed.

"See you tonight?" she asked.

He nodded. "I'll call if for some reason we won't make it back in time."

"Thanks. See you later."

She left him and felt instantly less happy. This was getting ridiculous, but she couldn't help it. If she didn't know better, she would have thought she was darn near falling in love with the prince.

Chapter 9

Over the next few days their sessions were a little hurried, but generally productive. Damian was getting better and better at following oral instructions through the transmitter and Sara was getting better and better at giving them. Hope was riding high that he would be able to function at the ball at almost a normal level of confidence.

At the same time, she was getting to know the other members of the family a bit better. Count Boris was usually her breakfast companion, as Karina tended to sleep late and the duchess often ate at the many various morning functions she attended. The more she got to know Boris, the better she liked him. Underneath his English leisure-set affectations he was often funny and always kind.

One morning she asked him why he had never married.

"I've tried to get married. Somehow things never work out."

His melancholy look made her smile. "Maybe your heart just hasn't been in it," she suggested.

He considered that, then nodded. "You may be right. I came here this summer to get married, you know. My sister had planned for me to marry Princess Karina."

"Oh." That was a surprise. Somehow she couldn't picture the two of them together.

He sighed. "That little project fell through, I'm afraid. Another chap got in the way. Handsome Italian fellow by the name of Jack Santini. Don't suppose you've met him, have you?"

"No, I haven't."

"Well, Karina preferred him to me for some strange reason. Can't imagine how that came about. I believe he's currently been banished. Don't know why. Can't keep all these comings and goings straight, you know."

Banished. How interesting. She definitely had to hear the story on that.

"Are you nursing a broken heart?" she asked, prepared to be properly sympathetic.

"A broken heart?" He looked at her as though she'd suggested he try mud wrestling with panda bears. "What a ridiculous notion." He readjusted his napkin. "It *has* put a crimp in my marriage plans, however." He cocked an eyebrow her way. "I don't suppose you'd consider marrying a lonely count?"

She laughed, knowing he wasn't serious, and he went on.

"The hours are good. Not much heavy lifting involved."

"I'm afraid I'm booked up for the rest of the summer," she said with a smile.

"What a shame. Well, keep me in mind if something opens up."

"Of course."

Marry a count—what a thought. But if she'd had to pick a count, Boris would definitely be the one she would choose.

One good thing about Damian being off with Sheridan much of the time was the freedom it gave Sara to take a few hours off to do some things for herself. She took the opportunity to run up to Mandy's to see how her sister was doing, stopping off at the duke's office before she went.

"Hello," she said brightly when he opened the door and peered out at her. "It's Sara Joplin," she reminded him, because his vacant stare didn't make her feel recognized.

"Of course it is," he said, breaking into a smile. "Come in my dear. I've been avoiding you, you know." He ushered her in. "Because I'm having the devil's own time trying to hunt down the ancestral connections on your mother's side. Things went so easily with the Joplin part of the family tree, I'm quite put out that it's taking so long to fill in the other side."

"I wish you wouldn't go to so much trouble," Sara said.

He brushed away her statement with a flick of his slender aristocratic hand. "It's no trouble, my dear, it's fascinating. I've joined a genealogy forum online. They've got a great chat group and I hope to gather more information from them."

It made her smile to think of the duke in a chat room. "Be careful," she warned him. "You know what they say about online deceptions."

He spent a little time showing her what he'd found so far, and when she explained that she'd come by because she was on her way to visit her sister and would like to take a copy of the Joplin family tree he'd worked up to show her, he acted like a proud artist loaning out his latest creation.

"By the way," she said before she left him, pulling the cassette out of her pocket. "I've brought this back."

The duke took it from her, turning it in his hand and noting the seal wasn't broken. "He didn't listen to it."

"No, I'm afraid not."

The duke nodded. "I didn't really think he would." He waved the cassette at her, handing it back. "Why don't you keep it? I have other copies. It's a series of readings of Damian's father's favorite poetry. He had most of it memorized himself, and tried to live by the idealism found here. I wanted Damian to know that.'' He gave her a sad smile. "It's hard for the young to understand that their elders need forgiveness, too,'' he said softly.

She didn't really understand, but she knew better than to ask for him to explain. It was really none of her business. Still, she couldn't help but mull over what the duke had said as she drove toward the mountains. Evidence would suggest that Damian resented something about his father. She certainly saw no signs of that resentment from Karina or Marco, and since Damian had only been eight when his father was killed, she couldn't imagine what could possibly have hurt him so badly. Surely he didn't blame his father just for not being there when he was growing up. That sort of resentment she could certainly understand, but it didn't seem to fit in Damian's case. Sighing, she gave it up and concentrated on her driving.

The trip to Pasadena wasn't bad as she'd picked a low traffic time and was lucky enough to avoid having to deal with an accident on the freeway. Pasadena had its own opulent neighborhoods, but the contrast to Beverly Hills was stark. The Westside was moneyed and trendy while Pasadena tended to let its Midwestern roots show. She pulled up in front of her sister's Spanish-style bungalow on a tree-lined street with a sense of anticipation.

Mandy was glad to see her. Confinement was making this pregnancy seem to last about twice as long as the calendar count reported. But her husband was home every night now and that made a big difference.

She was as thrilled with the family tree the duke had researched as Sara had been.

"You mean we really do have a place where we belong and people we belong to?" she said once she'd studied it. "I can't believe it. I've always felt like such an orphan."

"Our parents weren't very interested in making sure we knew about any of the extended family," Sara agreed. "It might be fun to contact some of our distant cousins."

"Definitely. Carrying this baby has opened up a lot of feelings for me that I never knew I had," Mandy said. "I want him to know as much about his background as we—or your duke—can dredge up."

Her duke. That made Sara smile.

"What's with the glow?" Mandy asked a little later as she and Sara sat in her kitchen talking.

"What glow?" She said it in all innocence.

Mandy suppressed a smile. "The one you're wearing, along with that goofy grin."

Now she was a little embarrassed. Was it really that obvious that she had a crush on a prince? "You tell me," she said defensively.

But Mandy only shook her head and began humming, "Fools Rush In."

"What are you doing all day to keep from going stark raving mad?" Sara asked to change the subject. "When you're not thinking up ways to torture those you purport to love, I mean."

"I've been watching a lot of television, of course." Mandy's face changed. "Oh, by the way, Mother and

Dad were on the *Gail and Reggie* show this morning. Looking tanned and rested, with the cruise-effect sea breezes still in their hair.''

They were both silent for a moment, thinking of their well-traveled parents.

"Good interview?" Sara asked at last.

"Great interview. They always do a great interview."

Sara nodded.

"I'm waiting for the day some interviewer asks them if they've ever had any children," she said, looking just a bit sly.

Mandy laughed. "Exactly." She made a pretend-father face. "And Dad says, 'No, regrettably, we've never been blessed.'"

Sara laughed. "And Mom says, 'Wait, Jim. Didn't we have a couple of girls living with us at one time? I wonder whatever happened to them.'"

They both laughed at their joke, but the laughter was edged with heartache. It would have been nice to have had real parents when they were growing up. It would be nice to have real parents now. It made Sara crazy to think they had been in Los Angeles and hadn't dropped by to see how Mandy was doing with her problem pregnancy. She only prayed that the sort of coldheartedness those two exhibited wasn't clomping around in her genes.

If I turn out like them, I'll jump off the Santa Monica Pier, she told herself.

But she wasn't going to turn out like them. She would never let herself. If she ever had kids, she would cherish them, she was sure of it. She would never, ever let her own children carry around a hard little lump of hopeless anguish deep inside the way she and Mandy did.

She was back in plenty of time for the afternoon session, and once they had finished their work, Damian surprised her by asking if she'd like to share his dinner with him. Sheridan had a meeting with his banker and wouldn't be back until later that evening. And Damian felt like pizza.

"The best pizza in town is Wong's Pizza on Santa Monica Boulevard," he told her.

"Wong's? Chinese pizza?"

"No, of course not," he responded with mock indignation. "Wong's makes Italian pizza with Chinese flair. You'll love it." He grinned at her. "The only problem is, they don't deliver."

"I'll run and get it," she offered.

He looked shocked at the very concept. "Don't be silly. One of the guards can go get it."

She shook her head. She had to admit, life with servants around was a different sort of animal.

"Boy, you people really live the life of Riley, don't you?" she said, her envy only half in play.

"'The life of Riley.'" Damian frowned. "I've never understood what that meant."

"Well, to me it means better than most people. Luxury. Whatever you want, you get." She looked at him out of the corner of her eyes. "Sort of like royalty. So I guess it fits."

He made a sound deep in his throat. "You know, you make too much of this royalty stuff," he told her, raising an eyebrow in her direction. "Being royal is just a line of work like any other. Only you get saddled with the job by birth rather than choice. And once in, there is very little opportunity to opt out."

"Would you opt out if you could?" she asked him softly.

He was silent for a moment, then turned to her with a slight smile. "Let's call in that pizza order."

The pizza was great and definitely Italian. They ate and talked and ate some more. She told him about Mandy and her pregnancy and he told her about when Marco's daughter was born and he'd been driving down from Denver, hurrying to get to the hospital in Flagstaff to see his newborn niece. A snowstorm threw him off the beaten path and he ended up halfway down into the Grand Canyon before he realized where he was.

"By the time I got to the hospital, Kiki was three days old," he said, the tragedy of it all written on his face, making her smile.

She liked that he'd felt compelled to rush to his brother's side at an important time like that.

They both ate too much, then sat on the couch and groaned.

"Now we should take naps and let our systems come back to normal," Damian suggested hopefully. "My bed is only a few steps away."

"Cute," she told him, a touch of sarcasm lacing her tone. "With such a smooth seduction line, I'm surprised you don't have women waiting in the wings.''

"Ah, but I do," he reminded her with a grin. "And I'd throw them all over for you, fair lady."

She sobered, knowing he was kidding but thinking it might be time she made tracks anyway. But before she could make the move, he spoke again.

"I hear your parents are these famous travel writers, the Joplins."

She stiffened. "That's right."

"The duke told me about them." He leaned back. "So what's it like to grow up in a typical California suburb with the typical California parents?"

"I don't know," she said calmly. "I've never done that."

He turned toward her, surprised. "What do you mean?"

She explained quickly about her parents' unique method of raising children by long distance. At first, she only meant to give him a sketchy idea of what her childhood had been like, but his perceptive questions got her going and to her surprise, she found herself baring her soul in ways she never had to any other living creature other than her sister.

Damian was a good listener, nodding as she told him things she probably shouldn't have.

"So," he said slowly, considering all she'd told him and digesting it. "Because your parents were emotionally blind to your needs you went into a profession where you could minister to others who were really blind."

"What?" She was so shocked, she stared at him, openmouthed, then threw a pillow at him. "Oh, that's ridiculous."

He took the pillow and tucked it away, looking smug. "You don't see the connection?"

"I see that you're as willing as anyone to resort to psychobabble when it suits your purpose," she said accusingly.

He grinned. "You should listen to what I have to say. I'm blind you know. That means my perceptions are sharper than those of others. I'm wiser than you."

"Hah! Sharper perceptions!" She looked around for another pillow to throw at him but came up empty and had to give him a glancing slug in the arm instead. "You phony. You were planning that diagnosis the whole time I was talking, weren't you?"

"You don't think that I can hear things in your voice that others can't hear?"

She hesitated, biting her lip. He couldn't be serious. Could he? "That can sometimes happen. But in your case I believe it's completely mythological."

"Then I would say you're the one who's a bigot, lady."

She was tempted to punch him again, but then she stopped, horrified at herself. What was she doing? She only wanted an excuse to touch him, didn't she? Her face burned crimson as she admitted it to herself and she moved farther from him on the couch, wondering if his sharper perceptions had caught that one.

"But it's understandable," he went on, being annoyingly generous. "After all, with parents like that, you must be an emotional wreck.'' His crooked smile teased her. ''Are you an emotional wreck under that facade of normalcy, Sara?''

''Not any more than the average mental patient,'' she said lightly.

He frowned as he considered her case. ''That could explain why you've never married.''

Now he was getting a little too close for comfort. She tried to think of a cutting reply that would take him down a peg or two, but she failed miserably.

''When was your last real date?''

''I don't know,'' she said defensively, rising to go. ''It's not something I keep track of, especially.''

''I wish I could take you out on a date,'' he said softly.

She flashed him a look that might have warned him off if he'd been able to see it. ''Well, you can't,'' she said crisply. ''You're engaged to Joannie Whatshername. You'd better take her.''

''Is that why you keep me at arm's length all the time?'' he asked her. ''Because I'm engaged?''

''That's part of the reason,'' she told him, starting toward the door. ''But there's a whole lot more besides. Thanks for the pizza. I'll see you later.''

''You can count on it,'' he said firmly.

She closed the door and sighed as she started down the stairs. She was going crazy. There was no other explanation. Only a crazy person would do what she was doing. Only someone who had lost touch with reality would let herself fall in love with a client—a client who was a prince of another land.

Maybe it was a passing thing, like a fever or a summer flu. That had to be it. One morning she would wake up and smile and realize she was over it. Cured. No more seeing Damian's dark face and blue-gray eyes everywhere. No more hearing his voice in her head, no more dreaming of his kiss. No more waking in the middle of the night to find herself aching for his hard body.

Sometimes she marveled at how she got through the day without everybody knowing. Didn't they see her dreamy look? Didn't they notice how she lit up like an overly decorated Christmas tree when he entered the room?

She had a feeling Damian knew. He was just being nice to her, pretending he didn't notice so as not to embarrass her. She'd never been in love before. How in the world did you get rid of it?

Maybe when she left it would fade away. There was only a week to go before the ball, and once that was over, she would be gone. There would be a new client. She would move on as she always did. But this time, she knew she wouldn't be able to keep herself from looking back.

The next night, Sara and Karina and the duchess ate dinner alone. The wine was flowing generously, and for once, the duchess loosened up considerably. The three of them had a regular gabfest, talking and laughing and telling secrets. Annie, realizing what was going on right away, excluded the other servants from the room and served them herself. Karina told a story about Damian's first date and the duchess regaled them with tales from her days as a young debutante in Nabotavia. Sara wished she had a wacky dating story to tell, but Damian's instincts about that had been right. She'd never dated much. She'd never much wanted to. Still, she enjoyed hearing the experiences of the others—though she noticed all the princess's stories concerned her siblings and not herself. What was the story on the mystery man Boris said had been banished?

After a light dessert of berries on vanilla ice cream, Karina took her to the library to show her the work she was doing on her mother's biography. She had tablets full of notes and reference books strewn around a long table. A number of them had pictures from the early years of her parents' reign. They were a very handsome couple. Sara could see where the children got their wonderful looks and sense of presence.

There was even a picture of Kari's mother, Queen Marie, with her sister, Lady Julienne, who was Sheridan's mother. The two women looked very much alike, though Julienne had a bit of a pout.

"Are you finding my brother an apt student?" Karina asked as they were putting the large volumes away.

"Oh, very," Sara told her. "He picks things up in no time at all."

She nodded. "I'm glad that you are satisfied with his cooperation. You never know with Damian. You may have noticed a tiny bit of anger in his outlook."

"Yes, but considering the circumstances…"

"Well, it's nothing new—though worse now, of course. It's always been there. Damian has always seemed to be the one hanging back a little, not joining in the general revelry when the four of us get together. It seems he resents something about the family, or about being royal, or something. I've never really understood it." She smiled at Sara. "And of course, I know him the least well of all my brothers. He was always living with Sheridan's family when we were young." She shrugged. "I suppose when we return to Nabotavia, things will be different. But then, he'll be married."

Sara twitched. She didn't mean to. But Karina's words touched a nerve. She only hoped the princess hadn't noticed.

"Yes," she said quickly. "I understand he barely knows the young lady."

Karina nodded, looking exasperated. "Disgraceful, isn't it? I don't know how he can do it. Damian of all people. He's always been so scornful of royalty and the things we're obliged to do because of it."

"Has he?"

"Oh, yes. He's always making fun of being royal, saying that we're no better than anyone else…not that we are, of course," she added hastily. Chagrined, she met Sara's gaze and they both began to laugh. "You know what I mean," she said, and Sara nodded.

"The one thing he said to me that gave me a glimmer of his motivation was…" She looked at Sara as though hesitant to tell her, but then she rushed on.

"The day he told the duchess he would do it, marry the Waingarten girl, he said to me, almost as an aside, that this was finally something he felt he could do for his family. I thought he was joking at first, because of how he'd always been about such things. But now that I think of it..." Her brow furled in thought. "He almost sounded as though he thought he'd let the family down somehow, and needed to make amends."

"That was pretty much the way he presented it to me, too," Sara said.

Karina shook her head. "I don't get it." She thought for a moment, then looked up. "I was supposed to throw my life away in a similar fashion. I suppose you've heard that the duchess wanted me to marry Boris? And I was prepared to do it. It was thought of as my duty." Her eyes got dreamy. "But I met another man and fell head over heels in love. And once that happened, I knew I could never marry poor Boris."

Watching her, Sara felt a wave of sympathy. This love thing was like a secret sisterhood, wasn't it? "What happened to this man?"

The princess turned and favored her with a slow smile. Sara could see that she was picturing the man she loved.

"His name is Jack Santini. He was working here as the head of security." Karina laughed. "Yes, look shocked. It's a shocking thing, isn't it?" She sighed. "I was ready to run away with him, and I would have, too. But he wouldn't do it." She shrugged. "So now I plan to devote my life to my country, Nabotavia."

"Oh, Karina..."

"But never mind all that. We need to talk about your gown."

"My what?"

"Your gown. You'll need one for the ball, of course. What style do you like? My seamstress will be here tomorrow and I'm having her bring along some gowns she has on hand. You can look them over, choose one you like, and we'll have her make any alterations you need."

Sara felt as though she'd been standing in a strong wind. "Wow. You do take over, don't you?" she said, laughing. "One would almost think you'd been born to rule."

Karina didn't laugh. She held her head high. "But of course," she said.

The next day was one of those days when everything seemed to go wrong. The transmitter practice didn't go as well as it had before. Damian got frustrated with it and pulled it off. He seemed annoyed and out of sorts, and that only got worse when Sara told him she was going out that night.

"I'm going to the movies with Boris," she told him. He'd asked her that morning at breakfast, and after an initial hesitation, she'd decided she ought to go.

"Boris!" Damian was horrified. "Don't go with Boris. I'll take you."

"You're going to Malibu with Sheridan. You aren't even planning to be home tonight."

He considered that. "I'll take you some other time."

She shook her head. "You can't go to the movies," she reminded him.

"Who says I can't?"

"Damian..."

"I can listen, can't I? Come on, if there's a film you want to see, let me take you."

She hesitated. It was nice he wanted to do this, but she had a feeling is was more dog in the manger than anything else.

"Damian, it's not the film."

He turned toward her, glowering. "You're not going to try to convince me you've fallen for Boris?"

"I—I just want to get out and do something. Go on a date."

His handsome face registered shock. "A date! Is that what you call this?"

"Yes." She held her head high. She was learning from Karina. "I think I can call this a date. Aren't you the one who told me I should go on dates?"

"Sure. But they were supposed to be with me."

She wasn't going to remind him about the engagement again. He hadn't forgotten. She lifted her chin. "I'm going out with Boris and I'm going to have a good time."

"Fine. Go." He glowered some more. "I hope the film breaks," he muttered. His head came up as she moved toward the door. "I hope you get stuck to the floor with chewing gum."

She opened the door and looked back. "Bye," she said.

"I'll bet Boris talks through the whole movie," was his answer.

"Have fun in Malibu," she added, and then she closed the door. But she found herself grinning as she bounced down the stairs. Despite everything, she had a feeling he was actually a little bit jealous.

She ran into Tom coming out of the kitchen area with a frosted doughnut in his hand.

"Oh, Tom," she said. "I've wanted to tell you, I so appreciate what you're doing for the prince. He's having such a good time with his cousin and having you along makes it possible for him to go without worrying about certain situations."

"No problemo." He gave her a good-natured grin. "I enjoy it. They go to some really great places. Like, last night we hung out at the Silk Parrot on Rodeo. The place was full of rock star dudes. You wouldn't believe it. Too cool."

She laughed. "Tom, I like your enthusiasm for your work."

"What's not to like? The only time I've had any problems was when Lord Sheridan tried to ditch me at the Santa Monica Pier. But I was on to him and it didn't work out." His grin was cocky. "I'm not as dumb as I look, you know."

She frowned after him as he disappeared around the corner. Lord Sheridan tried to ditch him? She would like to hear more about that incident. Maybe later. Right now she wanted to be by herself and think about Damian being jealous. In her position, she had to savor the smaller victories.

Chapter 10

Sara was watching from her bedroom window as the three men drove off in the low-slung sports car a half hour later. Sheridan was driving. Damian was in the passenger seat and Tom was in the tiny excuse for a back seat. And just as they disappeared out through the gate, her telephone rang.

She stared at it for a moment. This was the first call she'd had on the bedroom phone. Picking it up, she half expected to find someone had dialed the wrong number. But Crown Prince Marco was on the line from New York.

"I need your help, Sara," he said. "We've had some bad financial news. A couple of backers we were counting on are getting cold feet. This makes it imperative that we keep the funding that's already been pledged. Damian has to impress our big contributors at the ball. If they see any reason to begin to lose confidence in us, we're dead.''

''I see.'' She bit her lip. ''Did you want me to tell Damian about this?''

''No. I'm telling you because I don't want him to know. I don't want to put more pressure on him at this point. But we need to pull out all the stops for the ball. So I'm putting you in charge of making sure that's done.''

''Marco, I want to help all I can, but I'm an occupational therapist, not a...''

''I know. And I'm sorry to do this to you. But with everything that's come down so hard on Damian, I don't want to add to his stress. He's already acting paranoid about the accident. I don't want to put any more pressure on him.'' He laughed shortly. ''So I propose to put it on you instead.''

''Gee, thanks.''

''I'm sorry. But you're the one training him for his appearance at the ball.''

''So you want me to make him work harder getting ready, but you don't want me to tell him why.''

''Exactly.''

She sighed. ''I'll do the best I can,'' she promised.

''Good. I'm leaving for Arizona soon, but I'll be back in California before the Foundation ball. I'm counting on you.''

She stared at the wall for a long time after she'd hung up the telephone. Now it was all on her shoulders. She had to work very hard to ensure that the

man she was pretty certain she was falling in love
with could marry another woman and leave the country for good. And she would do it, too. Because she
cared for him. This was all too crazy.

But as she sat mulling that over, another thought
occurred to her. Marco had said something about Damian being paranoid about the accident, and she remembered the first night she'd been here he had been
adamant about wanting the lake dredged for all re-
mains of the hydrofoil. He obviously suspected foul
play of some sort. That had to be what his brother
was talking about.

And then she began to remember other things, such
as Damian's original wariness of Sheridan's arrival.
And Tom saying Sheridan had tried to ditch him. Suddenly, she could ascribe sinister motives all around.

She pulled herself short. Now she was getting even
crazier. Sheridan was Damian's cousin and the closest
person to him, from what she could see. It would be
downright rude to begin suspecting him of wanting
to harm Damian.

So, rude she was going to have to be. Because now
she was very nervous about the fact that they were
off together—and very thankful she'd made sure from
the beginning that Tom would go along.

The afternoon stretched out before her, and the evening at the movies was no longer half as inviting. She
knew darn well she was going to spend most of the
time worrying, and being tempted to call Damian's
cell phone.

"No," she told herself firmly. "Kiss of death to do that. Don't you dare!"

But she groaned, knowing she was in for a full day of misery. Sheridan was leaving the next day. If he were going to do anything to Damian, it would have to be tonight. Wouldn't it? Would Tom's presence keep Damian safe? Or would Sheridan manage to lose him this time?

Her insides were churning. She was probably being ridiculous. After all, there was no proof that Sheridan had done anything at all. If she said anything to anyone, they would be calling in a team of professionals to calm her down. She really couldn't do anything. Anything, but wait. And go to the movies with Boris.

Damian moved through his room restlessly. There were times when being blind nearly drove him mad. He wanted so badly to be free of the restraints, to do what he wanted to do when he wanted to do it.

He and Sheridan had driven to their friend's in Laguna and had a nice dinner, but he'd begun to feel impatient to get back before they'd made it to dessert. All he could think about was Sara at the movies with Boris. At the first opportunity, he told Sheridan he wanted to go home.

His cousin didn't seem to mind. He was pretty moody himself tonight. So they had sped back through the night, and now he was waiting to catch Sara coming home—with Boris on her arm. Or vice versa. But if he stayed here in his room, he was very likely going to miss her. There was only one solution that he could think of. Reaching out to where he knew it stood waiting, he grasped the long white cane.

"Okay, friend," he told it softly. "It's time for you to show what you can do. I'm going to get down into the rose garden by myself, or die trying."

It seemed simple as he started out. After all, he'd been up and down the upstairs hall with the cane a dozen times by now. But judging that first step on the stairs was a little scary, and once he started down them, he lost count and had to feel carefully with the stick for the bottom.

But he made it. Turning, he began to negotiate the lower hallway. This wasn't so hard. Tapping with the sensitive tip of the cane told him a lot, now that he was experienced. It told him he'd come to a door. The only problem was, what door? He was hoping for a way to the outside, but for all he knew, this could be a closet. Pulling it open, he tapped with the cane and felt relief. It seemed to lead outside, and the cool air on his face confirmed that. In another moment, he was out on the driveway, heading toward what he hoped would be the rose garden.

Sara saw him as soon as she stepped out of the car and relief flooded her. All that worrying for nothing! She felt a twinge of guilt for having suspected Sheridan of all sorts of nefarious deeds. It looked like she'd been letting her imagination run away with her good sense, blowing things way out of proportion. Sheridan had come and gone and Damian was still in one piece.

The two large dogs that patrolled the grounds at night ran up and sniffed her, then Boris, and trotted off to check out the far side of the yard.

"I guess we passed muster," Boris noted. "Let me see you to your room."

She turned, smiling at him and offering her hand. "Thank you so much, Boris. I had a lovely time. But I see Prince Damian in the rose garden, and I want to have a word with him before I go in."

"Ah." Boris squinted toward the garden. "I enjoyed the evening as well, my dear. I think I'll stop in at the kitchen and see if Annie has left anything edible out for late-night snackers. May I bring you anything?"

"No, thanks," she said, shaking his hand and smiling at him with genuine affection. "I'll see you at breakfast."

He nodded and started toward the house, while she made her way toward the prince.

"About time you got back," Damian said as she approached.

When he'd heard the car, he'd wanted to stash the cane and stand there like a man, ready to compete with Boris for a woman he wanted. And he did want her. The wanting was getting stronger all the time. Hard as it was for him to do, he'd resisted the temptation to ditch the cane. He was blind. There was no way he could deny it. So he'd stood there with the cane in hand and waited as he heard the voices coming closer.

"I hope my presence didn't forestall the traditional good-night kiss."

She was so happy and relieved to see him in one piece she ignored the touch of acid in his tone. In fact, she felt like throwing her arms around him and getting in that good-night kiss now. But she restrained herself.

"Well, it did seem to inhibit poor Boris," she said, teasing him. "We had planned to make passionate love on the driveway, but once he saw you here in the garden, he seemed to lose his appetite for carnal activities."

Damian's glare dissolved into a grin. "I want to officially volunteer to take his place," he said earnestly. "Anytime. Anywhere." He grimaced. "Except here in the rose garden. I got here okay, but the damn thorns are poking me full of holes. I think I'm getting weak from loss of blood."

She laughed, taking his arm to look at the one obvious wound. "Ouch. We'd better go in to the butler's pantry and get that bandaged."

"Never mind," he said, being brave. "It's not really that bad."

She smiled, feeling warm and wonderful. She loved that he had come out to meet her. She wasn't sure why he'd done it, but she loved that he'd used the cane on his own.

"I'm so..." Could she say proud? Would he hate that? She searched her mind for another way to say it. "Pleased," she said at last. "Pleased that you used the cane and got down here all by yourself."

"Don't patronize me, Sara. I'm not a child."

His words were tough, but the look on his face showed her that he actually was pretty proud of himself and not really resentful of her praise. That made her grin.

"Sorry," she said. Her affection for this man was spilling out of her heart and running all through her body. She wanted so badly to do something for him.

"Damian, tell me what you miss most," she said impulsively. "What activity was your favorite before?"

He thought for a moment. "I'd love to ride again," he said.

"Horses?"

"Yes."

She fairly shivered with anticipation. "Okay. You get ready. First thing in the morning, I'll call someone I know who runs a stable that specializes in accommodating people with all sorts of disabilities. We're going horseback riding tomorrow."

He looked toward her, puzzled. "How can I do that?"

"You can. There are ways." She grabbed his hand and held it tightly. "Damian, blind people go mountain bike riding using echolocation and a leader. That's a lot harder. At least you know a horse won't take you over a cliff."

One eyebrow rose. "But he might just find a few low-hanging branches to try to brush you off with."

She chuckled. "Into each life a little rain must fall."

"I'm overwhelmed by your sensitivity," he responded, but his mouth was twisted into something coming very close to a grin.

"You should be." She wondered if he was looking for a way to get out of this little adventure. "If you really don't want to go…"

"Are you kidding?" He took the hand that held his and put a kiss on her knuckles, then held it close. "I might not be able to sleep tonight, I'm so up for this."

"Good." She pulled her hand from his and began to back away. "I'll see you early in the morning, then," she reminded him.

He nodded. Taking the white cane, he began to make his way back toward the house. She watched him, knowing he knew she was watching, loving him for his cool composure under the scrutiny. This was a man like no other she'd ever known. Deep in her heart, he would always be hers, even if that dream couldn't ever become a reality.

The sun was golden and the sky was blue. A cool breeze was holding back the summer heat. The smell of hay and horses was just strong enough to enhance the outing. Perfect. Sara wanted to dance in the grass.

It had taken a few days to set this riding session up, days which she'd used to work Damian hard, keeping Marco's admonitions in mind. Progress was good, she thought, and he deserved to have fun today. They had spent a half hour in the corral while her friend Bonnie ran them through the fundamentals and techniques for blind riding. Now they were alone and

Damian had mounted the large mellow bay and was beginning to ride slowly down the trail. Sara watched for a moment, nervous but confident in Damian's ability. Then she climbed up on her tan mare and began to follow them.

They planned to spend at least three hours at this. Annie had packed them a fat bag full of picnic goodies. They were going to ride up to a corner of Griffith Park, have lunch and then ride back down. Fresh air filled Sara's lungs and she threw back her shoulders. She felt so good, so free.

Suddenly, that feeling fled. Ahead of her, Damian was falling. She didn't see why, and for just a second, she thought it must be something else, that what she was seeing couldn't be happening. But it was, and Damian slumped to the ground with a thump and a groan, and she was out of the saddle and running toward him, her heart in her throat.

What if she'd killed him? He looked so lifeless, sort of twisted, like a broken doll. Oh, why had she made him do this?

"Damian!" she cried as she reached him. "Oh, my God!"

He turned and sat on the ground, and his face, though dirty, was laughing.

"Damian?"

"I'm okay," he said, still laughing. "It was so great to be back on a horse, but I screwed up. I know what I did. It's my fault...."

"Are you sure you're okay?"

"Certain."

She took his hands to help him up and when he rose, somehow he just kept coming and then his arms were around her in a full body contact hug. She raised her head to tell him to back off, but before she could get a word out, his mouth had found hers.

The effect was electric. She slumped against him, conquered without him having to fire a shot. He felt so good and she'd wanted this for so long now. She responded without hesitation, accepting his tongue, opening to his exploration, curling her arms around his neck and arching into his body. Every part of her reacted to the long, strong muscles in his legs, the rounded hardness of his chest, the strength and maleness that made him who he was. He felt like a magical Greek statue, marble-hard on the outside, but alive and pliable to the touch, drawing her into his heat.

At the same time, his mouth was so soft, so hot, so delicious. She wanted more of his taste, but she was gasping for breath and she pulled away.

"If I didn't know better," she said, panting but trying to maintain a calm facade, "I'd think you planned this whole thing."

"No plan involved," he murmured huskily, his hands sliding down her sides. "Just doing what comes naturally."

She sighed. "Didn't anyone ever warn you that Nature is cruel?"

"I'll risk it."

He leaned close and kissed her again, and she sighed with regret. "Oh, Damian, we can't do this. You're engaged."

"Not really. I'm contracted to become engaged."

"Same difference."

"Forget about that," he murmured, nipping at her earlobe.

"I can't." She put the palms of her hands against his chest and began to push.

He lifted his head. "Just this once?"

"No."

He thought for a second, still resisting her rejection. "Okay, how about this? We won't be Prince Damian and his occupational therapist, Ms. Sara Joplin today. I won't be engaged. Today we are..." He frowned. "Okay, I'm Sam." He set his head at a cocky angle. "I'm a cowboy," he said with a drawl. "And you're Daisy."

"Daisy!"

He grinned. "I've told you that from the beginning. You smell like daisies."

She was melting. Resistance was melting. Her heart was melting. Her brain—yes, most especially her brain, was melting. She was going to go along with this silly plan, and she knew it from the start. Why? Because she wanted to. Oh, how she wanted to!

"Okay, I'm Daisy," she said, her fingers curling into the fabric of his shirt instead of pushing him away. "If you're a cowboy, what am I?"

He put his head to the side, considering. "Your daddy owns the ranch where I work the herd, of course. And you've ridden out into the countryside. And found me out here, hunting for strays."

She chuckled. "If I'm a good girl, I'd probably better hightail it back to the ranch."

His arms closed around her again. "No you won't, because we are secretly in love, even though your Daddy is opposed."

He felt so hard and strong against her and he smelled so good. She could die in his arms and still be happy.

"So we have to meet out on the range," she said, getting a bit breathless.

"You got it."

She laughed, shaking her head, then gathered her strength. "Come on, Cowboy Sam," she said, pulling away from him before things got out of hand. "We've got a fer piece to ride yet today."

"Okay, Daisy," he said, keeping a grip on her hand. "You lead the way."

She laughed again.

"What's so funny?" he asked as they walked toward where the horses waited.

"All I can think of when you say that is Daisy Duck with those funny little shoes."

He pulled her around to face him. "All I can think of is how much I want to kiss you again."

"Damian…"

"It's Sam. You can kiss Sam. And Sam can kiss Daisy."

She couldn't resist. He tasted clean and spicy and she was hungry for the feel of him in her mouth. She knew she shouldn't let this happen. But some things were just too wonderful to let slip through your fingers.

The horses were well trained and well mannered. Both were waiting very close by. Sara helped Damian remount and settle in more securely. She started him off, then hurried to her horse so that she could catch up with them. The rest of the ride up the hill passed without any more disasters.

They found the perfect place for a picnic on a hill overlooking the park, with oak trees all around. Spreading out a blanket, they set out the sandwiches and a bottle of wine. Nothing tasted better than a good lunch out in the fresh air. They ate and talked and laughed together. Damian recited some Shakespeare, then a little Keats and Coleridge.

"This is great," she told him, loving every minute. Listening to the beautiful language just went with the beauty of the day. "I didn't know you were so good at this."

"One thing about being royal, you definitely get a fine classical education." He said it with a twist of acerbity that made her look at him sharply.

"Tell me about your father," she said, leaning back into the grass.

"What's to tell?" he responded, moving closer to where she was. "He was the king." He touched her hair, which she was wearing loose about her shoulders, twisting it around his fingers. "He was big and he was handsome. And some think he was heroic."

She turned her head to look at his face. "But not you."

He raised an eyebrow. "Did I ever say that?"

"You didn't have to say it. It's written all over your attitude."

He shrugged. "Then I guess I'd better be more careful," he said softly.

She frowned, wishing she had the nerve to quiz him further along those lines. Whatever he had against his father didn't seem to bother the other members of his family. "What about your mother?" she asked instead.

His face changed, softening. "She was an angel. When I think of my mother I think of soft warmth and love and beauty. A refuge." He smiled. "And I can still hear her laughter. Like Christmas bells ringing. She was a lovely woman. And that's not just a child's memory. Everyone says so."

"Was she happy with your father?"

His smile faded. "She loved him."

Sara nodded. She recognized the "keep off" signals his tone of voice was conveying. She might as well change the subject for now.

"Sheridan's mother is her sister, isn't she?"

"Yes," he said. "They were twins."

"Twins. That is so interesting. That must have been a comfort to you when you were little and lived with her and her family."

"Why?"

"Well, weren't they very much alike?"

"Not at all. Though people often try to pretend they were. But there is no comparison. My mother was wonderful." But he smiled, thinking back.

"When we were kids, Sheridan used to try to convince me that we were switched at birth." He chuckled. "He was supposed to be the prince, and I was the one who should have been raised in the family of a baron." He shook his head, frowning slightly. "I actually went through a period where I halfway believed him," he added softly.

Sara looked out over the hills toward where a hint of the city could be seen through a canyon opening. For some reason, she always got a funny feeling when Sheridan's name came up. She didn't know him well enough to dislike him. And yet...

"So Sheridan's mother..." she began hesitantly.

"Hey." He reached for her, cutting off the question she was slowly formulating. "Would Sam and Daisy be talking about things like this? No."

She paused, then gave in and smiled. "Oh, really? And just what would that crazy fun couple be doing?"

He pulled her closer. "I'm glad you asked."

She turned toward him, expecting his kiss, reveling in it, kissing him back, tangling with his tongue and making a sound of sweet satisfaction low in her throat. She felt his fingers trailing along her collarbone and knew where they were going, but did nothing to stop him as he pushed aside her blouse and slipped beneath her lacy bra. When the tip of his finger touched the tip of her nipple, she cried out with a new need she didn't know she had inside her, her hips moving of their own accord. Damian groaned softly.

"Daisy my darling," he whispered very near her ear. "We've got the will and the need. All we lack is the proper place. Once we're alone somewhere private…"

"No." She pushed his hand away and shook her head. "No, Damian, you know that's impossible."

He pulled her close and kissed her. "Nothing is impossible for Sam and Daisy," he reminded her.

She smiled, touching his cheek with a love she'd never felt before. "Ah, but that's where you're wrong. You created a couple from an era where making love wasn't a casual thing. Daisy will resist. She wants a ring on her finger before she lets even the man she loves into her bed."

"What?" He looked like a boy who'd just lost his pony. "That's no fair."

She laughed, pulling him back into position for kissing. "Sure it is. I get to tease you into a frenzy, but you don't get anywhere near home plate."

"What if I turn the tables?" he asked, kissing her eyes, her nose, her ears. "What if you're the one driven into a frenzy?" he asked. "You can beg and you can plead, but Cowboy Sam has too much honor to sully the name of the woman he loves by making love to her."

"Oh, yeah?" She tickled him, making him laugh, but deep down she wished she could challenge that scenario. She didn't think old Cowboy Sam would last two minutes if she really decided to test him.

Chapter 11

Sara had expected their pastoral ideal to be destroyed once they returned to the house in Beverly Hills, but she wasn't prepared to have it shattered quite so savagely. The moment they drove onto the property, they could both tell that something was wrong.

"Princess Karina has been kidnapped," the gate guard told them breathlessly. "The place is going crazy."

Damian was transformed in an instant, going cold and intense. "Tell me what happened," he ordered, getting out of the car and starting toward the house. Sara ran to take his arm and guide him, but he strode ahead as though he could see.

"It started this morning," the guard said, talking fast in a voice pitched high with nervous excitement and walking with them. "The princess left to give a talk at the Pasadena Library. Greg went along as her guard."

"Mr. Barbera was driving?" Damian asked, naming their usual chauffeur.

"Yes. They were still in Beverly Hills, just before turning onto Santa Monica Boulevard, when a group of men highjacked and overpowered them. Greg was shot. Mr. Barbera was hit too, I think."

"Who did it?"

"They say it must have been the December Radicals," he said, shaking his head.

"Damn," Damian bit out.

Sara remembered having heard that this group was considered one of the fiercest resistors to the Roseanovas returning. They had instigated a number of terrorist activities in Nabotavia in recent months.

"They're the worst," Damian said. "Who's on it?"

"Crown Prince Marco and Prince Garth are on their way here in the Learjet. The police have been called."

They had reached the house and the duchess came flying out the door. "Damian! Thank God you are back. I've got Tom bringing a car around. I've been going crazy waiting here, hour after hour. The FBI has been called in. I'm going to FBI headquarters to see if I can be of any help."

"I'm coming with you," Damian said quickly. "Sara, you stay here and man the phones so we can call in for news."

"Of course," she said automatically. She watched as Tom drove up and the two of them piled into the car and sped off. There was a huge hollow feeling where her stomach should be. If anything had happened to Princess Karina…

Going inside, she went straight to the kitchen, looking for Annie. She found her going over menu cards. There was something oddly reassuring about the efficiency of the woman getting back to her daily tasks.

"Annie, the others have gone into town. Where's Count Boris?"

"He left early for Santa Barbara for the day, visiting friends." She looked a bit disconcerted, which was certainly unusual for her. She hesitated, then added, "I've been trying to call him, but his cell phone doesn't seem to be working."

Sara thought a moment. "So none of the family is at home?"

"Only the duke, of course. Oh, my, I wonder if anyone has told him."

Something she could do. Sara felt a small flash of relief. "I'll go down and check."

She sped down the stairs and through the dark hallways, knocking sharply on his door. There was no answer, but the door swung open, and she went inside, looking into the corners and shadows for any sign of him.

"Hello," she called, walking over to his working desk. A Web page was up and open on his computer screen. It looked as though he'd been here recently. She turned to look for other signs of what he might

be doing or where he might have gone and noticed
that the big leather bound book he seemed to guard
so carefully lay open. She glanced down at it, appre-
ciating once again the beautiful illuminated letters.
The book seemed to be open to the family tree of the
current Roseanova family and she went closer to take
a look.

The duke came in like an Energizer Bunny, speed-
ing up and snapping the book closed so quickly he
almost caught her nose in it.

"Oops, no you don't," he said firmly, locking it
with the key around his neck. "Family secrets you
know, my dear. Not for the casual observer."

"What kind of secrets could you be hiding in
there," she said, half-teasing him.

"Oh, you'd be surprised. All families have their
secrets. Especially royalty." He nodded significantly.
"The royalty of the Western world is rather like a
far-flung small town, with the same sort of saints and
sinners, and the gossip to go with them. Sometimes
those secrets can topple thrones, or bring new stars
out of obscurity."

"Interesting," she told him, noticing that he
seemed to have a careworn look to him today. "But
I haven't come here to spy into your secrets. Actually,
I just wanted to make sure you knew about Princess
Karina."

He nodded. "I do know and I'm praying for her
safe return. If I were younger, I would be out looking
for her right now."

She looked at the older man. He had lived long and

he knew a lot. "Why?" she asked him, searching his face. "Why would these people do this to Karina?"

He sighed, looking suddenly even more haggard. "The old country ways die hard with some of these groups. They are just so Nabotavian."

She smiled. "But you're Nabotavian."

"Of course. Like many immigrants, we live a slightly schizophrenic life, one foot in the old world, one foot in the new. Hopefully, we usually take the best from both worlds."

Hopefully. She left him, hurrying back upstairs to wait for news. But so much was swirling through her head and her heart. Her morning with Damian had been so wonderful, so perfect. If only she'd had a few days to digest it. Instead, there was this awful kidnapping.

"Concentrate on Karina," she told herself softly. "That's all that's important now."

The afternoon seemed to drag on interminably. A couple of officers arrived to watch over the compound and make sure no other attempts were made. Damian called to let her know they had gone to the Los Angeles airport in case anything could be found out there, but had come up empty and were going back to the FBI headquarters. Marco and Garth arrived, both making phone calls and preparing to take off as well. Sara only had a few minutes to note that Garth was just as handsome as his two brothers, though he did look a bit more the playboy. There was something rakish about the set of his mouth, the look in his eyes. But the two men were very grim and Sara realized just how serious this was. For all they knew, their sister might be dead.

But she wasn't. The call came just as they were about to get into the car. The princess had been rescued!

"How? What?" Sara looked to Garth, who had the cell phone to his ear and was grinning broadly.

"It was Jack Santini," he told his brother with a note of triumph in his voice. "I told you calling him was the right thing to do."

Jack Santini. Sara frowned. Wasn't that the security guard Karina was in love with?

Quickly, Garth outlined how Jack Santini had stormed up the ramp of the airplane the kidnappers were using for their getaway and grabbed the princess right out of their clutches.

"It was down at an airport in Orange County, so it will take a few hours for them to get back here."

In the relief and celebration that gripped everyone on the compound, Damian and the duchess came up the driveway and had to be filled in on it all. Sara watched, feeling a bit of an interloper. But when Damian had heard the entire story, she was the one he turned to, and that filled her with quiet satisfaction.

The family all went into the sitting room to wait for the princess's return. Sara hesitated, thinking she should go up to her room and not intrude, but Damian turned, asking for her and making it clear he expected her to wait with the rest of them. Garth looked at her curiously a few times, but Marco seemed to accept her presence without a second thought, and the duch ess was so overcome with all the emotion of the day, she didn't seem to notice.

Dr. Manova, the family physician, arrived and the duchess was happier since that gave her something to do. She installed him in a room upstairs, ready to look Karina over for injuries once she returned. And then Count Boris came in, completely unaware of the entire adventure and stunned to hear the news. Someone called the hospital and found out that both Greg and Mr. Barbera were doing well. That was a relief.

Finally, the big moment came. They all rushed out to greet the princess, even the kitchen staff and the groundskeepers joined the family. Sara watched as the two emerged from the car, the tall, handsome law enforcement officer and the delicate princess who clung to him. They were so in love, it shone in their eyes and vibrated from their bodies. The sight of them together brought a lump to Sara's throat.

Karina did look a bit worse for her experience. There was a bruise along her jawline and her clothes were rumpled and a bit torn. But she seemed to be fine and resisted being inspected by the doctor until Jack promised he would still be there when she came back down.

Sara smiled. True love was a heartwarming sight.

Marco, Garth and Damian talked among themselves for a moment, then invited Jack into the den for a conference.

Sara's smile widened. Damian had already confided in her. They were going to offer Jack a knighthood in appreciation for his actions in saving the princess. And once he had that, he would be eligible to court Karina. The fact that the two would now get married seemed to be an accepted state of affairs all of a sudden.

"Good for you, Jack," she whispered to herself as she climbed the stairs to her room. She noticed that they had to make him a knight for it all to end happily. What would happen if she saved someone? Would they make her a princess? Unfortunately, she didn't think it ever worked that way.

A celebratory atmosphere settled over the dining room that night as dinner was served. Laughter filled the room and banter flew about the table.

"The king himself was kidnapped once, you know," the duchess told Sara and Jack, as the two newcomers to the story. "It was the year between when Garth and Damian were born. I remember it so well...."

"They kept him for over a month," Garth explained. "It was the December Radicals then, too, hoping to destabilize the country. They've made a lot of trouble over the years."

"Yes, he was treated very badly." Karina hesitated, then winced and went on painfully. "He was tortured and kept on mind-altering drugs the whole time. They say it was really awful."

"We didn't know if he was alive or dead," the duchess added. "The poor queen...." Her eyes filled with tears and she looked more human than Sara had ever seen her before.

"How did you get him back?" Sara asked.

Karina grinned, casting her aunt a significant look. "My aunt was afraid you would never ask," she said teasingly. "My uncle, the duke, rescued him."

"The duke!"

A slight smile curled the corners of the duchess's mouth. She looked out dreamily and was almost beautiful for a moment. "Yes," she said simply. "My brave husband. He was very much a dashing man in his younger days."

"It was quite a scene, they say," Marco contributed. "Guns blazing and blood flowing. You'll have to get him to tell you all about it some time."

"I'll do that," Sara said, laughing softly at the thought of that scholarly man doing a John Wayne scene. She glanced at Damian. He didn't seem to be enjoying the story the way everyone else was. His face was set and there was a look almost of pain around his eyes. Her own smile faded and she wished she knew what she could do to make him happy again.

"By the way, Damian," Marco said suddenly. "The duchess tells me the county office called this morning while you were out riding. They've dredged the lake more thoroughly and found all the missing parts. And your suspicions seem to be vindicated. The engineer thinks there's evidence to suggest someone tampered with your boat. I'm going out to look at it tomorrow. I'll let you know what I find."

If she hadn't noticed the pulse at his temple, she might have thought he hardly heard his brother.

Everyone started talking at once, and then things had
to be explained to Jack. There was speculation as to
who might have done the tampering, and the consen-
sus seemed to be the December Radicals, but Damian
didn't give his opinion, and she knew he had his own
theory. Even when Jack volunteered to make a police
report about the incident, he didn't speak.

It was only later, when Damian and Sara were
alone in his room, that he gave vent to his feelings.

"I am so damn sick of being shut behind the walls
of this darkness," he told her, emotion vibrating from
his tone. "My hands are tied. I can't do anything. I
can't even look into the accident. I have to let others
do everything for me." Suppressed rage seemed to
fill him. "How am I going to defend myself? How
can I keep the ones I love safe?"

His voice cracked on the last word. She didn't try
to answer. She knew he didn't want to hear platitudes.
So she sat very still and let him rage, and at a certain
point, she reached out and took his hand in hers. And
listened. He laced fingers with hers and went on ex-
pressing all the anger that had been building up in
him for weeks. And when he was finished and tired
from his fury, she stood, bent down to kiss him softly
on the lips, and said good-night. He reached out and
pulled her back and kissed her hard, with pure passion, but she broke away and left him with tears in
her eyes. They weren't playing Sam and Daisy games
now. It would be much too dangerous to stay.

The day of the Foundation Ball arrived and her
heart seemed to have taken up permanent residence

in her throat, beating wildly. This was it. Do or die. Had she earned her keep, or not? Coordination was going smoothly. Damian seemed cool and confident and ready. But she knew only too well how many things could go wrong at the last minute.

The authorities were now investigating the accident at the lake. Damian seemed calmer than she'd ever seen him. Apparently his diatribe of the other night had cleared something in him and left him open to a certain peace. They had spent the past few days working very hard on using the transmitter and preparing for all contingencies. Marco had taken a quick trip back to Arizona, but he called Sara every night for a progress report and to make sure she understood how important success was to his fledgling administration.

Luckily, Damian had thought to have Jack Santini watch them go through their paces a few days before, and he'd had some ideas that had helped immensely. He'd also shown them a small microphone that Damian could wear unobtrusively like a body wire where he could communicate back to Sara, making the success of the entire operation seem that much more possible. Now all they had to do was arrive early in order to set up their speaker systems in the control room. That was it. So why was she so nervous?

Maybe it had something to do with the plans she'd finally decided had to be made. Excitement about the ball filled every moment of the day, but behind it all, she knew there was something waiting to be dealt

with. Once the ball was over, she had to leave. The
decision wasn't easy. Though her fears for Damian's
safety where Sheridan was concerned had pretty
much faded, Karina's kidnapping proved that anything could happen at any time, and she hated to leave
him vulnerable. Still, what was she going to do?
Spend the rest of her life watching over him? That
was hardly realistic. There was really no choice.
She'd stayed too long and let herself get too close to
her client as it was. She had to leave before something
worse happened.

And then there was the specter of the engagement
announcement to come. That was one element of the
ball no one had talked much about. The plan called
for the announcement to be made during the midnight
supper. Sara wondered if she would be able to maintain her composure long enough to get out of there
once the deed had been done. She really had no idea.
She'd never been in a situation like this before.

But she was getting ready, arming herself emotionally and preparing herself for anything. The silver-
blue gown Karina had ordered for her fit like a glove
and the seamstress even improved on that at the last
fitting. Just after lunch, the princess called for Sara to
come join her and Sara went, not sure what Karina
had up her sleeve now. She arrived to find a hairdresser had been hired just for her. She protested
weakly that she was used to doing these things for
herself, but Karina smiled and led her into a chair
beside her own.

"We're going to do this together," she told her sunnily. "Get used to it."

Getting used to this sort of luxury was just exactly what she kept telling herself she couldn't afford to do. But in this instance, she sighed and let the pampering begin. And before long, she was loving it. The manicurist did her nails and the hairdresser's assistant washed her hair and a makeup artist came by to make a list of what she thought she would need. Then Karina's special friend, Donna, who always did her hair, arrived and trimmed them both, chattering away the entire time, making them laugh.

Karina was riding on clouds these days. She and Jack were scheduled to get married almost immediately. They were leaving for the castle in Arizona for the ceremony right after the ball.

"It's mostly because of the media," Karina confided. "After the kidnapping and all, we thought it best to get the wedding done quickly before the gossip rags pick up on it."

"Not to mention the fact that you want to make sure he doesn't get away again," Donna teased.

Karina grinned. "You'd better believe it!"

When Donna left the room to get supplies, Sara turned to Karina and smiled at her, thinking of what a different life she led from that of most young women her age. If she hadn't been such a sweetheart, Sara might have been just a little resentful. So much beauty, so much wealth, and now so happily in love.

"Tell me what it's like to be a gorgeous princess

who's desired by every man within a ten-mile radius,'' she asked musingly.

"Don't be silly," Karina answered with a laugh. "It's not like that at all." She leaned closer. "I'll tell you a secret. Jack Santini was the first man I ever saw that I knew I could love. And I knew it right away. The moment I first saw him."

"That's quite romantic. But you're so beautiful, I'm sure he felt the same way about you."

Karina smiled happily, confirming her statement without words needed. "You're beautiful, too," she said firmly.

Sara flushed. No one had ever called her that before—at least, no one who could see. "Karina, please…"

"You don't think so? Oh, Sara, your doubts are all in your head. Get rid of them!" She waved her hand as though that would do the trick.

"If only it were that easy."

"But it is. Take tonight, for instance. You're going to be stunning. Damian will be speechless in your presence."

Ignoring the implications that the princess knew how she felt about her brother, Sara shook her head and smiled ruefully. "That doesn't make any sense. You know he can't see me."

Karina laughed. "Sara! It has nothing to do with what he sees. It has everything to do with what you feel about yourself." She sighed. "Don't you know that beauty is a fantasy? Use that fact to your advantage. I always do."

Easy for you, Sara thought, but didn't say aloud. Still, she had to admit she was beginning to feel prettier than she ever had before. That probably had a lot to do with having expensive attendants dolling her up. But maybe, just maybe, it also had something to do with being in love. That made her shiver. Being in love was scary enough in and of itself, but being in love with a prince was enough to send her into orbit. Very soon she was going to have to leave him, and then she would find out what it was like to live with a broken heart.

The limousines arrived to take them to the hotel by midafternoon. They had reserved a whole section of one floor and that was where they would don their gowns and do the final work on their makeup and hairstyles. Once she'd checked in, Sara took advantage of some extra time to go down to the ballroom and check on logistics. She was going to be ensconced in the projection room. From there, she could see most of the floor. While she was scouting around she found Marco doing much the same.

"This night is so important," he told her. "What do you think of our chances?"

She put her head to the side, considering. "I think they're pretty good," she said at last.

He nodded, though he didn't look convinced. "I've been more worried about this than I've let on," he said.

Sara cocked an eyebrow. "Really?" she answered, then hoped he didn't hear the irony in her tone.

"Yes. Many times I've been tempted to take over

and make Damian sit this out. If he hadn't been so adamant that he could handle this, I would have.'' He gave her a sheepish look. ''I knew taking this away from him might destroy what confidence he seemed to have left after the accident. And I couldn't do that to him.'' He shrugged and looked worried. ''Now I only hope he doesn't fail us.''

Sara swallowed hard. She thought she understood what he meant. Failure tonight might threaten Damian's chance to repair his spirit and begin to build his life back up again. Her heart hardened with purpose. Damian would not fail if she had anything to do with it. That was a promise.

''One thing we do have going for us is the way Damian looks,'' Marco noted. ''He doesn't have that faraway stare most blind people seem to have. If you didn't know better, you'd think his eyes were tracking.''

''Yes. He's unusual in that.''

He was unusual in a lot of other ways, too. And tonight was her last night with him. Had she ever felt such a deep reluctance to leave a patient before? No. Never. Leaving was usually a relief. This time it was going to be a heartbreak.

Two hours later, dressed in her blue gown with her hair piled atop her head and her makeup in place, she looked pretty darn good. She had to admit it. And others seemed to think so, too.

''Oh, my word,'' Boris said when he saw her.

''Hey, you clean up real good,'' Tom said in his clumsy way.

"Sara Joplin, you look like a princess yourself," the duchess told her, looking startled to have made that assessment.

Even the duke had been dragged to this affair—because it was vital that they all give everything they had toward wooing the investors—and he said, "A vision. You do us credit, my dear."

All this praise was beginning to work. She actually felt beautiful. Maybe Karina had the answer after all.

She went down into the ballroom early and set up her equipment in the projection room, getting comfortable. Damian came in as she was finalizing things, his dark splendor enhanced by the wonderful black tuxedo. Her heart nearly stopped when she saw him.

He took her hand. "Wish me luck," he said.

"I wish you all the luck in the world."

"No, not like that." Pulling her toward him, careful not to muss her in any way, his lips unerringly found hers. "Like that," he whispered, and then he kissed her again.

Steps heard outside the door forced them apart. Sara turned away while Jack entered and began to install the wire inside Damian's shirt. She closed her eyes and held the feeling of his kiss in her soul. If only…

Once wired up, Damian went downstairs to try the system out. Looking down from her perch, Sara smiled as she watched him stroll about the floor, carefully avoiding the workers putting the finishing touches on the decorations. She turned the transmitter on quickly, ready to help guide him through the maze.

"Testing, testing. Can you hear me okay?"

His head rose. "Well hello, beautiful," he said in his most sexy voice.

She felt her heart jump and she began to answer him, but before she could get a word out, she faintly heard a feminine voice saying, "Hello yourself, handsome."

Darn. She hadn't noticed the very attractive event manager walking past him at the most inopportune moment.

"Oops," he murmured into the microphone. "You're going to have to give me better warnings than that."

"Sorry," Sara said nervously. "I'll get the hang of this. I promise."

A few minutes of practice took care of the jitters. And then it was show time. The royals all went into a lobby from which they would emerge, two at a time, to be announced over the loudspeaker system once enough of the important people had arrived to make it worthwhile. And Annie joined Sara in the booth. Since she knew most members of the Nabotavian community on sight, she was going to help identify them.

The large double doors opened and people in finery began to stream in.

"Here we go," Sara murmured, giving Annie a quick smile. "Damian? Can you hear me?"

"I hear you," he said. "The head of the Carlington Financial Group was just announced. I'm going to go out to greet him. Ready?"

She took a deep breath. "I'm ready."

"Let's go."

Chapter 12

Damian knew very well how dangerous it was to get cocky, but he couldn't help it. He was feeling pretty good about this. The ball was going splendidly. The music never stopped and dancers spun past him all the time. But he hardly noticed all that. He'd spent most of the last hour discussing business and he hadn't tripped up yet.

He'd felt awkward at first, out of his element. It reminded him of the time as a kid when he'd gone swimming in a muddy lake and lost his way underwater. Swimming with his eyes closed.

When he'd first come down the stairs, he'd turned and almost fallen over a potted plant set in his way. Luckily Jack had been beside him and had caught him before he'd hit the ground. Funny. Just weeks before

he would have felt humiliated by such a gaffe. Now
it didn't faze him at all. He'd righted himself, laughed
and gone on, forgetting it to all intents and purposes.
What had made the difference?

Sara said something in his ear and he grinned. Sara
Joplin had happened. That was the answer. Sure, he
was more in control. He'd practiced until taking instructions over the wire had become almost second
nature. He'd learned a lot about how to handle himself without his eyesight. He had a certain confidence
now, a sense of certainty that he hadn't had before.
He could do things.

If the ball had been held two weeks ago, he would
have arrived, been led into a chair and sat there the
entire evening, letting people come to him, feeling
stiff and awkward and helpless. Instead, he moved
around the room like a natural man. In some ways,
he had his world back.

And why? Because of Sara.

"Large man coming in on your left," Sara said in
his ear. "It's Grover Berrs of Venngut Industries. His
hand is out...hold it...hold it...now!"

He turned and put out his hand to meet that of the
industrialist. Sara's timing was perfect. "Grover," he
said cheerfully. "It's been a long time."

Grover wanted Nabotavian importing rights for his
large kitchen appliances line. Damian had it all memorized. He could call up what each businessman
wanted, and exactly what Nabotavia was going to re-
quire in return in order to accommodate them. So far,
things seemed to be going well. Everyone was hope-

ful about the new regime. Everyone wanted to get in on the action.

He and Grover came to an understanding, and he turned away, waiting for his next direction from Sara. Their hard work had certainly paid off. They meshed like a professional dancing pair, each anticipating the other's move.

"You know what?" he said to her through the microphone. "We make a great team."

"Woman coming in on your right," she said instead of answering, speaking fast. "Tall, curvy, red hair...oh, Annie says it's Gilda Voden, an old flame of yours. She's lifting her arms and puckering. Better reach out for her waist and hold her off or you'll be wearing her like a necklace."

He did as she suggested and his laugh was meant for Sara, but Gilda took it as her due and began gushing about how much she'd missed him. He smiled and nodded, but he was hardly hearing her. His mind was on the evening, on how this much-dreaded event was turning out to be a triumph. He hadn't had a drop of alcohol, but he was feeling the kind of high that only success could bring.

Extricating himself from Gilda's clutches, he made contact with another businessman, then overheard a conversation as Sara had him moving toward the bar, heading for a drink of water.

"I thought he was blinded in some sort of accident," an unfamiliar voice said as he passed.

"Oh, no. Look at him. I think it did impair his vision somewhat, but he's managing beautifully."

He grinned. "I'm managing beautifully," he reported to Sara. "I just heard someone say so."

"Be sure to remind him that you owe it all to your occupational therapist," she said tartly. "Now pay attention. Ten steps straight forward. One, two..."

He reached the bar, asked for water and followed Sara's instructions in order to grasp the glass at just the right time. Taking a long drink, he sighed with satisfaction and thought about Sara for a moment. She'd been with him for days now, constantly in his ear. And he liked her there. In some ways, she'd become a part of him, a part of his head...and even a part of his heart. Maybe it was because of the way she lived in his ear, but he seemed to have taken in a bit of her outlook, her optimism. Her goodness.

He coughed, choking on his last sip. Had he really thought that word? *Goodness.* Sara was loaded with it. Was it catching? Maybe. Would it last? Maybe.

"Leggy blonde coming up behind you. Annie can't identify. She's definitely zeroing in...."

"Damian! Darling!"

He knew the voice. Thana Garnet, beautiful film star. Funny how uninteresting she seemed now. He turned to greet her as though it were a chore he had to get out of the way before he could get back to business. Times had certainly changed.

"You'd better try dancing with her," Sara said.

"What?"

"You might as well. You're going to have to dance with the Waingarten girl when she gets here. Better practice now."

"Oh, all right," he grumbled.

"Damian, who are you talking to?" Thana asked suspiciously.

"My better nature," he told her smoothly. "He's telling me you are dying to dance. Is he right?"

She giggled and gurgled and made him want to snarl. Funny how silly this sort of woman seemed now that he was used to Sara. But she danced with him and it all worked reasonably well.

Shortly after he left her in Boris's capable hands, they had their first technical difficulties. Sara spoke, but all he got was static.

"I'm losing you. There's something wrong with this frequency."

"Okay," she said, barely coming through the static. "I'm switching to the other line. How's that?"

"Scratchy. But I can hear you."

"Let's get you out of the action until we get this cleared up. Go toward the coatroom. Turn to your right. Two steps, now left. Go...go...go...now stop."

He stopped, but had a sudden the sense of company. Listening to the breathing, he felt surrounded.

"Sara," he muttered into the receiver. "I seem to have joined a crowd. What have we got here?"

Nothing sounded in his ear. He was on his own. Smiling, he turned his head from side to side. "Hello," he said. "What's going on?"

"You tell me," a gruff male voice responded. "I got instructions to come over here."

"So did I," another old-timer agreed. "Better wait and see what we're supposed to do next."

"Me, too, right in my ear," said a timorous voice. "'Go toward the coatroom,' it said. 'Turn to your right. Take two steps.' It was very explicit." He paused, then added in a hushed voice, "Do you think it was God?"

Damian groaned. "Tell me," he said carefully. "Do you fellows by any chance all have hearing aids?"

"Well, yes."

"Of course. Just like yours."

"Hmm," he told them. "I think it was a test. And I don't think God was involved. Why don't you all just go back to where you were?"

Turning away, he spoke into the mike. "Sara. Can you hear me?"

"Yes. I'm back on the original line."

"Good. Whatever that frequency was that you were using, don't use it again. Everybody with a hearing aid is converging on my position. Next thing you know we'll have dogs howling all over the neighborhood. I'm going to try to escape. Give me directions, quick."

Sara was laughing in his ear, but she also got him out of his predicament.

"That poor bunch of men is still milling around the coatroom, wondering why they were called to meet there," she told him. "But you've got Ludwig Heim coming straight at you. Get ready for a bear hug."

The bear hug nearly crushed his bones, but he'd been ready for it and he laughed, greeting the financial officer of one of the largest industries in Nabotavia. Deep down, he felt a quiet sense of satisfaction. Whatever the problem, Sara always came through. Thank God he had her.

Sara was beginning to feel exhausted. Almost three hours of guiding Damian had just about worn her out. But when Annie hissed at her and announced, "Here's Joannie Waingarten," adrenaline pumped back into her system and she woke up, craning her neck to see what the young woman looked like.

The girl and her father were announced and a hush fell over the crowd as everyone turned to stare. What they saw was a short, plump and balding man with a very pretty daughter who looked like a teenage Shirley Temple on his arm.

Sara's heart sank. She hadn't known what to expect, and she hadn't known how she would react. She'd thought she might be able to take it calmly. After all, she'd always known Damian was never going to belong to her. But devastation swept through her. It took all her strength to keep the agony out of her voice as she continued to guide him. And then she had to listen as Joannie broke away from her father and ran to meet her prince.

"Prince Damian! Daddy told me to wait until he could bring me to you, but I just couldn't stop myself. I had to come see you. You're even cuter than you were last time I saw you. I'm going to be such a happy princess. I can hardly wait."

She didn't want to hear what Damian said back but

she couldn't abandon him. He sounded merely friendly at first, and then charmed as Joannie inquired into the condition of his sight and babbled admiringly over his ability to rise above it. They danced, with Sara helping, working hard to harden her heart so that she could go on. She would have given anything not to have to listen to their banter. It was pure torture.

But then came something even worse.

"I'm turning you off," he said softly into the microphone just after he'd asked Joannie to accompany him to a room off the main floor where they could have some privacy. "You can't see me in there anyway. Bye."

And his line went dead. Sara sat staring at her monitor for a long moment, trying to come to terms with this. He'd shut her out and gone to be alone with the girl he was going to marry. Nothing unusual about that, was there? No, nothing at all. So why did she feel tears stinging her eyes?

"Well, there they go," Annie said as though it were somehow satisfying to see Damian and Joannie disappear into a private room. "At least the girl was smart enough to get a marriage proposal. Most of these silly twits would trade their futures for a smile from a royal, much less a night of passion. They get ground up and spit out, like so much cannon fodder. You have to be crazy to think a royal will give you a tumble without something substantial coming their way."

Looking up, she met Sara's surprised gaze and

flushed as though she hadn't realized she wasn't just talking to herself.

"Sorry," she said quickly. "Listen, why don't you go take a break while you have the chance. I can watch things until you get back."

Sara jumped at the offer, thinking she would head for the rest room to hide. But she'd barely made her way down the stairs before she was snagged by Prince Garth.

"Ah, the lovely Ms. Joplin," he said, smiling rakishly. "May I have the honor?" He presented his arm.

Sara hesitated. The music sounded wonderful and dancing would certainly be better than crying in the ladies' room. Deliberately, she lifted her chin, pasted on a smile and accepted his offer. Soon she was whirling about the room with one gallant swain after another, and if only her heart hadn't been broken, she would have been having the time of her life. She laughed. She exchanged clever banter. She threw a few flirtatious looks. And things did seem a bit brighter.

And then, suddenly, it was Damian, helped by his brother Garth, who was cutting in and taking over. His arms came around her and she felt how hard and muscular he was beneath the tuxedo jacket, and her heart began to pound.

"I'd better get back up in the projection room," she noted breathlessly.

"Why?" he said, holding her close, his warm breath against her temple.

"So I can guide you," she said.

"Sara," he said patiently. "You can guide me much better this way. Just don't let go."

"But, aren't you going to be making the announcement soon? I'd better…"

"No," he said.

She stopped, frowning. "What do you mean, no?"

"No announcement."

"But…"

"I'm not going to marry her."

She drew in her breath with a sharp gasp and for just a moment, she clung to him, afraid her legs would give way from underneath her. "Why?" she whispered, looking into his beautiful face.

"I don't love her. And she doesn't love me. So it's off."

"Just like that?" She still couldn't get it through her head. "But Damian, why?" she repeated.

"Why?" He smiled, then dropped a light kiss along her neckline, nuzzling hungrily into her soft skin. "I'll tell you why. These last two weeks with you have really opened my eyes—metaphorically speaking, of course. And tonight has taught me something, too." His jawline hardened. "You know what? I've got a lot to offer my family and my country. I don't have to sell my soul just to do my part."

He was talking about the engagement. Sara gazed at him in wonder. She hadn't realized he had felt he was letting his family down with his blindness, that he needed to make it up to them somehow. But she could see that he'd become a new man tonight. He held himself with more presence, more confidence.

She might almost, she admitted to herself with a half smile, have called it arrogance. Almost, but not quite.

"You did great tonight," she told him, her eyes shining as she looked up at him. "Most people knew you were blind, but they didn't see a figure of weakness when they saw you. They didn't see a disabled person. You held your own. You carried it off. And the people you dealt with admired you for it, I could tell. They are going to deal with you. They trust you."

He nodded slowly. "I think you're right," he said simply.

"So you're not going to marry Joannie?" She just needed it confirmed one more time.

He smiled again, then pressed his cheek to the side of her head. "How can I marry Joannie," he whispered near her ear, "when you're the one who is opening my eyes?"

She gasped, then looked at him quickly, sure that he was teasing her. There might be many reasons why he would break off with the girl, but their relationship couldn't possibly loom large enough to be one of them. "Oh, Damian, don't..."

"Too late," he murmured. "Much too late to stop now."

He was acting like he meant it. Sara shivered, caught between guilty joy and abject despair. What could she say? What could she do? It was all so impossible. She wanted him so badly and she knew she couldn't have him. Pretending any different wouldn't change things. And she knew very well that he knew that, too.

He was pulled away by others before she had time to say any more to him. The midnight buffet had been opened and people were streaming in to get food. Sara hurried back to the projection booth and joined Annie. Replacing the headphones, she began guiding Damian again, but her mind was on escape. She knew very well she couldn't stay. She had to leave before she let him win her over. Because a growing part of her ached to have him sweep her off her feet and take her to a magic place where common sense didn't exist and she could let herself reach for forbidden fruit. To protect herself—to protect them both—she had to go.

The excitement of the ball still shimmered through the air around the Roseanova estate the next day. Everyone felt things had gone extremely well and everyone couldn't stop saying so. Sara came in for her share of the praise.

"We couldn't have done it without you, my dear," the duchess told her. "That earpiece scheme was the foundation for everything else."

They all chimed in with agreement and she felt very much a part of the family. Funny how that happened on the very day she knew she had to leave it.

Damian spent the day fielding phone calls from people who wanted to get in on funding the new Nabotavian regime, and Sara spent the day preparing for her departure. She had already arranged for one of the best occupational therapists she worked with to take over her duties with the prince. He was arriving the next morning. She'd packed her bags and cleaned her room. There were just a few little things she had to take care of before she left.

First, she had a long talk with Jack Santini. As the future head of security for the country, she thought he was the one she should consult with. She wanted to make sure someone was going to look after Damian's safety.

She knew it was the height of arrogance for her to think her leaving might put him in jeopardy, but still, she had to make the effort to take care of things. Jack assured her that the accident was being investigated by the best people, and that all the family, including Damian, were under constant protection from the family security staff because of the threat from various exile groups, including the December Radicals. Tom, he revealed for the first time, was an expert bodyguard, well-trained in protection methods and hired specifically because Damian was more vulnerable because of his blindness. That reassured her but she still had one concern.

She hesitated to bring up Sheridan. After all, in some ways it was none of her business. And all her fears about him had pretty much proved to be bogus. Besides, the man was in Europe now. Still, she knew Damian had been a little suspicious at one time and she wanted to make sure someone was aware of it. So she told Jack.

Maybe it was because he was almost as new to the family as she was that he took her apprehensions seriously. He didn't laugh, didn't scoff, didn't tell her she was being ridiculous. What he did do was tell her he would keep her comments in mind. And really, there wasn't much more she could hope for.

The last and hardest thing she had to do was tell Damian she was leaving. He took it much more calmly than she expected.

"It's time for me to go," she told him, trying not to appear as breathless as she felt. She'd been dreading this, sure that he would try to argue her out of it. "I just wanted to say goodbye."

He sat still for a moment, and then he nodded. She couldn't read his emotions in his face. "Are you going back to your apartment?" he asked.

"Of course."

He nodded again. "I've got your number, don't I?"

She hesitated. "Damian, I think it would be best if we didn't see each other anymore," she said, talking so quickly her words spilled over each other. "It's been interesting and exciting and we've had a lot of fun. But we both know that our places in the grand scheme of things don't allow for anything more. You may think you want me around, you may even think...well, romantically about me...but that is very common in cases like this. It's just transference. It happens all the time when two people work closely together like we have. It doesn't mean a thing and it needs to be snuffed out quickly before it becomes something unhealthy."

He nodded, looking serious and thoughtful. "I see. It doesn't mean a thing but it needs a knife through the heart right away before it takes over my life. Got it.''

She looked at him suspiciously, but there didn't seem to be any humor in his face at all. Or any anger. Or anything at all.

''Yes. Well, I'm going.''

He nodded again. ''Drive carefully,'' he told her. ''And thanks for everything.''

She stopped at the door, looking back. This was it? Not even a goodbye kiss? She didn't know if she was angry or just plain bewildered. ''Bye,'' she said, feeling desolate and lonely. And then she left.

Chapter 13

Everything was going to be okay. Sara was very cool now, very calm. It had been almost forty hours since she'd slipped away from the estate in Beverly Hills and moved back to her own apartment in Westwood. She was managing just fine.

She loved where she lived. An older area of town, it had a small business district mixed in with residential zoning, so she was able to walk to a small grocery store, a deli and any of a number of good restaurants. She knew a lot of the merchants by sight if not by name. She felt at home here, a part of the community.

And she was back. No more dreams of castles and kings.

She'd left feeling desolate but she'd convinced herself it was all for the best. And she'd told herself that

what she was doing was the only wise and professional path she could possibly take. If she'd stayed,
she knew she and Damian would have become lovers.
And what Annie had said in the projection room was
spot on. Only brainless twits became lovers with royalty and expected it to go anywhere serious. She was
just too smart to let that happen.

But oh, how she missed him! Deep inside, she was
grieving. She went about her normal chores, but her
heart was broken and her spirit was difficult to rouse.
She wanted to go to bed and pull the covers up over
her head and cry her eyes out. If she let down her
guard just a little bit, she knew that was exactly how
she would end up. So she stiffened her spine and got
to work giving the place a long-needed cleaning and
airing out the rooms. And that night she was planning
to go up to Pasadena and begin staying with Mandy
and Jim, helping them prepare for the arrival of the
baby.

A part of her was disappointed. She'd thought Damian would call and try to talk her out of what she
was doing. She'd prepared some strong arguments to
give him, to let him know she wasn't going to change
her mind. But it had been almost two days since she'd
left and she hadn't heard anything from him.

Well, probably he'd thought it over and arrived at
the same conclusion she'd come to. And her own disappointment was just childish. Except that she
couldn't seem to shake it. Had his claim to love her
really been so shallow?

Yes, of course, and a good thing, too. He's royal,

for Pete's sake! To a man, those royals are spoiled
and prone to living for today, forget about tomorrow.
You wouldn't want a man like that in your life. It
would be crazy to fall in love with a royal. Suicidal.

But it had its moments.

No. The romance of it, the wonder, is all an illu-
sion. Don't fall for it.

She wouldn't. She hadn't. She was here, wasn't
she? All alone and feeling very virtuous. What was
that poem about virtue being a cold bed partner? No,
she wouldn't think about that. She'd done the right
thing. She was sure of it.

The doorbell rang and she jumped, then made herself relax. It was probably her neighbor checking to
see if she was really back. She went to the door and
threw it open. And came face-to-face with the man
she couldn't get out of her mind.

"Damian!"

"Hi. May I come in?"

"Oh. But..."

He didn't wait for her permission. Suddenly he was
inside, kicking the door closed behind him, throwing
his white cane to the side of the room and turning
toward her with a smile that curled her toes. He
seemed to fill the place, his shoulders so wide, his
form so tall and straight.

"Sara Joplin, I have missed you every minute since
you left."

"Oh." She tried hard to think of the arguments
she'd had ready but for some reason her mind had
gone blank on the subject.

He took a step toward her and reached out to take her by the upper arms, surprising her again. "If you've got any company, you'd better ask them to leave," he said quietly, his fingers moving against her skin as though he were soaking in the feel of her.

"Why?" she asked breathlessly. "What are you doing?"

He pulled her closer. "I'm preparing to make long, slow, sweet love to you, Sara," he said, his voice low and husky with desire.

"What?" Her own voice squeaked in her ears. "Now?"

"Right now." He dropped a kiss on her lips. "Right here." His arms curled around her. "On the floor if you don't take me to the bedroom."

"Oh, Damian..."

His mouth stopped the words of protest and her muscles felt like day-old spaghetti. There was no use resisting. His kiss was going to turn her own body against her. She sighed, relaxing in his arms and beginning to take her own measure of pleasure from the feel of his sweet lips, the rasp of his hot tongue. She was so hungry for his smell, his taste, the feel of his body against hers.

"The bedroom," he reminded her softly.

"Th-this way," she stammered, feeling drugged by his potent seduction. Thoughts of resistance had fled and she didn't miss them.

He began to shed his clothes on the way in, first his shirt, then his belt, his shoes and socks. Sitting on the bed, she let her gaze linger on the rounded muscles of his wonderful chest, then slip down to watch as his long, beautiful fingers worked with the closure on his slacks and let them slide casually to the ground. He had the most gorgeous body she'd ever seen. Watching him, she felt tears well in her eyes.

"No one should be allowed to be this beautiful," she muttered, more to herself than to him.

"What?" He turned to her, his naked body shining in the rays of evening sunlight that slanted in through the window.

She didn't speak. Not only had she forgotten anything she might have wanted to say, any ability to articulate thoughts seemed to have left her. Thoughts were gone. Only feeling remained. Feeling, and emotion so deep and strong, it was almost a form of pain.

She touched him, let her hands run down his golden skin, exploring his hard muscles, but avoiding the one place she was still shy of until he took her hand and put it there. She could hardly breathe. He was so hard, yet smooth as butter, and she wrapped her fingers around him, holding tightly. His low groan of pleasure filled her with an excitement she'd never known before and when he kissed her, she reached up to take more of him, feeling bolder.

He came down on the bed, reaching for her. "Hey. We need to get rid of these clothes," he told her, sliding his hand up under her jersey tank top and curling his fingers around the edge of her bra.

"I…okay," she said, and her voice was shaking.

He stopped and seemed to stare down at her. "Sara, you're not a virgin, are you?" he asked softly.

She hesitated. "Well, not really."

He started to laugh. "What the hell does that mean?"

She wet her lips and tried to explain. "There was this one man I thought I was in love with a long time ago and we...well, I'm not really a virgin. But I wouldn't consider myself a full-fledged experienced woman, either."

He pulled her close, laughing. "Sara, Sara." He dropped a kiss on her lips. "Don't worry. We'll take it very slow."

His hands went back to help her undress. "This is going to take a long time, you know," he told her as he pushed her shorts down over her rounded bottom. "I've got to see every inch of you and I've got to do it all by hand."

"Oh!" She shivered deliciously. "Damian, I don't know..."

"But I do." He found her breast with his mouth, his tongue curling around the nipple, making her gasp. Her hips moved and he laughed low in his throat, loving her body, loving her response. They were floating in a fog of desire now, and every move was driving anticipation higher and higher.

"Just hold it back," he whispered. "The longer you can hold it back, the better it will be."

She didn't know if she was going to be able to do that. She was already trembling with desire for him and her heart seemed to have taken up beating down low between her legs, making her feel just a little crazy.

"Just wait," he told her. "I've only begun to explore your body. It takes a long time for a blind man to see, you know."

She groaned in sweet agony. "But, I can see every bit of you in one glance and you're so beautiful and..." She writhed at his touch, her body moving as though something had taken possession of her. "Oh, how can one man be so sexy?" she moaned. "I don't think I can wait...."

"That's okay," he told her as he trailed kisses down across her stomach. His hand slid down to caress her. "You go right ahead."

"No, I really need you." She shuddered, reaching for him and he laughed softly, delighting in her reactions.

"Please," she begged him, feeling she was about to go mad. "Oh, please..."

He gave in, coming to take her with a fierce deliberation, as though doing so was sacred somehow, full of sweet, hot lust, but also filled with promises and reverence, an homage to some ancient god of intimate relations, a gift to tradition, an honor to primitive passions that ran deep in the species and exacted their price. She quickly found her rhythm and held on, whimpering as wave after wave of sensation roared through her. He held back, biting down on his lip to keep from bolting, waiting until she'd drained the last drop of pleasure, then he found his own release, quick and hard and triumphant, claiming her for his own in a way he didn't know he knew.

They lay back, entangled in each other's arms,

panting for breath. And as she regained her senses, Sara began to laugh. He winced.

"Is my lovemaking really that funny?"

"No," she said, shaking her head. "It's just that…this is exactly what I swore would never happen. And now that it has, I wish we could do it again."

He smiled. "Don't worry. I'll be ready in a few minutes." His hand cupped her soft breast. "But we're going to have to pace ourselves."

"Why?" she asked innocently.

He touched her hair. "Because we're going to be doing this all night long," he informed her solemnly.

"Damian!" She laughed. He was so loving and yet so outrageous. She wished she could stay here with him forever, blocking out the world and all its problems.

He pulled her close. "I have to make up for a lifetime of being without you." All the laughter was gone and he sounded very serious. "You are so special, Sara. I've been starving for what you are. Now I'm going to savor all I can get of you."

She sighed. This was the way she'd always dreamed love could be. All you needed was the right man. And Damian was definitely the right one for her.

He went back to playing with her breast. "I'm planning on getting to know each one of your body parts intimately," he said, the humor returning to his voice. "And after each one is fully explored, we'll celebrate it."

"You're crazy," she said, but her affection for him was plain.

"For instance, this breast is so soft and delicious," he said, caressing it with his cheek. "Just when I think it's melting away, it surges back and fills my mouth with ambrosia. It's quite unique."

She made a sound of skepticism. "It's just like the other one," she pointed out sensibly.

"Oh, no, it's not. This one is very much its own body part. It's got a personality all its own." He kissed her nipple, pulling it up hard in a way that made her draw in her breath. "And the other one is going to take just as much study for me to define it and get to know its unique attributes."

She gave him a baleful look and pulled away from his hand. He was already reigniting fires she thought were out. "This is getting much too silly," she said, shaking her head. "What would Cowboy Sam say?"

"Cowboy Sam would be on my side. He's a lot like me, you know." He reached and touched her where it was guaranteed to make her gasp in quick ecstasy. "But if you want me to be more serious, you got it, babe. I'm ready." And he proved it by rolling up and sliding inside her and bringing her along with him on a fast trip to a climax so intense, she cried out and then bit down on a pillow to keep from screaming.

"Stop it," she said, panting for breath and feeling frenzied. "We can't keep doing this."

"Why not?" he asked, laughing at her.

"I don't know." She shook her head, grasping for a reason. "It just seems so decadent."

"Hey, decadence is my lifestyle. I'm the prince. It's *de rigueur*." His tone got more cynical. "Royalty by its very nature is decadent."

Her fingers tangled in his wavy hair. She loved this man. That was good enough for now. "It doesn't have to be, you know," she noted wistfully.

He went up on his elbow, stretching his beautiful body beside hers.

"You know, with you around," he said so quietly, she had to strain to hear him, "something other than decadence seems workable in a way it never has before." His hand touched her face. "Have I told you lately that I love you, Sara Joplin?"

She went very still, holding her breath. Had he really said those words? But maybe that was something he said easily. Maybe he didn't mean it the way she heard it. Maybe...

"Sara?"

She realized with a start that he needed verbal feedback since he couldn't see how she was taking his statement.

"Damian, I don't think you should say something like that. I'm a simple person and I tend to take things literally."

"That's how I want you to take it." He kissed her softly. "I love you. Want me to take out an ad in the paper? I love you." His hands went on either side of her face, holding her still. "I don't say that lightly. In fact, I've never said it to another woman."

"Never?" she asked tremulously, because she couldn't think of anything else to say.

"Never."

"Well, all right then," she allowed, her voice still shaky. "I guess you already know that I love you, so..."

He laughed, pulling her up into his arms and rocking her. "Sara, my love, how am I supposed to know that if you have never told me?"

"I thought you would just know."

"I don't know. Tell me."

She licked her lips. "Damian, I love you." Suddenly she was hugging him back, holding on tightly. "I love you, I love you," she said with building joy. Tears were flooding her eyes.

They spent another half hour talking softly, laughing, holding on to each other as if to let go would make them lose the magic. But little by little, the outer world did start to worm its way in.

"You know one thing you haven't told me," she said as the afternoon melted into evening. "I haven't heard how your family took you breaking the agreement to marry the Waingarten girl?"

He groaned and fell back against the pillows. "The reaction was a mixed bag. The duchess had a fit."

Sara nodded. She'd seen a bit of that before she'd made her escape. The duchess had been scowling while people were still eating at the midnight buffet once she realized the announcement was not being made.

"And Marco seemed a little annoyed. Mostly, I

think, because he feels responsible and doesn't like it when plans get changed on him. But Garth and Karina both said they were behind me. Of course, Ted Waingarten is threatening to sue. But we didn't have a legally binding contract, so I think he's just blowing hot air at this point."

She sighed. "When you cut off the wire and went into that room with her, I thought…"

"You thought things you should know better than to think," he teased her. "I'd decided to tell Joannie it was off and I didn't think it was fair to let someone listen in to that conversation."

"Of course. I'm glad you did that. There was no reason to humiliate her." She hesitated. "But just days ago it seemed so important that you marry her and secure the funding her father could provide. What changed?"

He was quiet for so long, she thought he wasn't going to answer. But finally he turned and stroked her hair and began talking in a low voice.

"I'll try to give you a background for what happened. So much of it is emotions, not tangible facts, so bear with me." He took a deep breath and went on. "In some ways, I've always felt like the odd man out in my family. Partly I guess it was spending a lot of time with Sheridan's people instead of in Arizona with my brothers or here with Karina. Plus, being the youngest boy in a family like mine wasn't always easy. I always felt like Marco and Garth had done everything already. I was just the tagalong."

He stopped and groaned. "Lord, I sound like a

whiner. But I'm just trying to explain this to you. And to myself, when it comes down to it. When we all went to Nabotavia last year to help with the revolt against the faction that killed my parents, the ones who've been running the country for the last twenty years, I had dreams of taking revenge and doing great things. You know, the usual warrior fantasies. But instead of doing a lot of hand-to-hand combat, I ended up negotiating with businessmen and making deals for funding. I didn't feel like I exactly covered myself with glory. Marco and Garth are the heroes of the return. I'm the money guy."

He sounded bemused rather than bitter, but she bit her lip, wishing she could comfort him and knowing any attempt to do so would be met with outrage. Still, she thought he was describing a pretty typical youngest son situation and she knew there was more than that involved.

"And then," he was continuing, "when I went blind…well, let's just say I thought my chances of doing anything great were very possibly pretty much over." He grimaced. "But I still hadn't done my part. I needed to do something to help my family and my country. So when they began hinting around that we really needed the Waingarten money and that I could guarantee that with a marriage proposal, I decided I'd better do it. It seemed like little enough to do when the others had all done so much more than I had. I didn't have much of a life to look forward to anyway."

He turned and threw his arm over her, pulling her closer to him.

"But that all changed when you came along." Leaning down, he aimed for her mouth but caught her ear and kissed it anyway.

"It's nice to know I've got life-altering powers," she said lightly, turning her face so that his lips could find hers. "And here I was just doing my job."

"You did your job and then some." His voice deepened. "Sara, you showed me that being blind wasn't the end of everything. In some ways, it was a new and better beginning for me. You've opened up my world." He cradled her in his arms, rocking gently. "And I want you in it."

She reached up to touch his face, her fingers gently outlining his cheek. Tears rimmed her eyes and she sniffed. "Damian, I'm so glad you've realized that there is infinite untapped potential waiting inside you. You can still do great things, you know."

"I know." He said it with firm confidence. "I've got resources I didn't know I had, right here." He slapped his hand against his chest. "And right here," he added, reaching for her again.

She loved him and loved being in his arms and in his thoughts, and she loved that he thought he loved her. But she knew this wasn't going to last. It couldn't. And as much as she told herself to let it be, just enjoy it while she had it, the practical side of her nature wouldn't be silenced.

"Damian," she began hesitantly, "you know, people often get attached to their therapists...."

He groaned. "Not that again. I thought over all you said when you left. I gave it two days of good hard thinking. And you know what I came up with?" He kissed her hard, stopping the words. "Sara, I love you. I want to be with you. I want to make love with you. Not my therapist. And as long as you want that too, why the hell should we deny ourselves?"

Did she have a good reply? No. All she could think of were things like, "Because it's the right thing to do," and "Because I know you'll break my heart no matter how much you think you won't." And they had gone way beyond that. It was too late to stop now.

Her fingers were tingling. She would love to revel in his devotion, but she still couldn't believe in it. And she couldn't do it on a lie, even an implied one.

"Damian, you don't understand," she said, and each word was painful. "I'm not really right for you. It's not only that I'm not royal or anything near it. I'm not like the women you're used to."

"Thank God." He said the words with heartfelt emphasis. "I don't love them. I love you."

"What I mean is…" Swallowing hard, she closed her eyes and made herself say it. "I'm not beautiful. I'm very ordinary."

He rose above her, his smile luminous. "You're the most beautiful woman I've ever met."

"No, that's just it, I'm not."

"Yes, you are." His fingers skimmed her face. "I know you, Sara. I can feel your beauty. I know it with my hands. But more than that, I know it with my heart.'' He gave her three tiny kisses along her jawline. ''You might as well face it. I love you and I'm not going to be argued out of it.''

She sighed. She loved him so much. If only she could see a future for them. But her idea of a future was very different from his, she was afraid. Even now she had a hard time letting go and just enjoying him. She felt she ought to be doing something, saying something, making a difference somehow.

''You know, I've never cooked for you,'' she said suddenly.

He raised one dark eyebrow. ''Is that important?''

''Of course it is.'' She half sat up. ''I have to cook for you.''

He could tell by her tone of voice that it really was significant. That seemed a little odd. He would rather make love again than eat. But suddenly he realized what it meant. Cooking for him was a gift—a gift of love. He wondered if anyone had ever given him a gift like that before—and if he hadn't noticed what it meant at the time. It had taken becoming blind to show him how much of life he hadn't been paying attention to.

''We've got to eat. You've got to keep your strength up,'' she teased him, rolling out of bed. ''I'll just run to the store on the corner. I won't be gone long. And then I'll fix you dinner.''

He lay back and ''saw'' her in his mind's eye. She was getting dressed. He could see a lot of her by the sound of what she was doing, of her breathing, of the little snatches of her voice. In some ways, he saw a lot more this way than he ever had before. Things he wouldn't have noticed now stood out loud and clear. And he liked what he saw.

"Come on," she ordered him. "Get up and I'll give you a quick tour of the apartment so you'll know what you're doing while I'm gone."

He rose reluctantly, but she took his hand and led him from one end of her place to the other, pointing out things to watch out for, letting him get the lay of the land. And surreptitiously filling her memory banks with the wonderful sight of his naked form.

"Here's your white cane in case you need it," she said, stashing it in the bedroom. "Oh, and I've got to remember to get some lightbulbs. The hall light is burned out and it's dark as night in here."

"Hardly a factor I need concern myself with these days," he said dryly. "But get a new bulb, by all means. You sighted people are such babies about being able to see, after all."

She laughed at him, made a quick list, gave him a kiss and was out the door. He listened to her leave, then got up and made his way to the bathroom. A nice cool shower would feel awfully good, he decided, and so he had one, and it did. He let the fresh water massage his skin for a good five minutes, then turned off the water and began to towel dry. A sense of peace and well-being filled him. Where was that hard ugly core of anger he usually held inside? It was gone for the moment, at least. And only now did he realize how cheerless it made him to carry it around.

Suddenly he saw it like a physical thing, a motley

clump of resentment and regret, his bitterness toward his father tangled with his agony at losing his mother lumped with his feelings of inadequacy and the sense of being alone in the world.

Time to let it go, he told himself. Forgive and forget. Don't worry, be happy. Whatever. Just don't go there anymore. It's not a pleasant place to be.

He pulled on his jeans, then lay down on the bed and closed his eyes, feeling happy—waiting for Sara to return and make him happier. He was half-asleep, almost dozing when he first heard it.

His eyes blinked open into his constant darkness and he held his breath. There was someone coming into the apartment and it wasn't Sara.

In a flash everything came flooding back, his accident, the suspicions he'd had, the official report that backed his fears, the knowledge that someone wanted him hurt, at least, and maybe dead. He'd avoided dealing with it and now that neglect had come back to haunt him.

Without thinking, his hand shot up to test the lightbulb on the bedside lamp. It felt cool—it wasn't on. Rising as soundlessly as possible from the bed, he touched the switch by the door. That light was off, too. Good. He'd have a better chance in the dark. That way, they would be even. Gliding like a ghost, he took a station just inside the door and waited for the intruder to come looking for him.

And waited. It was taking too long. The person was moving around in the kitchen, then walked over to look out onto the balcony. Every step he took was a signal, loud and clear, to Damian's newfound senses. He waited for him to turn and come his way, but it didn't happen. Frowning, he tried to think why.

It hit him like a thunderbolt. This person wasn't after him at all. He probably didn't even know he was here. He was after Sara. A sick knot formed in the pit of his stomach. What an idiot he was not to have thought of that sooner. Time was getting short. Sara would be back soon. She might be starting up the stairs right now. He had to take care of this jerk before she returned. He couldn't risk what might happen if he didn't.

He hesitated. What if he was wrong? What if this was someone who knew her and was just waiting for her to come back? What if this person was used to coming in at will?

He narrowed his eyes, concentrating. No. This wasn't a friendly visitor. The vibes he was getting were angry and evil. He was sure of it. This was danger and he had to take care of it. If the bastard wouldn't come to him, he would have to go out and make something happen. But he needed something. A weapon.

He felt on the nightstand. A small ceramic lamp and a book. Not very helpful. The top of the chest of drawers wasn't any better. Very carefully, he made his way to the bathroom and found something on the counter. It seemed to be a curling iron. It was too light, but it would have to do. Oh, for the good old days when houses were littered with items made from real iron.

Taking it in hand, he slipped down the hallway, flattening himself against the wall just inside the doorway to the living room. Then he made a deliberate scraping sound against the wall to attract the enemy.

All sound went dead in the other room. He held his breath, waiting to see what the intruder would do. Finally, he heard faint footsteps coming toward his position and he tensed, every sense alert, judging speed and distance.

He knew right when the visitor came through the doorway, and he struck at exactly the right time. At least, he hoped it was the right time. He only knew for sure that his weapon came in contact with human flesh and there was a yelp of pain and then a fist grazing off his jaw. But the man fell as he hit out, then scrambled to his feet and began to try to escape. Damian went after him with a flying tackle, but he missed him entirely and landed hard on the ground. Still, the intruder was moving away, heading for the kitchen. And at that very moment, the door swung open and Sara called out.

"Damian? I hope you like anchovies."

He could hear the man change course and head for the balcony.

"Sara! Get out! Go quickly!" Damian yelled at her, trying to make sure she got out of harm's way.

But he might as well have been yelling at the wall.

"What? What is it?" she cried, running toward the hall and grabbing him as he emerged into the living room. "What's happened?"

"Didn't you see him? The balcony..."

Whirling, she ran toward the balcony and looked down at the street. The drop was only about ten feet to the sidewalk, a jump that could be made easily by a man in halfway decent shape.

"Who was it?" she asked him, glancing at the curling iron he still held like a club. "He's gone now."

Damian wasn't sure if he was glad or sorry. His heart was thumping so hard he began to wonder what heart attacks felt like. Adrenaline was still coursing through him and he wanted to hit the guy again, harder and maybe even lethally.

"You don't have some boyfriend who comes in when you're gone, do you?" he asked, just covering bases.

"No. No one has a key to this place but me."

He nodded. He knew that already. Because he knew who the intruder was. And he knew that this wasn't over. He would be back. And next time he would probably be more prepared. It was all very well to glory in the new senses he could employ, but that still didn't give him even odds with someone who could see.

"Come on," he told her, turning back toward the bedroom and beginning to feel his way. "We've got to get out of here."

He grabbed his clothes and began to dress, all the time detailing for Sara what had happened.

"Ever had an intruder in here before?" he asked her.

"Never."

He nodded. "I'm afraid he was here because of

me," he said simply. "But that means he knows he can hurt me through hurting you. That's why we've got to go."

"Go? Go where?"

He hesitated. That was a very good question. Everyone at the Beverly Hills estate had left for Arizona and Karina's hurried wedding. That wouldn't be any safer than this was.

"We'll decide that in the car," he told her. "Right now I think we'd better get out. Come on. Grab an overnight bag and let's go."

They were out the door ten minutes later, hurrying toward where she'd parked in the open garage.

"How about your sister's?" he asked her very near her ear, hoping no one else could listen in.

She nodded, realizing what he was doing. "Sounds good," she said shortly. "I'll give her a call on my cell phone as soon as we are underway. Here, I'll show you the passenger side door...."

"Wait." He held up his hand and stopped her. They were only a foot away from the car. He frowned. "I don't like this."

"What? My car? It's an oldie, but a goodie. It runs, at least, and..."

"Wait!" He put his hands carefully and very gently on the hood of the car. Then he snatched them back. "There's a bomb in this car," he said firmly.

She wrinkled her brow and looked at her old jalopy. "How can you tell?"

"I don't know." He shook his head. There was no rational reason, but he knew it was true. There were

times when he really felt his blindness in the real
world did open up a new area of special insight that
was unexplainable. "But I can. I can feel it, smell it,
hear it." And if only he could see, he could do something about dismantling it. But as things stood, avoid-
ance was the best plan. He reached out and grabbed
her hand. "Come on. We can't take this car."

"How did you get here?" she asked, looking
around for a car she might recognize.

"I had Tom bring me over, but he's long gone.
We're going to have to walk to some place where we
can get a cab. Got any ideas?"

She had ideas all right, but she couldn't help but
look back regretfully at her car as they hurried down
the street toward the little deli where she knew the
manager and they could wait for a cab out of public
view. She found it very hard to believe he could sense
a bomb that easily. Still, he hadn't been wrong yet.
And as she walked along with her hand in his, she
knew she would trust him beyond anyone else in the
world—at least in the protection department.

"My hero," she whispered.

He squeezed her hand and grinned. "So far so
good. But save the accolades for when we get this
bastard locked up." He raised her hand to his lips and
kissed her fingers. "Then you can show me all the
hero worship you want."

She loved him, loved his teasing, but she was more
worried than she was letting on. He hadn't said who
he thought was trying to hurt them, and she wasn't
ready to ask for his theories just yet. She was afraid

she knew whom he suspected. She'd had her doubts about his cousin from the first. But she also knew that it was going to hurt him deeply if his suspicions panned out.

Chapter 14

Sara was nervous. How ridiculous! But she couldn't help it. What was Damian going to think of Mandy and Jim and their tiny little house in a modest neighborhood? What were Mandy and Jim going to think of her bringing a real live prince into their home? Two worlds were about to collide and she hoped the crash wouldn't take any casualties.

Jim opened the door when they arrived on the doorstep, gave them barely a glance, and dashed back into the house, saying, "Oh, there you are, forgot you were coming, come on in, Mandy's got contractions, we're going to the hospital, it's too soon, I'm packing the bag, ohmigod, my poor little Mandy!"

Sara looked up at Damian and shrugged. "Out of the frying pan, into the fire," she said wryly. "From

one maelstrom to another. That was Jim, by the way.
And now I'm going to introduce you to my very pregnant little sister Mandy.''

Mandy seemed sublimely serene for someone about
to be rushed to the hospital. Sitting on the couch,
holding her stomach like a huge melon in her lap, she
was the picture of calm in a raging sea.

"Prince Damian Roseanova, it is a pleasure to meet
you,'' she said, taking his hand in hers and smiling
up into his face. "I've been reading up on your family
and the history of Nabotavia. So much tragedy! I'm
so glad you are getting your country back—and that
your people are going to have your family back in
charge. I know you'll do great things.''

"Thank you for your support. I appreciate it.''

"Do you know that our parents actually have a
chapter on your country in one of their travel
guides?'' Mandy said.

"I'm sure they do.'' Damian frowned. "I suppose
they are coming for the birth of their first grandchild?''

Sara and Mandy exchanged a look.

"What would give you that idea?'' Mandy asked
wryly.

"Common decency,'' he said.

Sara was surprised at his vehemence, but warmed
by his interest.

"Sara has told me a little bit about them,'' he went
on. "I haven't really had parents since I was eight
years old, but it seems to me parents have certain
responsibilities. I don't understand yours.''

"Nobody does." Mandy sighed. "I think they're just people who should never have had children." She stopped, her eyes widening. "Oops, here it comes again."

She began to do her rapid breathing, lightly running her hands over her rounded belly at the same time, staring at a focal point and seemingly in another world for the duration of the contraction. Sara frowned, worried.

"How long has this been going on?" she asked Jim as he raced through the house, collecting his wife's overnight bag and stuffing it with all sorts of things.

"Going on?" He looked at her blankly. "Oh, you mean the contractions? I don't know. Hours, it seems like. Maybe days." He had a wild look in his eyes and she realized she wasn't going to get any information out of him that she could count on.

Luckily, Mandy was coming back to normal. "They started about an hour ago," she told her sister. "And they started very hard right away. The doctor says to come right in and that is what we're going to do, once Jim settles down and remembers where he parked the car."

Sara turned and caught Jim as he started through the room on another sweep. "Jim, let's go," she said firmly. "I'll drive. You help Mandy. Take her left arm. Damian will take her right."

"But I don't have everything she needs packed yet," he said fretfully, looking around the room with glazed eyes.

"Give me the bag." She took it from his submissive hands. "I'll carry it." She gasped when she felt the full weight of it. "You've got enough in here for a Mediterranean cruise. If you've forgotten anything we can always come back later. Now let's get Mandy to the doctor!"

Turning to Damian, she whispered, "The man is a brilliant biologist, but has no common sense whatsoever. You're going to have to keep tabs on him for me."

"Aye-aye, Captain," he told her with a grin. "I had no idea you ordered everyone around just the way you've always done with me."

"If I didn't tell you all what to do, you'd stand around like turkeys with your beaks open in the rain," she said, only half-kidding. "Let's go."

They went. Mandy was checked in rapidly and soon had a room with a drip set up in hopes of slowing the contractions, and perhaps stopping them altogether.

"Delivering her baby at this point wouldn't be a disaster," the doctor told them all. "But we would like to get another week or two under her belt before she lets that little angel out into the big bad world. I'd like to keep her quiet for a while. You all go out into the waiting room and I'll come by with an update in an hour or so, just to let you know what to expect."

They camped out in the overstuffed chairs of the waiting room, anxious but hopeful. Jim picked up a magazine, flipped through it without seeing any of the pages, and set it down. He got up, then sat down, then got up again. Sara shook her head, hiding a smile. It was cute how much he cared for her sister, but he wasn't much good in a crisis. Not like Damian.

She thought again of how he'd defended her apartment from...someone, even though his blindness made that darn difficult and dangerous and she had to reach over and touch him, just to make sure he was still real. She only wished he had something to do. He hadn't learned Braille yet, so he couldn't read. But there must be something....

Then she had an idea. She still had Mandy's overnight bag with her for some reason, and she dug into it, finding what she wanted right away—a personal tape player with earphones. Fumbling in her purse, she pulled out the tape of Nabotavian poetry that the duke had been trying to get Damian to listen to. Popping in the tape, she offered the player to Damian.

"Since you can't read a magazine, you might enjoy listening to this," she told him.

He took it from her and put the earphones on. She watched apprehensively, not sure how he would react once he realized what she'd done. He pressed the play button, and one eyebrow rose, but he gave no other indication that he heard a thing. And after watching for a few minutes and getting no feedback, she gave up and went back to her magazine. Either he was listening or he wasn't. In any case, she'd done her best to further the duke's good-hearted agenda.

Damian was listening. Most of this poetry he'd read at one time or another. The words were beautiful, full of ideals and values that highlighted another time, another place. A golden age. Were he and his brothers going to be able to bring it back?

Suddenly something flashed in his eyes. He held his breath. It had happened before, but just like before, nothing came of it. It had been so quick, so small, it might have been brought on by wishful thinking. Everything in him longed for it to be more than that. He'd learned a lot since Sara had come into his life, and he knew that his blindness was not the end of the world. But sight was such a miraculous gift. To be able to see, to be able to know Sara in that way, to be able to open up the world again…he would give almost anything to have that back.

Sighing, he went back to listening again.

A half hour later, he took off the earphones and handed the player back to her. "I've got a headache," he said.

She sighed. Oh, well, she'd tried.

The doctor came out a little over an hour later and told them nothing had changed and he didn't expect anything other than a slow response to the drip until morning. He okayed Jim's request that he be allowed to stay in the room with her. Sara and Damian got the house and car keys from Jim and drove back to the quiet neighborhood.

It was late. They lay together in the guest bed and talked softly, ready to fall asleep at a moment's notice.

"How's your headache?" she asked him.

He shrugged. "Still there. But it's not too bad. Once I get some sleep it'll be gone."

The truth was, once he got the situation under control with this thug on the loose who was trying to hurt him, it would be gone. At least, that was what she suspected. He'd called Jack in Arizona and got the name of someone on the force Jack trusted to look into the business with the car. By morning, they should know the truth.

"Why didn't you just call the police and report the whole thing?" she asked him.

He didn't answer and she turned and looked into his face. Despite his blindness, there was a haunted look in his eyes. Suddenly she thought she knew. "You think it's Sheridan, don't you?" she said.

He didn't speak for a moment. Then he nodded slowly. "It's been my worst fear from the beginning," he told her. His arm tightened around her and she waited, biting her tongue. "Sheridan is hard to explain. He's been my best friend, close as a brother, and at the same time, my biggest rival. He's smart and quick and a lot of fun to be with." He sighed, shaking his head. "But he's not always stable. I've seen him do some pretty crazy things. There was one time when his family almost had to institutionalize him." He grimaced. "Still, I can't believe he would hurt me," he said in a hollow voice.

She drew in a short breath, then said what she was thinking. "But if he really is the one who was in my apartment, he might have been behind your accident. You have to tell the police."

"I can't."

Rising up, she stared at him. "Damian, that's nuts. You're in danger."

"He's like a brother to me. Could you turn in your sister?"

She swallowed. "If I thought she was going to hurt someone...."

"But the only one he really wants to hurt is me."

"He's trying to kill you!"

"No." He shook his head vehemently. "No, I don't believe that."

"But..."

"You don't understand."

"Then tell me."

He turned his head in her direction and for a flashing second, he thought he saw her. Her outline, at least. His heart beat a little faster. This wasn't the first time it had happened. He'd been getting flashes of light periodically for the past few days. At first he'd thought he was imagining things, because he wanted it to be true so badly. But now it was happening more frequently. It was coming back. Just how good it would be was what he wanted to know. Just how long it would stay. But it was coming back. And that made all the difference.

He'd learned he could deal with life even if he were blind. Sara had taught him that. But he could deal with threats to his safety so much better if he could see. And now there was evidence that his sight was coming back. That gave him such confidence in his ability to handle Sheridan.

And Sheridan really was going to have to be dealt

with somehow, and soon. And in doing so, he was very much afraid the truth was going to come out, the truth he had been so carefully hiding from his own family for so long. The truth he was about to tell for the first time. How appropriate that it was Sara he was going to tell it to.

"When I say Sheridan and I are as close as brothers, I mean it, Sara. Because the fact is, we both have the same father."

Her eyes widened and she gasped. "Oh, Damian." She put a hand on his chest, fingers spread, as though that would calm him.

"My father and his mother...my mother's sister..." His voice choked for a moment.

"Oh, Damian, I'm so sorry." She'd known there was something about his father he hated, and now she knew what it was.

"You're sorry." He ran his hand through his hair. "Just imagine how sorry I was when I found out about it." He turned toward her. "My brothers and sister still don't know, by the way."

"But how did you find out?"

"Sheridan."

"He told you? How did he know?"

"He's got a very dysfunctional family. His mother and father hate each other. They fling accusations like weapons. He knew from the time he was very young. And he told me in order to prove how unfair it was that I was a prince and he was just considered a baron's kid, when we both had the same biological father." He grimaced. "He showed me proof. And I overheard his parents talking about it, so I knew it was true.''

She winced. ''How old were you?''

''About twelve, I think.''

She shook her head, sad to think of him being disillusioned that way. ''That's a very bad age to hear something like that about your father.''

''Yes.''

''But you've kept it from your siblings.''

''Yes. I didn't want them to go through what I went through over it. I want them to hold on to their view of the old man as long as they can.''

She frowned, gazing at him. ''You feel like you lost something when you found out the truth.''

''Of course.''

''Oh, Damian.'' She stroked his chest. ''I wish I could take away that pain somehow.''

He buried his face in her hair and breathed deeply. ''You do,'' he told her softly. ''Just by being here with me.''

She smiled and sank into his embrace. ''You know, this really doesn't change the admiration I've had for your father from the first. He was a great man.''

''Great men don't break the hearts of those who love them,'' he said gruffly, then winced as though he knew that sounded extremely naive.

''Great men have their strengths and weaknesses,'' she said softly. ''Perfection is a goal to reach for, not a state of being.''

Turning toward her, he laughed softly. ''Do you

have a comforting word to say for every single con-
tingency?'' he asked her.

"I do," she said. "You just wait and see."

He curled her close in his arms and in a few
minutes, his even breathing told her he had fallen
asleep. She sighed and snuggled closer. She was going to learn to appreciate what she had and not worry
about the future if it killed her.

Damian woke and stretched and blinked in the
morning sun that was streaming in through the open
window. And then he did a double take.

Was he dreaming? He closed his eyes and counted
to ten, then opened them again. Nope. This was real.
He could see.

Joy filled his chest so fast he thought he might
explode with it. He could see! The darkness was
gone. He was out of the twilight zone. Closing his
eyes again, he did a quick prayer of thanks for his
deliverance, then opened them again quickly. He
wanted to take in everything. He could see!

But why? What had he done? What shouldn't he
do in order to make sure it didn't go away again? He
didn't want to risk bringing the darkness back. He
was going to be moving pretty carefully for a while,
testing out this miracle.

Sara stirred beside him and he grinned, making
himself wait before he turned to look at her. Anticipation. He was going to really see her. He was finally
beginning to believe in it. He could see!

He made his move slowly, first looking at her slender foot with its pink toenails, then letting his gaze travel deliberately up her leg, taking in her delicate ankle, the smooth tanned skin, every freckle, every muscle, the great line of her knee and the way her skin turned soft and creamy as he reached her upper thighs. Lingering there, he felt his male instincts surge. He wanted her. He wanted to reach out and take her right then, but he held it back. He had to do this right.

She'd slept in a huge old T-shirt. He lifted the hem so he could see her lacy panties, the tempting heart-shaped darkness beneath the fabric, the fascinating curve of her bottom. He wanted to slide his hand under the lace, but he knew that would wake her. Desire was becoming an ache.

But there was still her cute little belly button to study. It lay quietly in the middle of a nice stomach area, just slightly rounded and guarded by two great hip bones formed to make the perfect resting place for lovemaking. He wanted to kiss the navel, to slide his tongue into that tiny maze and explore it.

Not yet, he told himself silently. We're not finished here.

Lifting the hem a little more, he could make out her beautiful full breasts, the nipples flat, relaxed and shiny pink. His breathing was coming faster now, and the ache was becoming an urgent need. He trailed his fingers along the length of one arm, modeled like a dancer's, and stopped his gaze at her collarbone. Was that her pulse beating there in the cusp?

Closing his eyes, he made himself wait a few seconds longer. It was time to look at the face of the woman he loved. He knew what to expect. He'd studied her often enough with his fingers. But this was going to be something special. The first real sight of Sara Joplin. Licking his lower lip, he opened his eyes and looked at her.

And fell in love all over again. Her skin was rosy, like a summer peach. Her lips were full and lush-looking. Her nose was small and slightly turned up at the end, like a snub-nosed teenager. Her golden eyelashes lay on her cheeks like fans from the flapper era and her silver-blond hair curled wildly about her face. All in all, she was the most beautiful thing he'd ever seen and love for her swelled in his chest and choked his throat.

He looked at her for a long time, filling his mind and heart with the sight of her and saying a quick prayer of thanks—for her, and for his sight coming back. Then he began to drop tiny kisses along her neckline.

"Mmm." She turned and smiled up at him, reaching to touch his cheek. "Good morning."

"You don't know how good," he murmured. "But you're about to find out."

She welcomed his lovemaking, joining him with an eagerness that only made his ardor come hotter and harder. He'd never had a woman be so responsive to him, so in tune with his moves. She was wonderful. She was his.

"Sara, Sara," he murmured, kissing her collarbone. "I've never known a woman like you before."

"Just too much woman for you, huh?" she teased, still groggy from the aftermath of lovemaking. "Do I scare you?"

He laughed low in his throat. "Damn right you do. You always have." He nibbled at her earlobe.

"Then we're even," she said softly, opening her eyes to look at him with all the love in her heart shining brightly. "Because you scare me, too."

He smiled. "I think I was scared of you from that first day you showed up in the front yard," he told her, stroking her cheek with the palm of his hand. "I knew right away you were going to do things that would change my life." He kissed her chin line.

"For the better, though," she reminded him just as his lips found hers and he kissed her long and hard.

"For the better," he agreed, wrapping himself around her.

She was so soft, so smooth, like velvet and whipped cream and cuddly kitten fur. All things loveable. All things touchable. As they lay back, still wrapped in each other's arms, he contemplated how he was going to tell her his sight was back. But he didn't have to.

She turned to him, frowning. "You can see, can't you?" she said.

He hesitated, then nodded with a sheepish grin, his joy exploding again now that he could share it with her. "How could you tell?"

She shook her head as she raised up on her elbow to marvel at him, her own eyes shining. "It was different. I just knew somehow." Laughing softly, she shook her head. "You can see! This is so wonderful!"

He nodded, grinning. "And you do realize what this means, don't you?"

She looked at him questioningly.

He put on a superior look. "I was right. I told you my sight would come back about now, didn't I?"

"You were right," she admitted, laughing softly. "I guess I'd better learn to defer to your greater wisdom in all things."

"Of course."

"You wish!" she responded, grabbing a pillow and hitting him with it.

He grabbed one and hit her back, and a quick pillow fight ensued, marked more by misses and laughing than by any direct hits and ending when he tackled her and kissed her into submission.

"So you can really see now." Looking up at him, she pretended regret. "I'm afraid it will never be like it was yesterday again."

"I'll start wearing a blindfold," he told her with a growl.

"Don't you dare," she said. She laughed, her own joy almost as intense as his. "How is it? How much can you see?"

He shrugged. "Everything. My eyes feel a little tired, and things are just a bit blurry. But that's all. It's almost like I just turned a page and I'm back where I was, sightwise at any rate."

She nodded, her own eyes shining. "It happens that way sometimes. Are you glad?"

"What do you think?" Touching her cheek, he smiled at her. "Just being able to see your beautiful face is enough to keep me happy for the rest of my life."

He saw doubt appear for the first time in her eyes, and he wasn't sure what that meant. But she kept up happy chatter as they got up and fixed themselves some breakfast. Damian made a few phone calls while she showered and dressed in some of her sister's clothes. She seemed to assume they would both go back to the hospital together.

"I'm afraid I can't go with you," he said. The joy of the morning was still in him, but packed away now. He had serious matters to deal with. "We've got a report on your car. There was indeed a bomb, tucked neatly where it was primed to explode when you turned the key in the ignition."

She gasped. Knowing it was true was much scarier than just thinking it might be.

"It wasn't much of a bomb. It would have made a lot of noise and not done much else. Obviously meant to scare more than to damage. But bombs are not nice things and this situation has to be dealt with." He frowned, thinking. "I'm going to take the next flight I can get to Arizona," he said.

"For the wedding?" she asked softly. She was beginning to feel excluded. It was an exclusion that couldn't be helped. But it was going to hurt anyway.

"To see if I can catch Sheridan there," he told her. "Everyone thinks I'm not coming, so his guard should be down."

"But Damian, if he is planting bombs in cars, and if he was the one who sabotaged your boat, he's too dangerous to confront on your own. Call the police. Let them handle it."

He frowned at her, surprised she didn't understand how impossible that was. "I can't do that. This is a family matter. A Nabotavian crime. We have to deal with it ourselves."

She gazed at him in horror. "You make it sound like something out of *The Godfather*," she said. "That's not what you do in a civilized society."

He found his own anger wasn't far from the surface. "Nabotavia is as civilized as any other country," he snapped. "Or she will be, once we get our administration up to speed." He made himself back off and calm down. "Sara, you just can't understand how these things are. I have to take care of this. It's a part of my culture. It's a part of who I am. And it concerns a member of my family. The most important thing is to keep it out of the media."

She felt rebellious. This just didn't seem right to her. "I beg to differ," she said, her eyes flashing. "The most important thing is to keep you alive."

He turned away as though it wasn't worth trying to explain any longer. She pressed her lips together, knowing there was nothing she could do to change his mind.

"Do you want me to come with you?" she asked hopefully.

He hesitated. "No, you'd better stay here and help your sister. I'll be back very soon. And don't go anywhere near your apartment or your car until I get back and can go with you. Okay?''

She nodded, but deep inside, she was dying. He had his sight back. He didn't need her anymore. That was wonderful of course, but it was going to change everything. And he'd seen for himself that she wasn't a beauty queen like most of the women he'd dated. She was just plain old ordinary Sara Joplin. Maybe he was disappointed.

Maybe? Of course, he had to be. But she'd always known this would happen sooner or later, hadn't she?

''I'll drive you to the airport,'' she told him stiffly. ''But I really think you should see a doctor first. Just in case.''

He shook his head. ''No time. I promise I'll go first thing when I get back.''

Promises, promises. She knew better than to count on them.

''At least be sure to wear your sunglasses.''

''I plan to do that. And I'll take my white cane.''

''Your white cane? Why?''

''Nobody in Arizona is going to know I can see.''

''Ah.''

She dropped him at the airport, where he was meeting Tom who was to accompany him, and he kissed her goodbye, but his mind was already on what he had to do in Arizona and she felt as though he hardly remembered who she was.

Tears spilled down her cheeks on the drive back, making her furious with herself. What was she crying about? She'd always known it couldn't last. She wasn't exactly princess material. When you came right down to it, she wasn't even concubine material. She'd been living a dream made possible by a temporary blindness. That was over now. And so was the dream.

Drying her tears, she was able to muster a cheery face to greet her sister with at the hospital.

"I've stabilized," Mandy told her happily. "I've got to stay under observation for the rest of today, but tomorrow, I might get to go home."

"Oh, I hope so." She gave her sister a hug. "I can hardly wait to see this little guy, but it would be best if he gets a little stronger before he arrives."

"Speaking of guys, where's your prince?" Mandy asked, looking behind her in case he was lurking there. "He is so super gorgeous. I'd give him the throne on looks alone."

"He had to go to Arizona."

"Arizona! Whatever for?"

She hesitated. "It's a long story." She didn't want to get into all of what had happened in the past few days. Mandy didn't need any more stress or worry to add to what she already had. "He'll be back."

Mandy shook her head. "If I were you, I wouldn't let a hunk like that out of my sight for any longer than I had to. Some other babe is likely to try to snap him up." She made a face as though she regretted her silly joke. "Only kidding. From what I saw, I'd say the two of you are pretty tight right now." She looked at Sara hopefully, waiting to see if she was going to get the straight scoop on this little romance.

Sara saw the look and laughed. "You won't believe this," she said, feeling suddenly shy about it and actually blushing a bit. "He says he loves me. Isn't that wild?"

Mandy's eyes widened with delight. "It's not wild at all. You're very loveable."

"No I'm not." Sara frowned fretfully. "And I'm not beautiful like the women he's used to. You know the type. They all look like they were born on yachts."

"And haven't had a decent meal since," Mandy agreed. "Yes, I know the sort you mean. You don't look like that. But you have your own style of beauty. In fact, I think you get more beautiful all the time."

"Right. I've got a lot of character in my face," she said with an ironic twist to her voice. "I've been told that before."

"Oh Sara…"

"Anyway, you know it won't last. He's just sort of…infatuated right now. But that will change."

Her sister opened her mouth, then closed it again, her cheeks turning bright red. She took a deep breath and spoke very carefully, but firmly. "Listen to me, Sara. Just because our parents couldn't manage to hang around long enough to love us doesn't mean no one else ever will."

Sara groaned. "Don't try to psychoanalyze me."

"Somebody's got to set you straight," Mandy said. "I've noticed this in you before. You don't trust love from other people. You've really got to snap out of it. If you want him to love you, you have to open up your heart.''

"Just because I open my heart doesn't mean I have to let my brains fall out of my head,'' Sara said cynically.

"Oh!'' Mandy cried out in frustration. "You just don't want to be happy, do you? It's your turn, Sara. You've helped him get his confidence back. Now you should return the favor.''

Sara frowned. "Which means?''

Mandy hesitated, then said softly, "Let him love you.'' Tears were suddenly rimming her eyes. "Don't try to hold him off now because someday he might not want to love you any longer. Be brave enough to trust him.''

Sara stared at her, wishing she would explain why she thought it was that easy to do. But there was no explanation. Because it wasn't true.

She went down to the hospital cafeteria to get a cup of tea and a young intern sat at the table with her and tried to chat her up. He was looking at her with obvious admiration of a sort. She put him off, but she had to wonder—had she changed after all? Something had changed. Because men didn't usually look at her like that.

Male attention was nice, but it didn't make up for heartbreak. When she actually thought about it, she wasn't sure why she was feeling so pessimistic. Damian had told her he loved her. Why couldn't she accept it? But he had acted a bit distant toward the end—once he got his sight back, she remembered uncomfortably. And after getting his sight back, he'd turned what should have been one of the happiest days of his life into something a little angry, a little edgy. And she had to admit, she'd been on pins and needles, too. Maybe it was just not meant to be.

She agonized for another day and a half, telling herself it might be for the best to consider her short affair with a prince null and void. Best to make a clean break and make it quickly. It was going to happen. Why not get it over with? She remembered what Annie had said about silly girls who thought royals would marry them. Annie was right. It would be the height of foolishness to expect a prince to pledge his life to a plain and ordinary woman such as she was. She was too smart to let herself get caught up in dreams like that. Wasn't she?

She kept busy visiting Mandy and helping her move back home, then going in to the office and filling out her report on her work with Damian. She contacted Dr. Simpson to tell him about the return of the prince's sight, then had to turn down a request from her agency that she start a new assignment right away. Damian called, but she wasn't in and he left a message on the answering machine, giving her the number at the castle. She stared at it for three hours before she got up the courage to call.

She asked for Damian, but the butler didn't seem to have any idea where he might be.

"Well, is Princess Karina available?" she asked.

"Of course. May I tell her who is calling?"

"Sara!" Karina cried when she came on. "It's so

good to hear from you. Are you coming to the wedding?''

"Oh, well, I don't know...."

"Oh, that's right, Damian said you have to stay to help your sister. How is she?"

"Fine, actually. She came home today and her husband is taking time off work to be with her, so I don't actually have to stay any longer."

She rolled her eyes. She couldn't believe she was actually fishing for an invitation to the wedding like this. And if she got one, what was she going to do with it? She didn't know. But Karina took her up on the hint and insisted she was to come to Arizona right away. And by the time she hung up the phone, she'd promised to do just that.

"And we won't tell Damian," Karina said happily. "Let it be a surprise!"

"Ohmigod!" she cried once she'd put down the phone, covering her face with her hands. She couldn't get out of it now. What was Damian going to say when she showed up? She groaned and peered through her fingers at her own reflection in the mirror at the end of the hall. The expression on his face when he saw her would speak volumes, she was sure. But if he looked sorry to see her there, a little embarrassed that he was going to have to find a way to let her down gently—she would never be able to smile again.

Chapter 15

"You just do so well, for someone who's blind and all that."

Damian smiled in the general direction of the little blushing maid who'd made the statement, feeling like a louse and a con man. Everyone he'd met here at the castle seemed to want to fall all over themselves telling him how brave he was to venture out when he couldn't see—and the irony was, he probably would have come even if he were still blind. But this way, he was garnering false praise and he felt like a hypocrite.

But it couldn't be helped. He knew Sheridan and he knew he would show up at some point. And he didn't want him to know the situation had changed drastically.

The Roseanova castle had been built in recent years very near Flagstaff, Arizona, but it managed to look as though it had been ensconced in the red rock hills since the Middle Ages. Usually a sleepy, resort sort of feeling permeated the atmosphere here, but right now it was buzzing with people and activity, everyone intent upon doing in a few days what usually took months—prepare for a formal wedding. Since mostly family had been invited, he knew just about everyone he saw, but he had to pretend not to know who they were until identities were pointed out to him. It was odd the way people acted, thinking they couldn't be seen. The funniest were little boys who made outrageous faces at him, but grown women gave him looks they never would have dared had they thought he could see them. It took all his self-control to keep from laughing at times. He was learning a lot about human nature.

He'd spent some time discussing different aspects of the Sheridan problem with Jack, being careful not to actually name his suspect. His soon-to-be brother-in-law was happy to take time out from wedding plans to talk about crime and criminals.

"Karina actually wants me to help pick out the colors for our monogrammed bath towels," he'd said, looking at Damian with puzzled wonder. "Bath towels. As long as they dry your body, who gives a damn what color they are?"

"Women," Damian said, nodding in sympathy. "The strangest things are important to them."

He'd tried to talk to Garth, but his brother couldn't

concentrate on anything other than his own problems. It seemed he had a love-hate thing going on with a beautiful young woman named Tianna who had hired on as a nanny, but seemed to actually be a princess and distant cousin of theirs from the White Rose side of the family who Garth was supposed to be betrothed to. Apparently, she was still acting as a nanny. At least, she was carrying a baby around who might or might not be Garth's. Or something like that. He didn't feel he'd had the straight story yet. And when he tried to ask Garth, his brother growled at him like a sulky bear.

Marco had his children with him, a little boy and an even smaller girl. They were adorable and he looked very proud when he was with them. Made Damian wonder what a combination of his and Sara's genes would result in. And that brought up a new dilemma. Was he going to marry her?

If he weren't royal, there would be no question. He loved her, wanted her with him at all times. But he had responsibilities to higher authorities, and a country to think of. He wished there was someone he could talk to about it. Karina was too tied up in the wedding. Garth was busy glaring at the nanny-princess and pretending he wasn't madly in love with her, which anyone with eyes could see. Marco seemed to be distracted by an argument with his mother-in-law, the parent of his beloved wife who had died two years before. The duchess was impossible to talk to. Boris had disappeared. That left the duke.

His dear old uncle had been trying to waylay him

since he'd arrived and he'd been avoiding him. He knew what he wanted to talk about. His father. But that wasn't what Damian wanted to talk about. He wanted advice on defending himself against the whirlwind he would certainly kick up if he let them all know how much he loved Sara.

So when he found the older man alone, sitting on a chair at a table on the upper terrace, he decided to give it a try.

"Good afternoon, Your Grace," he said, tapping loudly with his cane as he approached, then pulling up a chair and sitting across from him. "I hope you will allow me to join you."

"Of course." The duke looked up with a bittersweet smile and didn't seem to question Damian's sudden ability to identify him this easily. "I was just thinking about you. It's time we talked."

Damian started to protest, then sighed and let it go. After all, if he wanted something from the duke, he had probably better give a little first.

"I think you know what I want to talk to you about."

"My father."

"Yes. Of course. I want you to understand what happened. I don't think you've ever been told the full story."

Damian winced. "I don't want to know the full story."

"Yes, you do. You don't know it, but you do."

Damian held back his temper and managed an even tone. "Fine. Lay it on me. Let's get this over with."

Nodding, the duke moved in his chair so he could look his nephew fully in the face. "I've come to understand, from comments you've made, that you know of your cousin's parentage. I believe you are the only one of your generation who does."

"Besides Sheridan."

"Yes, of course. There is Sheridan. But you've made it clear that you hold it against the late king. As we haven't spent much time together, I haven't had a chance to explain the truth of the situation to you. It's something that can't be explored in front of others, as to do so would be to let the cat out of the bag, so to speak."

Damian looked at the handsome man with a mixture of amusement and indignation. He was a loveable old scoundrel, but he did rattle on. "I understand," he said simply, suppressing his impatience and resigning himself to a lecture. "Why not do so now?"

"I intend to." He took a deep breath. "You know that your mother, Queen Marie, and Sheridan's mother, Lady Julienne, were twin sisters."

"Yes. Everyone knows that."

"Both women, as teenagers, fell in love with your father."

"That's apparent."

The duke's head came up at his snarky tone. "Mind your manners when talking to your elders," he said sharply. "And please let me tell my story without your constant interjections."

Damian's temper was getting more difficult to control, but he managed. "All right," he said through clenched teeth.

The duke sighed. "Marie and Julienne were both so beautiful and accomplished, and they looked alike, but they were very different. It was pretty much the classic good girl, bad girl pattern."

"Are you saying one of them was an evil twin?"

He shot Damian a look. "No, not that bad. But Julienne was sprightly. A real handful. The kind of girl who had to have excuses made for her more often than not. Your mother was an angel, good as gold. Butter wouldn't melt in her mouth." His eyes glazed, remembering. "Well, they both flirted with the king outrageously. Julienne pulled some tricks that are best left in the dustbin of history. But for a long time, it wasn't evident which one he might choose. Then Julienne made the mistake of her life. She became pregnant."

Damian reacted with shock. "With my father?"

The duke looked affronted. "No, of course not. Actually, it was thought at the time to be one of the horse wranglers. Someone totally unsuitable for her to marry. But now that marrying the king was completely out of the question, she had to marry someone. That was when Baron Ludfrond stepped up and offered her a safe haven. She took it gratefully at the time. But the baby was stillborn, and the baron was sterile. She was stuck in a loveless, childless marriage to a baron, while her sister married the king and had one beautiful baby after another."

"The proverbial wages of sin," Damian cracked.

He knew his aunt Julienne and only felt vaguely sorry for her.

The duke frowned his disapproval. "Still, you can understand her bitterness."

"Definitely." He'd lived with the family enough to know of her bitterness firsthand. "So far you really haven't told me anything I didn't pretty much know."

The duke rolled his eyes. "The impatience of youth," he said to himself. "Well, let me see. Oh yes. The years went by. Julienne and Marie grew estranged, mostly because Julienne made things difficult. And then came the time when the December Radicals kidnapped your father and held him for a month in a dungeon."

Damian nodded. "I know that story, too. It's a legend among us." But he frowned as he remembered that the duke had been the one to rescue his father. Was it possible he was really going to learn something new?

"You know that the radicals wanted him to give them details of a secret alliance our government had made with the Alovitians. They thought there was a stash of hidden gold somewhere or some such nonsense. And when they couldn't torture the information out of him, they put him on psychedelic drugs, hoping to loosen his tongue in that way."

"Yes."

"You know all that. What you don't know is that Lady Julienne, true to her rebellious spirit, had been somewhat sympathetic to the radicals. I suppose it made her feel young and exciting to play with their

sort of fire. She was rumored to have let them hold
secret meetings at her estate, to have given them funding, any number of things. At any rate, feeling she
was one of them, they brought her in to help with
your father.''

Damian sat up straighter and didn't say a word.
This, indeed, was new.

''Your father was drugged. She stayed in the dungeon with him, pretending to be your mother and in
his semidelirious state, he bought it. And that is how
your cousin was conceived.''

Damian sat frozen. ''How could she do that?'' he
said softly.

The duke shrugged. ''Perhaps she still loved him.''

''No,'' Damian said bitterly. ''She doesn't love
anyone but herself and her son. I've lived with them,
I know.''

There had been a time, when he was young, that
he had tried to love her. He'd had fantasies of her as
a mother figure. She was his mother's twin, after all.
Longing for his own mother, he tried to transfer those
feelings to her. But Lady Julienne had never treated
him as anything but a burden she was forced to carry.
She quickly killed all efforts to reach out to her and
made it very clear that her own son was her only
priority. He hadn't thought of those days in years, but
now he remembered how hurt he'd been as a little
boy that the woman who looked so much like his own
mother rejected him.

''She did it out of spite,'' he said now, sure of his

judgment. "She's a traitor and should be prose-
cuted."

The duke put a hand on his arm. "This happened
long ago, Damian. Everything's been forgiven."

He stared at the older man. "No it hasn't. The ram-
ifications are still being felt." And Sheridan is trying
to kill me, he could have added, but didn't. "What
happened when my father realized what she'd done?
Did my mother know?"

"Oh, yes. Lady Julienne made sure she knew."

"You see? Spite."

"Perhaps. At any rate, your mother forgave her.
Though your father never spoke to her again." He
smiled. "And of course, you were conceived within
days of Sheridan. That alone should tell you something."

Damian shook his head. He was stunned by this
revelation. "I wish you'd told me this story sooner,"
he said.

"I didn't realize you knew about Sheridan's parentage until fairly recently," the duke told him sadly.
"And when I tried to talk to you, you brushed me
off."

Damian winced, knowing he was telling the truth.
"I've been a fool," he said.

The duke groaned. "I wanted you to know so that
you would stop beating up on your father," he said.
"Now don't start beating up on yourself. You
couldn't know the truth until you were told. Let this
be an end to it."

Damian rose to go, then turned back and leaned

down to give the older man a hug. "Thank you, Uncle," he said. Straightening, he thought for a moment,
then quoted, "'To give mercy is to earn forgiveness,
and that coin will do you well in heaven.'"

The duke looked up with delight. "You listened to
the tape of Jan Kreslau's Nabotavian poetry, then,"
he said. "I thought you never would."

"I listened. Sara tricked me into listening." He half
smiled, thinking of her.

"Great girl, that Sara. Tell her I'm still working on
her mother's family tree. It's a tough one, but I'll get
it to her soon."

"I will. And Sara is wonderful. She knew listening
to the poetry would help me put things into perspective. There's a lot of wisdom in it."

"Yes. Your father knew most of Jan Kreslau's poetry by heart and would recite it to me whenever he
got the opportunity," he said with a chuckle. "It used
to drive me mad. And now I would give anything to
hear his deep, rich voice uttering those words again."

Damian touched his shoulder with affection, then
left the terrace. Emotion was flowing in his veins and
he wished Sara were with him. On his way downstairs, he stopped off in the hall of portraits and
looked long and hard at his father's face. A lump rose
in his throat. It was such a relief to be able to love
him again.

Sara took a cab from the airport. A gate guard
called up to the house and talked to Princess Karina
to verify her invitation before he let her in. She left

her luggage there with a pile of others to be brought up to the castle later, and began the long trip up the curving driveway, looking up at the beautiful castle as she walked toward it. Dusk had just fallen and lights were coming on in the windows. The scene looked magical.

She was so anxious to see Damian, and yet terrified of what she would learn when she saw him. And how was she going to find him? The grounds were filled with people strolling in small bunches, talking and laughing. She didn't see anyone she recognized. At first glance, it seemed more like a theme park than a home. There were layered terraces overlooking rolling lawns that swept out from the castle. Gardens filled one area of the estate, while a series of ponds connected with small waterfalls covered another.

The entire setting seemed out of place in the stark purple beauty of the nighttime Arizona desert, where the rumble of distant thunder was warning of lightning storms coming. She couldn't help but wonder if they had tried to recreate a little bit of Nabotavia for themselves here.

But she really needed to go inside and find Damian. She'd put it off long enough, wandering around the yards and gardens, watching the workmen beginning to set up the tables where she supposed the ceremony and reception would be. Turning to go, she was startled when a hand shot out of the shadows and grasped her arm.

''Well, look who's here,'' the owner of the hand

said, a slice of sarcasm spicing his tone. "If it isn't Ms. Sara Joplin."

Her heart skipped and then tumbled into her throat to beat loudly in her ears. "Sheridan," she said, shocked and alarmed. She could barely stutter out a normal sentence. "I thought you were in Europe."

"I was. But I'm back."

"Oh." Of course, she knew that. But did he know she knew? "Have you come for the wedding?"

"Yes." He didn't release her arm and she didn't like the way he was looking at her. The crowd had thinned and there was really no one within earshot. She began to worry. He was acting strangely. Maybe he knew what she suspected.

"I never miss these family functions."

"That's nice."

Keep acting naturally, she told herself, though with her heart beating so loudly, she could hardly hear what he was saying to her. She'd taken a woman's self-defense course once. She'd done pretty well, too. But that had been over five years ago and she couldn't remember one thing that she'd learned there. And even if she had, he was big and strong and tall and she knew darn well she wouldn't have a chance against him.

"Well, I've got to go tell Damian that I've arrived," she said with a smile, trying for a cheery, breezy tone. "You haven't seen him anywhere, have you?"

"Sure," he said. "I'll take you to him."

"Oh, that won't be necessary," she said quickly.

"I think I can find my way if you'll just point me toward the entrance."

He paused, staring at her. He was thinking something over. She could almost see the wheels whirring. And suddenly, a more friendly smile curled his wide mouth. "Sara, you know what?" His grip relaxed on her arm, his fingers moving gently. "I'm really glad I ran into you tonight. You're going to be my angel."

"Angel?"

He grinned. "Don't look so startled. I'm not going to make you put on wings. But I am going to ask you to help me."

"Help you?" She knew she was echoing everything he said but she didn't really see much of an alternative.

"Yes."

He looked uncomfortable and suddenly she realized he'd dropped his hold on her entirely. She could attempt a run for it if she wanted to. His hands were both shoved into the pockets of his slacks and he looked perfectly normal, though slightly embarrassed. She blinked, wondering what she was missing. Was he or was he not a menace?

"You see, I came here tonight with lots of plans but now that I'm here, it all looks so impossible." He ploughed his long fingers through his thick hair, standing a portion of it on end in an endearing way. "What I need is a chance to talk things over. Get your perspective. Maybe even a bit of advice." He looked into her eyes. "Will you take a walk with me?

Just for a few minutes. And let me run some things by you?''

She searched his face. There was nothing there she wouldn't have expected to see in the Sheridan she'd known at the Beverly Hills estate. He was restless, edgy. But hardly dangerous. Could it be that they had made a mistake?

"I'd really like to say hello to Damian first. Why don't you come with me?"

He nodded, looking troubled. "You see, that's not going to work. Because it's Damian that I want to talk to you about. I...I need help." His voice had a slight break as he said the last word, as though it was very hard for him to say it, as though a deep emotion was involved.

She hesitated. His gray eyes looked so like Damian's. He was a fellow human being—in distress of some kind, it would seem. If he was sincere, if she could help him... Damian had been adamant about not going to the authorities about his cousin. And she was a therapist, for heaven's sake. Maybe she *could* help him. Maybe all he needed was some good advice and an understanding listener.

Besides, what if he wasn't the guilty party at all? He didn't look very guilty right now, his eyes so sad and tortured. He'd had a lot of unhappiness growing up just as Damian had. Maybe he just needed someone to help him deal with things. And maybe she was that person.

"Why can't we talk right here?"

He looked around the area. A threesome was coming toward them, talking animatedly among themselves in Nabotavian. One of them hailed Sheridan and he nodded an acknowledgment.

"That's why," he told her. "Too many people know me. Someone will be interrupting us every moment." He looked into her eyes. "Please, Sara. I won't take up much of your time. But I've got to talk to someone."

She hesitated, but it was to the point of seeming churlish if she didn't give him a chance.

"All right," she said, wondering if she was being a friend or a fool. "I'll walk with you for a little while. I'd like to hear what you have to tell me."

He smiled and actually did look relieved. "I really appreciate this, Sara," he said. "Let's go toward that stand of cottonwood trees." He nodded toward a small charming forest of trees with shimmering leaves. She could see the outline of purple mesas behind them. But the trees didn't seem very far away. "There's a bench out there where we can sit down." He gave her a quick grin. "And you'll still be visible from the house."

"All right," she said, and gave him a quick smile of her own. "Let's go."

"Hey." Karina grinned at her brother as she gazed at him from the doorway she'd just opened after he'd responded to her knock. Her wedding was the very next day and she was walking on air.

"Were you surprised?"

He gazed at her in bemusement, then remembered to unfocus his eyes. "Surprised about what?"

"About Sara, of course."

He came alert and serious in an instant. "Why? What happened to Sara?"

"You haven't seen her?"

"Kari, would you please stop asking questions and tell me what this is all about?" he demanded.

"I talked to the gate guard over an hour ago. He was letting her in. She was supposed to come up and surprise you." Karina frowned. "I wonder what could have kept her?"

A cold hand gripped Damian's heart. "Has Sheridan arrived yet?" he asked her, his voice harsh.

She looked at him in surprise. "Not that I know of. Why?"

"I've got to find her." He rose and, abruptly abandoning all pretense of being blind, strode for the door, his heart hammering in his chest. Protecting Sara was all he cared about now.

Searching for Sara, he felt like he was walking in quicksand. He made a quick survey of the public rooms, then a look outside. No one had seen her. There was no trace of her existence. Thunder rumbled ominously out along the mesas.

What now? He couldn't very well call for a massive search when there was no sign that Sheridan was anywhere nearby, though he did call the gate guard, first to ask if he'd seen Sheridan, which he denied, then to warn him not to let any cars leave until further notice.

Over an hour Karina had said. Despair gripped him. Sheridan could have grabbed her and driven miles away by now. In what direction? Where could he turn? He was going to have to call the police. But what could he tell them? Did he actually have any hard evidence to show them to prove that she'd arrived? He knew he could exert some influence and make them come and take this seriously, but he also knew they would only do so if he used his royal position. And in doing that, he was asking for the media to get wind of it.

"Too bad," he told himself fiercely. "I'll have to risk it." Because something told him Sheridan had her. And the only chance he had of getting her back unhurt was to get the police involved.

He reached in his pocket for his cell phone and flipped it open.

"Damian and I spent every Christmas vacation here when we were young," Sheridan said, his eyes staring at the sky but focused on that past. "We used to count off the days before we would be allowed to leave our boring old prep school and board that big silver plane for Arizona." A smile of memory played on his lips. "Summers, too. We lived like wild things, riding out over the desert, camping out, hunting, tracking cougars, visiting the Hopi reservations, only coming back to the castle when we needed food." He sighed, shaking his head. "Those were such good times. Sometimes I feel like that kid in that book,

Catcher in the Rye, wanting to stop all kids from growing up.''

"Did your parents come here, too?" Sara asked. She was sitting beside him on the bench facing the red rock canyons out beyond the Roseanova's property. Here and there a flash of lightning cracked the purple sky, reaching down to touch the tops of the mesas, then retreating back into the clouds.

"My parents? No." His laugh was short and harsh. "My parents wouldn't come to Arizona on a bet. They need firm reservations at a five-star hotel before they'll set foot out of the old baronial mansion.''

"So you two were pretty much on your own here."

"Absolutely. Sometimes the others were here, sometimes not. But Damian and I didn't care. We lived in a world of our own.'' He grinned, remembering.

"It sounds like the ideal boyhood. Sort of Tom Sawyer goes to the desert.''

He nodded. Then he looked at her as though he was suddenly remembering why she was with him. "Damian and I were very, very close," he said, almost defensively.

She smiled at him. "Like brothers," she said.

"Yes." He looked at her sharply, as though to see if she knew more about that than she should. "Like brothers,'' he repeated.

"And you still are close," she reminded him.

He hesitated, something flickering in his eyes. "Yeah," he said reluctantly. "But..." He looked out at the horizon. "You have to help me, Sara. I want to go in and talk to him but I can't."

"Why not?"

He swallowed hard and grimaced, then turned to look at her. "You don't understand how much I love Damian. He's all I've got, you know. My mother only cares about stoking the fires of her bitterness. And the baron spends most of his time drunk. But I've always got Damian. He's my brother." His face darkened and he looked away. "Only, he has so much more. He's got the other guys, and even Karina. He's my only brother. But I'm not his only brother." He looked back at her. "Do you get it?"

She nodded. She got it. It explained a lot. But an explanation was not an excuse. The most important issue was lurking there in the shadows. If this conversation was going to do any good at all, someone was going to have to bring it up, and she was beginning to realize that someone was going to have to be her.

"If you love him, why do you try to hurt him?" she asked softly.

He shook his head, looking shocked that she would say such a thing. "No. He's the last person on earth I want to hurt." Staring at her intently, he went on. "I just want to win sometimes. Can you understand that?"

"To win?"

"Yes. To win. To be the best."

She shook her head. "Is that why you sabotaged

his hydrofoil? So you could win? Didn't you know it might kill him?''

"No." His expression was distressed. "I never meant to hurt him. That's what I have to explain to him. You have to help me."

She stared at him. There it was, a full admission that he had been the one. Her heart began to beat a little faster. Did she have any idea what she was doing here? No. But once begun, this was hard to stop. "Why did you break into my apartment the other night?"

He looked at her, then away, biting his lip. "I... I saw you leave. I didn't know he was in there, I swear. If I'd known..."

"And my car. You planted a bomb on it."

He looked worried. "I was going to put it in your apartment, but I didn't have time. I had to put it somewhere. It wasn't a very big bomb. I just wanted to scare you."

She gasped. He was admitting it all. "Why?"

"Why?" He stared at her blankly. He didn't seem to know the answer to that himself. "Because I had to. I don't know how to explain to you how awful it feels sometimes. I just have to do something to make things better. You know?"

"Sheridan."

Damian's voice seemed to come out of the blue and both of them jumped at the sound of it, turning to see him standing in the small clearing behind them.

"Hi." Sheridan bounded to his feet, a trapped look in his eyes. "Uh...I've just been talking to Sara."

"Damian...." She rose, her hand outstretched. The look on Damian's face told her there would be trouble unless she could forestall it. "We've just been talking. He hasn't done anything to me."

"I wouldn't hurt her," Sheridan declared earnestly.

"Wouldn't hurt her?" Damian repeated coldly, his face a mask of stone. "Putting a bomb on her car could have killed her."

"No," Sheridan insisted. "It was just..."

"He was only trying to scare me," Sara cut in quickly.

Damian took another step closer, seeming to grow bigger all the time. "And why exactly was it so important to scare her?" he ground out.

Sheridan blinked at him, as though looking into a bright light. "Because you can't have everything, Damian," he said, his voice rising. "Because it isn't fair that you always win."

Damian caught himself, holding back the natural urge to reach for his cousin and break him in two. Taking a deep breath, he made a conscious attempt to ratchet down a notch on his emotional state. "I don't always win," he said. His kept his voice soft but his hands were balled into fists.

"Yes, you do. You know you do."

"Sheridan, that's ridiculous. You've beat me at plenty of things."

Sheridan's looked petulant, and then his face cleared. "I beat you once right here. In a horse race. Remember?"

"Sure, I remember," he said, gazing at him levelly.

"My horse stepped in a rattler's hole and went lame."

"That's not true." Sheridan's voice rose a bit more. "I was already ahead before that. I beat you fair and square. It was the Christmas of tenth grade. Remember?"

Damian looked hard at his cousin. This was the man who had caused him to spend weeks blind. This was the man who had broken into Sara's place, put a bomb on her car and generally terrified them. Anger boiled hot in him, along with the need to take revenge, to punish somehow. Sheridan deserved it. The bastard had put him through a lot of agony that hadn't been necessary.

But this was also his cousin, his brother, the man who was probably closer to him than any other man had ever been. For just a moment, he thought he understood a little of the pain that had brought Sheridan to this extreme. He probably knew better than anyone the demons that drove him. But he had to be dealt with. He couldn't be allowed to threaten people the way he had.

He nodded slowly. "Sure, I remember now. You got me on the turn down by the corral."

"Right." Sheridan's face lit up. "I'm glad you remember that." He almost smiled. "You don't always win, you know."

Damian stared at him as though he was seeing him clearly for the first time in a long time. "Of course I don't always win. Sheridan, you have always been my biggest challenge. I have to work harder with you than with anyone.''

"Right.'' He sounded almost pleased, then he remembered what they were here discussing and his eyes shifted. "Look, I'm sorry about all this stuff that's been going on. I didn't want you to go blind or anything. I just wanted you to understand that you can't always be the winner at everything.'' His face changed as his mind jumped ahead. "I mean, why is it always okay for you? Here you go blind, and you're still on top. You get accolades from everyone.'' His voice turned bitter again. "You can't lose, can you? No matter what I do, you are always there first.'' He ran his fingers through his hair, making it wild. "You've got everything. You've got that whole family. Everybody loves you. Even Sara loves you. You can tell by the way she looks at you.'' He shook his head. "And I've got nothing.''

"Sheridan, you're not thinking straight. You've got plenty of good things in your life.'' Damian looked at Sara, then back at his cousin. "Let's go back to the house and talk it over. I'll bet I can think of a whole list of things you have that you haven't thought about.''

"Yeah? Name one.''

Damian shrugged. "You've got me,'' he said.

Sheridan stared at him hard. Suddenly his eyes were shimmering with moisture. "Really?'' he said in a broken voice. "Really, Damian?''

"Really.'' Damian took another step and reached out to put an arm around Sheridan's shoulders.

"Come on. We'll go in and have something to eat and…"

"Wait a minute!" Sheridan shrugged out of his embrace and stared at him. "You can see, can't you? You're not blind anymore."

Damian nodded. "I got my sight back a few days ago. So you see, it's not the end of the world. You didn't damage me for life."

Sheridan stared at him. He didn't look as though he thought this was a good thing.

Damian reached for him again. "Come on, Sheridan," he began.

"No!" Sheridan flung his arm away and a stream of ugly obscenities came out of his mouth as though they'd been ripped from his soul. "Damn you! You can't even stay blind!"

"Sheridan…"

Damian tried to reach for him but his cousin was striking out, losing control, and when his flailing fist hit Damian along the side of the head, his anger boiled over and his control stripped away. He grabbed Sheridan with both arms and they went down, rolling in the grass and dirt, grunting as each tried to hit the other. Despite his anger, the situation felt so familiar. How many times had they fought like this as boys? There had always been so much affection between the two of them, and so much resentment, too.

His head hit a rock and for a moment, he was afraid he might black out. He felt his strength fading and he lost control of his arms. But the moment passed and he went back harder, pinning Sheridan to the ground, rising over him and giving him a slashing blow to the head that left him groggy and unable to fight on. He stayed above him, panting, feeling incredibly drained in his body and his soul.

The timing was good. Others from the house were arriving, Marco and Garth and Jack. They would take care of Sheridan. Damian rose and stumbled away, turning to look for Sara.

But she was already there, throwing her arms around his neck, hugging him close, tears of relief streaming down her face.

"My God," he murmured in her ear. "I was so afraid he'd hurt you."

"But he didn't," she assured him. "He just wanted to talk. He loves you so much and somehow that seems to hurt him so much." She shook her head. "I don't know what you can do to help him."

Help him. The anger still seared his soul, but he knew she was right. He loved Sheridan—like the brother he was. And they were going to have to find some way to help him.

But right now, all he wanted to do was hold the woman he loved close and feel her heart beat. Maybe later he would think of something to do with Sheridan.

Sara sank into his embrace and reveled in it. She looked at what she could see of his face, shadowed by darkness. Was it possible to keep loving him more every time she saw him? Yes, it was not only possible, it was the way she was going to be living her life. At least for the time being. He looked up and met her gaze and smiled. She couldn't detect any hint of second thoughts or regrets. He seemed to be genuinely glad to see her. A tiny flicker of hope took root in her heart.

Maybe, just maybe, Mandy was right. Maybe, if she was brave enough to trust him, he would love her forever. She knew darn well she would be there, loving him. So maybe…

Chapter 16

"I suppose you're wondering why I called you all here tonight," Crown Prince Marco said in a mock mystery character tone.

"Are we suspects?" Princess Karina asked playfully. "I say it was the duke in the library with the candlestick. Confess!"

Her uncle gave her a baleful look. "I can understand that we are all a little giddy tonight," he said generously. "But I believe His Majesty called a royal family meeting to take care of some loose ends before your wedding tomorrow. And as the time is almost midnight, I say let us get on with it."

"Hear, hear," the duchess said, agreeing with her husband for the first time in recent memory.

The six of them were clustered in a corner of the

library. All were quite used to these meetings. They
had them whenever enough Red Rose Roseanovas
came together in one locale. It helped to keep the flow
of family affairs under control.

"Next time we have a meeting like this, Jack will
be with us," Karina said, smiling joyfully. "He'll be
one of the family."

"I wouldn't count on it," her brother Garth teased.
"Perhaps we'll decide to expel *you* instead."

She stuck her tongue out at him and the duchess
sighed painfully, rolling her eyes and fanning herself
with a pamphlet she'd picked up.

"The first order of business involves Count Boris,"
Marco informed them, glancing at his notes. "He
called me tonight to let me know he and Annie were
married this afternoon in Las Vegas."

The duchess looked thunderstruck. The fanning
was suspended in midair. "What?"

The duke turned to her and took her hand. "It's
true, my dear. I knew all about it." He patted her
hand. "He tried to hire her to come back to Europe
and take charge of his household staff for him, but
she held out for a ring. Wise girl, that Annie. Knows
what she's doing."

"But she's a housekeeper," the duchess moaned.

"She'll take charge of more than his household,"
Damian said. "Unless I miss my guess, she'll be the
power behind the Commerce Department in no time."

Garth nodded. "And a good thing, too. Boris is
helpless with figures."

"Yes," the duke said. "I think we'll all benefit

from this move." He looked at his wife. "Though I know the duchess is heartbroken. She wanted a princess for him, you know."

"There were so many who would have jumped at the chance," she murmured mournfully, still too shocked to respond with her normal fire.

"This is hardly a surprise," Karina noted. "It's been brewing for a long time. It's been obvious for ages that those two were mad about each other."

"Now to a more serious subject," Marco said. "We need to decide what to do about Sheridan. He's being guarded in a local health clinic right now, and he's okay. But we either have to contact the police and bring charges against him, or take care of this ourselves."

A brief discussion ensued, filling everyone in on what had happened just a few hours before. Everyone was very surprised and saddened to find out that Sheridan had become such a menace. Marco suggested he be sent back to Nabotavia and confined to one of the better mental health institutions. There was general agreement to the plan.

Damian was relieved. He had no interest in taking any sort of revenge. He just wanted Sheridan where he couldn't harm others, and hopefully, where he could learn to understand himself and his own motivations better. He looked around at these people, his family, and affection swelled in his chest. He'd been hard on them lately and he knew he ought to apologize.

Rising slowly, he nodded to Marco, who gave him the floor, and then he turned.

"First I want to let you all know that, yes, my eyesight is fully restored. I visited an eye specialist in Flagstaff this morning and had it confirmed. And I want to thank you all for accommodating my disability while I had it. You were all very helpful and generous and I appreciate it, even if there were times when I didn't show it very effectively."

Karina made a smart remark and the others laughed. He gave her a look, but went on with what he had to say.

"Just recently I had a chance to hear some of the poetry of our father's favorite, Jan Kreslau. One of his last poems was 'Fresh Eyes for a New Age.' I think that pretty much wraps up my life with a bow on it. In some ways, being blind was good for me. I learned a lot about myself, and about things in this world I'd been ignoring." He smiled. "And about us. I saw us with fresh eyes. And it may surprise you to hear that I like us. But we're changing. I love Nabotavia. I love the Roseanova family, its history, its traditions. I believe in us. I think we're going to do a great job ruling Nabotavia." He shifted his weight from one foot to the other. "It's the old system I'm a little shaky on. Traditions are important. They give a culture depth and richness. But often a culture will start to follow meaningless and outdated restrictions masquerading as traditions. We have to be open-minded enough to have the strength to throw those fakes aside and move on. I realize we won't always agree on which are good and which are ready to be discarded. But this long, boring speech is my way of letting you know, that I am ready to follow the path that tradition has set for me. Still, at the same time, I'm going to ask Sara Joplin to marry me.''

A buzz rose and fell in the room, and then they were listening again.

"I don't know if she'll accept. She might not relish living so far away from what she's used to. But I'm going to do my best to convince her. Because I love her very much and I think she'll bring something fresh and vibrant to this family. I just wanted you to be prepared.''

''I've heard about enough of this nonsense,'' the duchess cried, her jaw jutting out. "I don't know why you're even bothering to inform us,'' she went on sarcastically. ''It's the new trend. Everybody's doing it. First Karina marries a policeman. Now Boris is wed to our housekeeper.'' She shrugged and said as an aside, ''Where we're going to get someone good enough to replace her is beyond me.'' Sighing, she went on. ''And you,'' she said accusingly, pointing at Garth, ''I hear you are refusing to marry Princess Tianna of the White Rose Roseanovas, a beautiful girl you've been betrothed to for years and years. A girl who tired of waiting for you to do right by her and had the gumption to come here incognito to find out what the holdup was.''

Karina made a face. ''Well, that wasn't exactly what happened,'' she began, and Garth growled,

"Aunt, you don't know what you're talking about,"
but the duchess wasn't listening.

"So why shouldn't Damian marry his occupational
therapist? Everyone else is doing it. At least Marco
did what was right when he married," she said, turning to look at him with reverence and not noticing
that he was avoiding her gaze. "And now he's betrothed to Princess Illiana in Dallas and I'm sure he'll
do his duty. He's the only one of you who still remembers what that is."

The meeting disintegrated into squabbling. Damian
smiled. Typical family meeting, he thought, feeling
nothing but love for all of them. He knew they would
all have to know about their father being Sheridan's
biological father as well eventually. Sara had convinced him that learning of the truth at their ages
would be very different from the way he'd found out
at such an impressionable age. Realizing that had
helped lift a burden from his shoulders. He no longer
felt as though he had to be the guardian of their happiness. They wouldn't be devastated by it as he had
been. He wanted nothing but happiness for them all,
but he couldn't be the one to make that happen. Still,
he loved them.

He was full of love tonight. Bursting with it. And
he knew where he wanted to go to express that feeling. Glancing back at the argument still going on, he
made his escape.

The halls were dimly lit and quiet. It was late. Most
of their visitors were asleep. He found the room Sara
had been given quickly and eased the door open. The

moon had finally made an appearance, lighting the room enough for him to make out her form on the bed. He looked down at her for a long moment, then touched her cheek.

"Sara, wake up."

"What?" She blinked up at him, confused. "What are you doing here?"

"I couldn't wait until morning. I have to talk to you now."

"Why?" she asked, but she moved to make room for him and he lay beside her.

He stroked her hair. "You're sleepy, right? Your guard is down?"

"I suppose," she murmured, staring at him through eyes squeezed into slits.

"Good." He took her shoulders in his hands and smiled into her face. "This is it, then." He took a deep breath. "Sara Joplin, will you marry me?"

Her jaw dropped slightly. She stared harder, then seemed to find the answer. "Oh, wait a minute. I'm dreaming, aren't I?"

"No. This is the real deal. I want you for my wife."

She made a noise of derision low in her throat. "A dream. I knew it was too good to be true. Princes don't ask women like me to marry them."

"Who told you that?"

"Everyone knows. It's one of those conventional wisdom things." She yawned and punched her pillow and looked like she would drop back to sleep.

"Hey. Don't go to sleep. I'm proposing to you."

"No, you're not." She shook her head. "You can't ask me. You're royal. Royalty doesn't do things like that. Annie told me all about it. Stay away from those royal guys, she said. They're only after one thing...."

He laughed at her, cradling her face in his hands. "Then I guess it will surprise you to know that Annie and Boris were married in Las Vegas today."

Her eyes finally opened wide. "Yes. Yes, that surprises me very much."

"So what do you say now to my proposal?"

She thought for a moment, frowning. Then she looked at him with a faint smile and began to wriggle out of her nightgown.

"Come on," she said. "Let's make love. And if you still want to ask me after you have had your way with me, then I'll believe you."

Damian laughed and began to shed his own clothes, racing with her and then wrapping her in his arms. "You're so beautiful," he said, looking from her rosy-tipped breasts to her happy face and brushing her hair back so that he could kiss her. "I loved you when I was blind, but now that I can see you, I love you twice as much."

Tears filled her eyes. "Damian, you make my life worthwhile."

He kissed each eye, blotting out the dampness. "Remember that first day, you came when I told you that I didn't need you?"

She nodded. "I remember it well."

"I was blind."

She laughed. "Yes, I know. Remember how I told

you I would only be with you for a short time and then I would be gone?"

"I remember something along those lines."

"I was blind, too."

He laughed softly. "Tell me now. Will you marry me?"

She put on a Regency face. "Not until you've sated your desire for my body, my lord. Only then will I know I have the truth of your undying affection for my heart and my mind."

"Okay. Have it your way." He began kissing her, one square inch at a time, but he stopped when he got to her navel.

"One of the first things I'm going to do is contact your parents," he said, looking up so that he could see her face.

She gazed at him, bemused. "Don't tell me you want to ask them for permission to court me?"

"No. The courting will continue apace, regardless." He looked serious. "I want to offer them a deal. I'll give them exclusive rights to produce the official tour guide to the new Nabotavia—on one condition."

"Which is?"

"I want to see them in the waiting room at the hospital when Mandy delivers her baby."

Sara began to laugh, reaching out to hold him in her arms. "I love you, Damian, Prince of Nabotavia."

"But will you marry me?"

"Not yet!"

He took her body and molded it with his hands.

His own body was taut and ready and he ached to thrust inside her and take her as high as they could reach, but he waited, learning to read her readiness from the glow of her skin, the trembling of her thighs, the sound of her pleasure moans. And when it was exactly the right time, he came to her and she welcomed him, and they rose and fell together in a timeless dance that had traditions even older and more basic than those of the Nabotavian royalty. But these traditions he never wanted to change. And as they clung together in the slow downward spiral, he whispered in her ear, "Will you marry me?"

She pulled her head back and looked straight into his face, her eyes searching his, her own heart open to his exploration in return.

"Yes, Damian," she said loud and clear. "I will."

It was a hope and a promise and she meant it with all her heart.

*   *   *   *   *

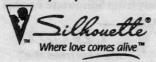

**Like a spent wave,
washing broken shells back to sea,
the clues to a long-ago death had been
caught in the undertow of time...**

Coming in
July 2003

Undertow

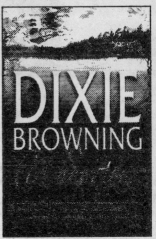

Cold cases were
Gray Hollowell's specialty,
and for a bored detective
on disability, turning over
clues from a twenty-seven-
year-old boating fatality
on exclusive Henry Island
was just the vacation he
needed. Edgar Henry had
paid him cash, given him
the keys to his cottage, told him what he knew about
his wife's death—then up and died. But it wasn't until
Edgar's vulnerable daughter, Mariah, showed up to
scatter Edgar's ashes that Gray felt the pull of her
innocent beauty—and the chill of this cold case.

Only from Silhouette Books!

Where love comes alive™

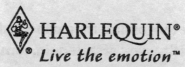

New York Times bestselling author

DEBBIE MACOMBER

weaves emotional tales of love and longing.

Look for the second book in her celebrated NAVY series

Carol knew her stubborn, honorable ex-husband would be
the perfect man to father the child she so desperately wanted.
But could she convince Steve?

Available this June wherever Silhouette books are sold.

We're proud to present two emotional novels of
strong Western passions, intense, irresistible heroes
and the women who are about to
tear down their walls of protection!

Don't miss

SUMMER
Gold

containing

Sweet Wind, Wild Wind
by *New York Times* bestselling author
Elizabeth Lowell

&

A Wolf River Summer
an original novel by
Barbara McCauley

Available this June wherever Silhouette books are sold.

Silhouette®
Where love comes alive™